KU-683-229

CHILDREN OF FIRE

PAUL CW BEATTY

The Book Guild Ltd

First published in Great Britain in 2017 by
The Book Guild Ltd
9 Priory Business Park
Wistow Road, Kibworth
Leicestershire, LE8 0RX
Freephone: 0800 999 2982
www.bookguild.co.uk
Email: info@bookguild.co.uk
Twitter: @bookguild

Copyright © 2017 Paul CW Beatty

The right of Paul CW Beatty to be identified as the author of this
work has been asserted by him in accordance with the
Copyright, Design and Patents Act 1988.

All rights reserved. No part of this publication may be
reproduced, transmitted, or stored in a retrieval system, in any form or by any means,
without permission in writing from the publisher, nor be otherwise circulated in
any form of binding or cover other than that in which it is published and without
a similar condition being imposed on the subsequent purchaser.

This work is entirely fictitious and bears no resemblance to any persons living or dead.

Typeset in Minion Pro

Printed and bound in Great Britain by CPI Group (UK) Ltd, Croydon, CR0 4YY

ISBN 978 1912083 466

British Library Cataloguing in Publication Data.
A catalogue record for this book is available from the British Library.

To Sue for her patience, advice and tolerance, and all my friends from Writers, Inc. for listening to me read sections of Children of Fire *which were far from finished.*

I

BEGINNINGS

February 1841

You must remain calm. Panic betrays you. Breathe deeply. Walk deliberately. Count your steps. One at a time. Think of nothing except your steps. Only your steps. Have the metal wheels begun to turn? How many revolutions before the rollers catch and spark? How far away do you have to walk to be safe? Safe at this range? More to go?

The explosion rips the corning-mill apart. You feel it through your feet as the ground shakes. The shockwave makes you gasp. Compelled to look, you turn to see your handiwork.

The detonation has formed into a terrifying pillar of smoke, flame and debris. The bodies of the men who were charging the mill are flying through the air within this fountain of destruction. You have killed before in combat but this seems so much more cold-blooded. You are comforted by the thought that they would have known nothing.

But the macabre play is only in its first act. The sheet of flame that follows is uncontrolled. It forms into a single ball and, caught by an indolent wind, drifts downhill close to the ground.

Three men, brave men, appear from other buildings and run towards the explosion hoping to rescue their comrades but they cannot see what you see. The ball of flame reaches the press-

1

house, which in turn disintegrates. The explosion transforms these would-be rescuers into blazing Roman Candles. Two fall to the ground and, wreathed in private palls of oily black smoke, writhe in pain. One of them makes it to the river and plunges in. You taste the vomit in your throat. You have done a dishonourable thing. They were not your enemies.

But the last act is yet to play. A time almost too short to be perceived, then, simultaneously, the glazing and charge houses explode. Their combined blast throws you to the ground and sets your ears ringing.

When you come to your senses, men, appearing from all parts of the site, run past you towards the bodies. One man stops and drags you to your feet.

'Get up! Get up! Come and help!' he screams, his cheeks purple with rage. Then a frown passes over his face.

Blood pounds in your ears. Has he recognised you as a stranger? Your stomach tightens. You touch the pistol in your coat.

'Coward!' he yells and runs on.

Move your feet. Do not think. Do it. Your lips are dry but you cannot moisten them. Only a few more steps. It is done. You are free, safe.

June 1841

'Left, right! Left, right!' Constable Josiah Ainscough marched on, the high leather stock digging into his neck, his reinforced top hat, heavy and hot. More scare-crow than scare-criminal.

'Look Mama, soldiers!' shouted a small girl.

'Not soldiers dear, policemen,' corrected her mother.

'Ooo! Po-lice-men,' she said, hearing the word for the first time. Then she waved enthusiastically.

For the hundredth time, Josiah wondered what had ever

possessed him to join the police. He didn't feel like a police officer. Even his squeaking boots were giving him blisters.

'Well now, that's progress and no mistake,' said Constable Howcroft next to him. 'In the Army they used to jeer at us rather than cheer.'

Howcroft waved at the child without so much as losing step, a feat quite impossible for Josiah. If he had attempted it he would have fallen flat on his face.

The truth was that his fellow officers would have been a more presentable body of men without him. The police force would be much more capable of impressing the sceptical Stockport populace, who had never wanted it in the first place. Without him, it would have been easier to show that the promises from the Mayor and Corporation, that the police would make the town safer, were not just the meaningless prating of civic worthies.

'Left, right! Left, right!' shouted Constable Giles as the company swung out of Hillgate and into the yard behind the Lamb and Flag.

'Company, hal-t.' They came to attention with a unified stamp of boots, unified except for Josiah.

'Right-turn.' Another stamp with, for once, Josiah in unison.

'Company ten-shun.'

'Thank you, Constable,' said Sergeant Smith. 'I'll take over from here.'

'Yes Sergeant!' There followed a whole series of stamps by Giles as he returned to his place in the line. All those stamps meant nothing to Josiah.

'Gentlemen you all have your tasks for today. Move to them promptly and in a business-like fashion. Be courteous at all times as you go about your duties. Constable Ainscough, see me after dismissal. Company dis-miss.'

As Josiah walked over to the sergeant he wondered what was about to happen.

'You wanted to see me, Sergeant?'

'Yes, Josiah. You are to report to Mr Prestbury urgently. You'll find him at the Magistrates' Court. It sounds to me that he has a bee in his bonnet, so I'd get down there sharpish if I were you.'

Josiah saluted and set off towards the centre of the town; it was definitely not the best start to a day. If he was a fish out of water marching, then in the next few minutes, he was likely to find himself a fish in a frying pan. The last thing he wanted to do was to have an interview with Mr Prestbury.

Ruefully he considered again how unsuitable he was for his occupation. Smith, Giles and Howcroft, like the majority of his fellow officers, were old soldiers. Smith had been wounded in the Opium Wars and Giles had been at Waterloo as a drummer boy. In their company, Josiah, even in his early twenties, seemed to himself no more than a child. True, at five-foot eleven he was the tallest officer in the group, but the rest were thickset, mature men while he was spindly.

But there was no way of escape for him from the force. A lot of his reason for joining the police had been to reduce discussion about his future, especially to prevent having to confess his lapse in morality in Spain. In other circumstances he could have asked his father to help him out of this mess. Every inch a generous parent and Christian gentleman, The Rev. Thomas Cooksley would be shocked but would forgive his adopted son. But Josiah realised he would never be able to withstand seeing the pain of disappointment on his father's face. There was nothing to be done but to play the cards he had and hope. At least, to cheer him up, he had three hundred yards to walk to the Magistrates' Court through the core of his hometown, its beating heart and his favourite place, the Market Square.

Most of the buildings in the centre of Stockport made up a confusion of cheap houses, brick-built shops and factories. Serendipity was the only discernible principle of design. Cotton mills crowded at the River Mersey's edge where they could get power from the water. Brinksway to the west was now dominated by one of the new wonders of the age, the brick-built, twenty-seven arch viaduct that would take the Manchester railway on to Crewe, Birmingham and eventually to London.

But despite the pace of change all around them, true natives of Stockport considered the market, in all its marvellous topsy-turvydom, their favourite place. On his way home from school Josiah had often diverted his steps to come this way rather than go straight home. He'd seen many things on those walks.

Once, on the steps on the parish church of St Mary's, he'd seen a well-dressed lady, accompanied by her maid, engaged in a slanging match with a pedlar from the country over the price of an Indian shawl. When the lady had not got the price she wanted she'd started to lay about the pedlar with her umbrella, to the great amusement of the traders and the embarrassment of her maid. The fact was that at some point all the people of Stockport, rich or poor, came to the market and bartered, argued or plain fought for what they needed.

'Well look at that,' a voice said in a strong brogue. 'How smart and proper the lad looks. What a stalwart upholder of the law. To think when I first met him he was nothing but a scrawny grammar boy.' Michael O'Carroll came over.

'I am guessing that you still might have reservations about becoming a Bobby?' He took out his short clay pipe from his pocket and started to clean out its bowl with a small, wooden handled knife. He scraped at a particularly stubborn bit of ash, spraying it across the patched sleeves and frayed lapels of his tweed jacket.

'Reservations is a very big understatement, Michael.' In fact, Josiah's world was firmly obscured by a black cloud of self-doubt.

'I'll be bound it'll have been a disappointment for Mr Cooksley,' said Michael. 'I remember how disappointed my Ma was when I said I'd not be offering for the priesthood.' Josiah smiled, finding the idea of Michael as a Catholic priest slightly amusing, though not totally implausible.

Michael returned the knife to his jacket and took out a pinch of tobacco from a waistcoat pocket. He packed the leaves into the pipe, then he found a match and struck it with his thumbnail and lit up. After a few puffs he gave Josiah his full attention.

'Your family will understand. They love you and they'll realise that you'll not have made your decision lightly. You were wise to take the time to travel, there's a tradition in Ireland that youngsters should see a bit of the world before settling.'

Josiah wondered how Michael would react if he understood all the reasons behind the decision. What would he say then? His friendship with Michael had been a surprising one, established years before Michael and his wife Mary were the respected members of the town's Catholic community they were now.

They had first met when Josiah had been on one of his excursions through the market on his way home. He came around a corner to be confronted by Billy Green, a boy two years older than him, who already helped on his father's stall. Billy had snatched the books Josiah was carrying and held them high in the air.

'Now what are you going to do, mammy's boy?'

Desperate to get the precious books back, Josiah had jumped at Billy, trying to reach his hand. But no matter how he tried he couldn't make himself tall enough or strong enough.

'What a whelp,' shouted Billy. 'No wonder your mam up and died. It must 'ave been for shame of 'aving you.'

Any mention of his natural mother or father was Josiah's Achilles' heel. Whether Billy knew it or not he was playing with fire. Josiah flew at him intending to knock him over, sit on his chest and bang his head on the cobblestones but he never got the chance. A powerful arm caught him in mid-dash and swung him into the air.

'That's enough, Billy. Playing games with books is one thing, insulting the memory of a woman as good and kind as Mrs Ainscough is another. Josiah found himself on his feet. 'Give those books back to Josiah and make peace with him.'

'I'll do no such thing. Who are you to give me orders, ye bog trotting Irish tinker,' said Billy.

'Well if you don't, I'll tell your da what you said and he'll give you a leatherin' big as you are. Mrs Ainscough was a friend to many around here, him included.'

Reluctantly Billy came over, gave Josiah back the books and they shook hands. When he had gone, Josiah considered his saviour. He was shabby, his hands gnarled and his face dirty. He looked very disreputable but Josiah knew one vital fact about him.

'Did you really know my mother?' Josiah whispered.

The man looked down and smiled. 'I certainly did though not for as long as I would have liked. She was a fine woman.'

'Can you tell me about her?' Josiah started to cry. 'I can't remember her, I was too young.'

The man smiled. 'Of course I will lad.'

'Good luck, boy, and remember you can always count on Mary and me.' Michael's voice brought Josiah back to the present.

'Thank you, Michael. You've always been a good friend.'

2

MR PRESTBURY

Josiah walked briskly down the steep, narrow alley of Vernon Street under the shadow of the high walls of the Castle Mill.

The impressive two-storey façade of the Magistrates' Court faced onto the busy thoroughfare of Underbank, but the Court could only be entered from Vernon Street by a small side door. This rather compromised its gravitas, especially when visitors realised that the Court only used the upper floor and shared the rest of the building with the town's cheese market.

But Josiah was not interested in the main entrance. There was a second menial doorway with certain advantages. Just inside it was the two small cells used to hold prisoners going into court. The cells had a permanent bouquet of urine and stale humanity, which combined to pungent effect with the ripe smell of cheese. But it was the quickest way in since it led to the stairs that came up in the dock. Unfortunately, that morning as Josiah came up the steps, he found himself face to face with Mr Prestbury who was sitting at the Clerk's table, furiously drumming his fingers.

'Constable Ainscough, at last. I was beginning to think that the distance from here to the other end of the Market had been miraculously elongated or that you had been robbed of the ability to walk quickly.'

At the best of times, Mr Prestbury was a daunting prospect, but at eye level from a courtroom dock he looked particularly fierce. He had a hawk-like look as he peered over pince-nez firmly clamped to a Roman nose. All Josiah could do was tuck his hat under his arm and stand to attention feeling he was, in all but name, the accused.

'I am sorry that I have kept you waiting, Mr Prestbury.'

'Well I suppose I should be grateful for the small mercy that you're here now. I have no time to waste so let us get down to the matter for which I summoned you. You are one of those confounded Methody, aren't you?'

Josiah was surprised by the question and at once was on his guard. As the town's longest-serving magistrate and now chairman of the new Police Watch Committee, Mr Prestbury was a leading Anglican, some would say the leading Anglican in the town. As such it was well-known that he had a deep-seated intolerance of members of any other Christian denomination. It was the term Methody that had put Josiah on his guard. Methody could be used as a derogatory common name for members of the Methodists. Mr Prestbury was well aware that Josiah was an active Methodist.

Josiah had always suspected that Mr Prestbury didn't like having Mr Cooksley's son as one of his officers. But Mr Cooksley's reputation, as well as Methodists making up an important proportion of the town's population, meant Prestbury could not be seen to discriminate against them in recruitment.

Josiah had considered several possible reasons for Mr Prestbury to have summoned him but anything about his religious leanings had not been on the list. Puzzled, he hesitated 'Yes, Sir.'

'So, you are prone to such things as camp meetings and worship in the outdoors?'

'It is true I have attended such meetings, Sir.'

'Normally I would consider that an unforgiveable lapse into non-conformist radicalism but in this case, it might be helpful. What do you know about the Children of Fire?'

Josiah was astonished, what could Mr Prestbury know or care to know about such a small religious group. 'Not very much Sir. They are an independent sect.'

Prestbury smiled in a sneering sort of way. 'Extraordinary, a Methody calling someone else's meeting a sect. Do you know any of their members?'

'No Sir.'

'Have you ever been to one of their meetings?'

'No Sir. But several members of the Tiviot Dale chapel have attended.'

'And what do they say about them?'

'They have been greatly taken by the preaching of their leader.'

'Ah yes, the flamboyant and charismatic Elijah Bradshawe. Do they note anything specific about him?'

'That he's very inspiring. They make reference to his concern for the mill workers, especially the children. Pardon me for asking Sir, but why are you interested in the Children of Fire? They are based at Long Clough which I thought was outside our jurisdiction.'

Prestbury looked at Josiah and scowled. 'Do not be impertinent, Constable. I do not need to be reminded by you about the geographical limitations of my authority. I will content myself with pointing out I am your employer and I can dismiss you at any time.'

Time to be a little more cautious thought Josiah. It would not do for him to give Prestbury an easy way of dismissing him.

'Beg pardon, Sir.'

Momentarily Prestbury looked pensive. 'The fact is the matter is unofficial but I suppose I must share the details with you if you are to aid me effectively. I have been contacted by an old friend of mine, Steven Hailsworth. He is not in good health and he is very concerned about his son, Abram, who is the owner of the Furness Vale Powder Mill.'

The name stirred Josiah's memory. 'Was that where there was a bad explosion earlier in the year, Sir?'

'Yes. There were several deaths, and the Mill was put out of production for three months for rebuilding and repairs. They are just about to start production again.'

'Is there a connection between the Mill and the Children of Fire?'

'There has been long running tension between Bradshawe and the local cotton mill owner Mr Celeb Arlon. As the members of your chapel noticed, Bradshawe preaches against child labour in the cotton industry. He has often attacked Arlon on those grounds but he has recently ranged his rhetorical guns against the younger Hailsworth in connection with the powder mill. Mr Steven Hailsworth is worried that the Children of Fire are stirring up discontent against the powder mill that might threaten its reopening. I'm minded to send you to find out if his fears are justified.'

Josiah was surprised. 'Why me, Sir?'

'Because as the most recent recruit to the force you are the least likely to be recognised as a Peeler and you are the one who can be most easily spared,' and dismissed if it all goes wrong, Josiah thought.

Prestbury continued. 'Go there incognito, make contact with the Children of Fire, get to know them, especially Bradshawe, and then report back to me so I can advise my friend what is to be done.'

Josiah's heart sank, but he did his best to put on a good face. 'Thank you, Sir. How long may I take?'

Prestbury thought for a moment. 'Let us say a week. Finish today's duties and start for Long Clough tomorrow.'

Josiah saluted and half turned to go but Prestbury had not finished. For a moment, he seemed unusually unsure of himself and spoke softly.

'Do it all without revealing the involvement of this force or me. You are not even to make yourself known to the Hailsworths. Do I make myself clear?'

'Yes Sir.'

3

THE ROAD TO LONG CLOUGH

He is lying with his back to a sycamore tree. The sky is alive with twinkling stars; the constellations of Orion, the Great Bear and Cygnus are all visible. The camp is in a clearing. It is the day he finished the pilgrimage to Santiago de Compostella. In his mouth is the taste of stewed rabbit, olives, herbs and red wine.

Figures are coming and going in the soft light of a fire; the Egyptian folk with whom he travels. Somewhere off to his left a guitar starts to play. The women rise to dance before the fire, arms outstretched, tossing their heads and swirling their hips in the flamenco. He takes another mouthful of wine.

The scene shifts to midday in the piazza in front of the cathedral. Everywhere movement, life and colour. The bells are ringing to welcome the pilgrims at the end of their quest. He is happy, proud and relieved to have decided that he will serve God as the minister his father wants.

Back to the clearing. Maria is standing in front of him, pretty, sad-eyed Maria. The next moment she is dancing, backwards and forwards, hair swirling, hips swaying, fingers sensual and expressive. Her movements become more intense and thrilling as the music and singing grows in pace. She kneels before him and, taking his hands, pulls him to his feet.

He knows he should stop her; he has seen what this gesture means. Maybe it is the wine or the sense of relief in having made his choice. He gets to his feet. She dances round him, getting closer and closer, her hair and body brushing him, pushing against him. The music stops, she draws him to her, kisses him and pulls him away into the soft, warm night, out of earshot or sight of the camp.

The dream disintegrated. Faces, his adopted father and mother Martha and Rev. Cooksley, his long dead natural father and mother, Mary and Michael O'Carroll, even Mr Prestbury were screaming one word at him over and over again: fornicator.

Josiah woke with start. His heart was pounding and he is sweating. It had taken him a minute or so to calm down, to control the sense of panic.

He couldn't sleep again. For the rest of the night he was either wracked with guilt about Maria or fretting about his unsuitability for his assignment given him by Mr Prestbury. Only as the clock on St Mary's chimed six and Sergeant Smith knocked on his door to make sure he was ready to go, was he able to put the dream behind him and concentrate on his journey to Long Clough.

'Stick to the plan we've discussed,' Smith had advised him. 'Take your time. You should get to the Children of Fire's place at about midday. The sun came up fair as anything this morning, so it's going to be hot. When you get there, you should easily pass yourself off as a traveller interested in a bit of casual work. Asking for water's always a good ruse to get your foot in a door. They'll be in the middle of haymaking and in need of extra help so it shouldn't be too difficult.'

'Thanks, Nathaniel,' Josiah had said.

'Josiah, the thanks I want is seeing you succeed. Remember, if you need help, especially if you don't want Prestbury to know about it, then give a note to my brother. He comes through Marple on the mail coach from Sheffield twice a week. He'll pass on any messages you might need to send. Now get going and good luck.'

Josiah had picked his way through narrow back streets of

the town until he found the turnpike to the southeast. As he had walked, his surroundings gradually changed. The air became less smoky, the road became more country than town.

By mid-morning he was resting in the shade of trees next to a stream at the bottom of the steep hill up to Marple. He was now only a few miles north-east of Long Clough and the walking had been steady and relatively easy, though it would be a bit more hilly from here. He wiped his neck and face with a kerchief he'd wetted in the stream. Then he picked up the light travelling pack and the thumbstick he had with him and started up the hill.

He found Marple its usual busy self. He walked up the short main street and made for the bridge that went over the canal junction. At Marple, coal from mines to the south met limestone from the Peak District. This confluence had made Marple a major centre for making quicklime. He could see all the chaos, filth and noise of the process from the bridge.

The quicklime kilns belched a combination of steam and black smoke into the blue sky. The soot from the kiln fires polluted everything it touched so that the chimneystacks, the tops of the kilns and the roofs of the sheds were blackened. In contrast, the white dust from breaking the limestone into small enough pieces to be fed into the kilns, gave a dazzling white patina below the soot-line.

In the canal basin that served the kilns, the lime dust touched the bargemen and women as they struggled to keep their boats in the queues for offloading stone or taking on the lime. They looked like old people, their faces, hands, clothing and hair all grey with the lime dust. Children could only be distinguished from the adults by size and the quickness of their movements. Even the barge ponies looked prematurely aged.

The last detail in this dreadful scene was the cacophony from the basin. It was a continuous blend of the noise of the machinery used to crush the limestone with disputes and arguments between the bargees. It struck Josiah that if Dante had seen the Marple lime kilns, they would have featured in the *Inferno*.

He walked on along the canal. In no more than half-a-mile, he found a footpath that went down through trees to the bank of the River Goyt.

Here, the river flowed slowly over broad, flat, shelves of rock and meandered round lazy bends. On one bend was a stone bridge that curved in a shallow arc over the river. When he arrived, the bridge was occupied by three packhorses, led by an old man. The horses were making slow progress, despite the attentions of a boy who brought up the rear and encouraged them along with an occasional prod from a switch of hazel.

The man led the first two ponies off the bridge as Josiah watched, but the boy was having trouble with the third, which had got to the centre of the bridge but then stubbornly refused to move. It seemed that it had been mesmerised by the flowing water. While they waited the man nodded to Josiah. 'Good day,' he said.

'Good day,' Josiah replied.

'Goin' far?'

'Long Clough,' said Josiah.

The man spat into the river. 'Visitin' the Children of Fire?'

'As it happens, yes.'

'You be careful, lad. Them's a rum lot to my mind.' He jabbed his thumb in the direction from which he'd come.

'The old packhorse route goes hard by their farm. Since I came that way last, them's built a great big cross 'bove Pulpit Rock. I don't hold with such things; crosses on churches perhaps but not on any old 'ill.' He spat into the river again.

The boy had stirred the third horse into motion. It came slowly but carefully down from the bridge. The man got the horses back in line and they set off upstream.

Josiah crossed and followed the packhorse route. The continuous passage of many horses over the years had worn the track down to the bedrock. Its surface was rough and strewn with loose stones and small boulders. The fact was that the packhorse track was falling into disrepair, practically all of its traffic having been taken long ago by the canal.

As well as the feeling of dilapidation, the path was hot and oppressive in the midday heat. It was hemmed in by trees on one side and dry-stone walls on the other. Josiah had no view of the hills in front of him or even the river behind, nothing to lift his spirits. Discovering this fracture in his resilience back came the memories: his unfitness and a policeman, his guilt about Maria. It was if he was being unfair to himself. He had a positive reason for joining, something he had witnessed which had convinced him of the need of an organisation such as a police force before he had ever heard of one.

At last the track released him and he suddenly emerged onto flatter, open grassland. A boundary wall drew his eyes to a small knot of trees which sheltered a farmhouse at the base of a jagged, stone cliff running roughly north-south. The face of the cliff was canted backwards so it looked as if a series of slabs of different sizes had been placed irregularly against a massive wall. About half a mile or so to the south of the farm, about twenty feet up, a large overhang with a flat top intruded through the slabs, Pulpit Rock. Above it a further sixty feet up, on the edge of the cliff, was a huge wooden cross, beside which, was what looked like, a bell mounted on a trestle.

It was the perfect place for outdoor preaching with plenty of places to sit amongst the rocks at the feet of the preacher. The dramatic cross, betrayed a mind that appreciated a spectacular gesture, to go with natural perfection.

As Josiah studied his objective, he disturbed a small brown bird from the shade of a wall. It hopped away from him and then took to the air. It circled round and round, rising higher and higher. Then it shortened its wing beats and started to hover and it sang, churring and jarring to the whole of the Furness Vale.

Josiah was captivated by the skylark as it sang, hovered and ascended. He watched, eyes shaded against the sunshine, as the bird became no more than a barely visible dot. Finally, when it was far above the level of cliff and cross, it gave a flourish of song, stiffened its wings and glided back to earth in quick silence.

As Josiah traced its dive as it bisected the view he had of the cross. The momentary thought came to him that the bird was like a pilgrim who had flown heavenwards to know God better and offer its praise more directly. Part of his reason for travelling had been to do the same. His effort had failed and he felt a pang of jealousy for the bird, comparing its perfection to his fallen state.

4

THE COMMUNITY

Long Clough was bigger than Josiah had appreciated from the view over the fields. It was not simply one farm, more a small hamlet. The farmhouse was an imposing building. It was solid and full-square, with four mullioned windows on the first floor and two larger ones on the ground. It had a central front door with a portico on carved doorposts, all built of the fine-grained, pink sandstone of the area.

Next to the farmhouse stood a small chapel, above the door of which was a black plaque with white letters: Bethel J T 1801. Whoever JT had been, it was a fine memorial to him and his faith.

The downstairs windows of the farmhouse were open, and a girl was happily singing a hymn. The voice was light and the singer happy; who would not be in such a place? Swallows flicked and skidded their way round house, chapel and under the trees. The hedges had more than their fair share of finches, warblers and throstles. Josiah pushed open the garden gate and walked down the path. He knocked and the singing stopped. After a few seconds the door opened and there was the girl.

She was not the down to earth, bucolic milkmaid, used to hard physical labour he had expected. Though she was flushed from the efforts of her work and there were wisps of untidy hair floating over her oval face, that was as far as earthiness went.

This girl was tall and slim, with dark golden hair and hazel eyes. The hands she was wiping had long fingers. He guessed that like him she was in her early twenties or perhaps a little younger. She was beautiful and the increase in his pulse rate indicated that it wasn't merely an intellectual assessment. She wore an inquisitive look, accompanied by a friendly smile.

'Can I help you?' she said.

'Well I was passing and it's a hot day. I wondered if I could beg some water.'

'Of course, our pump is in the backyard. You are welcome to come and drink or wash if you need to get the dust of the road from yourself. We pride ourselves on our hospitality. All are welcome to Long Clough.'

Inside, the house was as unexpected as the girl. The front door did not lead to a corridor between living rooms but directly into a stoutly flagged, capacious kitchen. On the right was a black metal range with a fire. Hooks to the ceiling held a variety of iron and copper pans. Opposite the door was a fine oak sideboard, heavily carved and decorated with mouldings. Daylight came in from leaded windows in the back wall.

The girl led him up two steps into a second, high-beamed room with a long table. From this room was a corridor that led to storerooms and finally a washhouse, complete with a steaming copper and a basket of washing.

'You are welcome to whatever you need,' she said, indicating a sunlit door at the end of the corridor.

Josiah emerged into a cobbled courtyard with a pump over a trough. Taking off his pack and putting down his walking stick he pumped out water with one hand as he ladled it into his mouth with the other. It was cold and tasted slightly earthy but it was clear and pure. Having slaked his thirst, he rolled back the collar of his shirt and drenched his head under the full force of the pump.

'You look as though you needed that.'

He had not heard her coming, probably because his head was under the water. He did not know how long she had been watching him, which made him feel uncomfortable. Perhaps his attraction was far too visible to her.

'Yes,' he said. He laughed awkwardly and cursed himself for his sudden nervousness. He had negotiated his way into jobs on farms dozens of times while on his travels. He had chatted happily with young women in exactly these circumstances without embarrassment and he'd done it in French or Spanish. Now, being aware of his attraction to Rachael made him nervous and uncertain despite his desire to be seen as confident and experienced.

She smiled and handed a towel to him. 'When you've dried yourself would you mind helping me hang out the washing?'

'It would be my pleasure,' he said. He held out a wet hand to her. 'My name is Josiah. What is yours?'

'I am Rachael, Sister Rachael.'

'Sister? If I may say so, that's a strange way for a young woman to describe herself.'

She laughed. 'I suppose it is. I'm so familiar with it I suppose I don't notice that it might sound odd to a stranger like yourself. I am a member of a religious community here in Long Clough. We're called the Children of Fire. We're intent on living from the land, praising God and serving our neighbours. We call each other Brother and Sister. You may have heard of us?'

'No, can't say I have. I'm not from these parts. Just passing through, searching for work and seeing the country.'

She fetched the washing basket from inside. 'The clothes lines are round the corner,' she said when she came back. Josiah took the basket from her and followed her out of the courtyard. In a paddock beyond a gate several lines of washing were already hanging to dry.

They started to peg out the contents of the basket. 'Are you travelling to anywhere in particular, Josiah?'

'No, I'm footloose.' He groaned inwardly as the words came out flat and rather forced.

'So if there was work to be done here for a few days, you could stay?'

'Is there any work?'

'We're hay making. We are in great need of extra help. Although it looks that it's going to be fine for the next few days you can never really tell up here in the hills.'

'Do you pay well?'

'No,' she laughed, 'but we'll feed you, give you a comfortable bed in the barn and send you back on your road with our prayers and blessings when you leave. Are you interested?'

Josiah took the time to try look as though he was thinking it over. If he had not been under orders from Mr Prestbury and free to take himself off leaving these people in peace, he would have done it. 'It is very tempting, Sister Rachael. This is a wonderful spot and I am in great need of a peaceful place to think things through.' Whatever else were lies, there was the truth, voiced despite his intent.

'I should warn you that even if you decided that you want to stay for a while it will not be my decision whether that happens; that will be up to our leader, Brother Elijah. He and the rest of the community will be in from the fields in a few minutes for some food. Stay, eat, wait a little to meet more of us, before you make up your mind.'

When the basket was empty, she asked if he'd mind taking in some other washing that had already dried, while she went back and tidied up the washhouse.

The wet washing had been general household laundry but the dry washing included girls' dresses, and boys' cotton shirts and britches. He took the washing back to Rachael who was setting the long table for food. 'You must have a lot of children in this community,' he said.

'No, there are no community children.'

He frowned and looked puzzled. 'Oh, I see.'

She laughed. 'We take in children's washing for the poorest in the vale. It's part of our service to our neighbours.'

There was a scraping of boots at the back door. Then in from the courtyard came a burly man of about thirty. He stopped immediately he saw Josiah.

'And just what would you be doing, if I might ask?' he said.

'Well timed, Brother Peter. This is Josiah, a traveller looking for work and needing water on his journey. The Holy Spirit has brought him to our door. I've bidden him stay for a meal with us and he has been helping me with the washing. I think we might be able to persuade him to stay to help with the haymaking. What do you think?'

Brother Peter scowled. 'That will be Brother Bradshawe's decision and no one else's.'

Gradually the other members of the Children of Fire came in from the fields. They were about thirty of them. A mixture of men and women aged from sixteen to fifty or so. The women wore simple printed dresses of various colours and the men the jackets, boots and leggings common to agricultural workers. If there was anything in their dress that marked them out as a religious community Josiah could not see it, unless it was that their clothing had a certain humility about it.

The last to come in was Brother Elijah Bradshawe. Even with a shirt covered in dust and pieces of hay from the fields, he cut an impressive figure. Over six foot six tall and broad shouldered he looked like a man used all his life to physical labour; though he carried its burden lightly. In his mid-sixties, he was still in the prime of life: hail, hearty and energetic. Unlike the other brothers and sisters, it was easy to see that Brother Elijah was consciously a man of God; his shoulder-length white hair gave him the look of an Old Testament prophet.

'I see we have a stranger within our gates,' he said to Sister Rachael as he came over to Josiah. 'Elijah Bradshawe,' and he enclosed Josiah's hand in a grip that exuded strength and confidence.

'This is Josiah, Brother Elijah,' said Rachael. 'I invited him to eat with us. He is in search of work but uncertain if he should stay with us.'

'Welcome, Josiah,' said Bradshawe. He looked at him with his head slightly cocked to one side and took his time. Josiah felt that he was being appraised in much the same way as when summoned to his father's study.

'Well, Sister Rachael, set a place for him near me. I need to get to know anyone the Lord sends us whether he is uncertain of us or not.'

When all the food was laid out and pitchers of fresh water from the pump put on the table, Elijah took his place at its head. Josiah was placed next to him with Rachael at Josiah's side, facing Brother Peter. The community stood, held hands round the table and sang the doxology.

As the prayer was offered, Josiah could feel Rachael's hand, smooth and soft from the washing. When he opened his eyes at the end of the prayer, he saw a tight-lipped Peter looking straight at him.

'So,' said Elijah, after bread, cheese and water had been passed round and the meal begun, 'what has brought you to our door?'

'I suppose it is pure chance.'

'I am afraid, Josiah, you are with people who do not believe in chance. We believe that on a man's path in life he is perpetually accompanied by providence. The choices he makes shape where he goes and who he meets. So it may seem like chance to you but from our point of view you have been sent to us. Do you agree that the choices people make are really important?'

How could he not agree? He was acutely aware how choices could change things forever. 'Yes, I do, Brother. I most certainly do.

Elijah looked at him steadily. 'I mean important to God, not just ourselves.'

'Yes, I know the choices we make are important to God as well as ourselves.' He was conscious how Elijah was drawing from him deeper truths than he wished to reveal. He must remember his objective and guard his tongue. He should put aside his guilt, and focus on the task in hand.

'But I am not yet sure I understand what you believe. I have met many for whom those words would mean different things. I might agree with you and the Children of Fire if I knew more about you.'

'Does that mean you wish to stay to get to know us better?'

'Yes, I suppose it does.'

'I will strike a bargain with you, Josiah. Help us bring in the hay and I will teach you about our beliefs. Is that agreeable to you?'

'I believe it is, Brother Elijah. I believe it is.' In the crude terms of his mission from Mr Prestbury, he had got over the first obstacle in his way. He was to be admitted to the Children of Fire.

5

THEOLOGICAL DISCOURSE

It was still dark when Josiah found himself being shaken awake by Brother James.

'Wake up, lubber, show a leg,' he said as he continued to shake Josiah. 'Breakfast's in the kitchen but you'll have to look lively.'

Josiah dragged himself into his shirt and trousers and staggered over to the farmhouse. He slumped down next to Brother James at table.

'You made it then,' said James far too cheerfully. 'Nothing to it really, just like getting up for the middle watch at six bells. It'll be fine when you're used to it.'

Josiah struggled with his conscience as he suppressed some desperately uncharitable thoughts about Brother James. 'Sailor then?' was all he managed to grunt.

'Aye, lad, been to sea most of me life. You?'

'Once,' James looked impressed.

'Which ship?'

'Nothing important. Worked my passage down the south Baltic coast. Never got used to waking up at six bells then either.'

Flimsy as the link to the sea was, it developed into a friendship with James which helped Josiah get to know the other members of the community. After three days everyone, except Peter, accepted him and conversations came easily. But he still had to complete the task Mr Prestbury had given him: assess what threat, if any, the Children of Fire were to the Hailsworths and the powder mill. But none of the conversations went deeply enough into the community's beliefs to be useful to him.

The exception were the conversations he had with Rachael. Those were more like conversations between old friends which he felt he could think of safely as a pleasant part of his emotional landscape. So, each evening, between the end of the evening meal and prayers, he was drawn to helping her clear up in the kitchen.

On one evening as Rachael was putting away the washed plates and dishes while Josiah was generally tidying up, she paused in what she was doing. 'You know you've never said the real reason you came here.'

'I am just a traveller, happy to have a few days of rest before getting back on the road.' He picked up some bowls from the table but as he turned to put in them in a cupboard Rachael stood in front of him and barred his way.

'You don't expect me to take that at face value, do you?' she said in mock annoyance. 'You must think me a very sleepy sort of country girl if you do.'

Josiah felt he must have missed a nuance in the conversation of the last few moments.

'I am what I seem to be, Sister Rachael. Nothing more.'

'Perhaps, but you are much more learned about the Bible and the teachings of the church than anyone else I have ever met, except Brother Bradshawe. That is hardly the background of any old ne'er do well itinerant traveller.'

Josiah relaxed a little. 'Rachael, believe me when I say I really don't think of you as any sort of sleepy country girl. If I know more about the Bible than you it's just that I may have had more luck in the past in my education. You are one of the cleverest young women I have ever encountered.'

She smiled and her eyes widened for an instant. The she

turned away from him a took a couple of steps, rather as a partner might in a country dance, before she turned back to face him again.

'And what, pray, most sweet tongued sir, was that education?'

'Grammar school and a home where books were common and reading encouraged.'

'And that Bible knowledge?'

'I was brought up in the Methodist way.' She looked dissatisfied, in a way that demanded more detail. He hesitated 'And I have been a preacher of sorts in the past.'

She grinned in delight and she clapped her hands together like a child who had won a simple parlour game. 'I knew it! I got it right! Brother Elijah didn't believe me when I said you'd been something like that. I shall take great pleasure in telling him he was wrong.' Her attention came back to Josiah.

'So, tell me, mister lapsed Methody preacher, what do you make of what we believe? How does it compare with Methody standards?'

'To be frank, though you've all been very friendly, none of you have told me enough for me to judge. What would you say you believe?'

'That is quite a challenge but Brother Elijah says we should all be ready to say what we believe when challenged so I'll try. We believe that our first priority is not to ourselves but to God and our neighbours. How is that for a start?'

'Very good. So you would agree with what it says in the bible "Thou shalt love the Lord thy God with all thy heart, and with all thy soul, and with all thy mind and thy neighbour as thyself"?'

'Yes, I would and so would all of us here at Long Clough.' She paused. 'Only there is something more perhaps than that. Not about our duty to God and our neighbour, I don't doubt that. It's about the difficulty of what loving means. The actions we take in this community are what define us, not just our beliefs.'

'Actions?'

'I don't mean dramatic things. Simple things like washing for our neighbours, taking care of the poor in the vale, living in harmony with creation, being at peace with all and friends to all without favour of rank or status.'

'For many that may be easier to say than do. You live in a self-contained community here. Methodist Chapel members are employed in cities and towns, or on farms if they are country folk. They might think you find it easier than they do to take care of their consciences. What would you say if they confessed they got angry with people in the hectic pace and difficulty of what can be a cruel world. They might be more than a little jealous of your privileged position.'

Rachael laughed. 'I would say they should try living in a dormitory with Sister Rose when she starts to snore!'

James' head appeared in the doorway. 'You two coming to prayers?'

'Yes,' Josiah and Rachael said in unison. They finished tidying up and went out towards the chapel.

As he walked next to her, Josiah thought about what Rachael had said about the beliefs of the community. Nothing he had seen while at Long Clough suggested any reason why Mr Hailsworth should be fearful of the Children of Fire. They might in some ways be considered a more radical sort of church than many; nearer to Primitive Methodists than his own softer and perhaps over comfortable Wesleyan form, but from the point of view of the law, they were essentially a peaceful group.

His only uncertainty surrounded Brother Elijah. He had not got to know Elijah as well as he had hoped, nor as well as Mr Prestbury had instructed him. With time running out, Josiah was thrown back on hoping that what Elijah Bradshawe believed would be clearer after Josiah heard him preach on Sunday.

6

A Sunday Sermon

The Sabbath was a strict day of rest in the community. It began with a prayer meeting in the chapel followed by breakfast. Then the brothers and sisters broke up into small groups to study the Bible.

In the middle of the day, food was available in the kitchen for those who felt the need of sustenance but there was no community meal. The most devoted and committed members of the community, including Rachael and Peter, fasted in seclusion with Elijah, and helped him prepare for his preaching.

At noon Peter walked up the path to ring the calling bell next to the great cross. It was a signal to all in earshot that Elijah Bradshawe would preach at two o'clock. Peter pulled on the bell for a good half hour and then returned to the inner circle around Elijah.

The rest of the community met in the rear courtyard at half past one. They formed into a line two abreast and started towards the track that ran under the face of the cliff. As they went along, they passed people waiting on the roadside. Most were simple folk: small groups of mill workers in their working clothes; farm workers in traditional smocks. But the well-off were there as well, sitting high up in their coaches or standing by horses held by grooms. As the community procession passed, all the onlookers fell in quietly behind them: rich mixed with poor; master with servant; landowner with labourer.

When they reached the rock, people dispersed and picked suitable places where they would be able to hear and see Elijah. At two o'clock the bell rang again, twelve slow strokes and suddenly Elijah Bradshawe, leader of the Children of Fire, was there on the edge of Pulpit Rock.

The congregation, including Josiah, gasped. Bradshawe was dressed in a black cassock, with a leather belt at the waist, white tabs and a clerical collar at the neck. Over the cassock was a long-sleeved multicoloured garment. It reminded Josiah of a cloak open at the front but it was fuller and covered the arms in such a way that if the arms were held wide and outstretched the garment would droop down in a semi-circle; it was beautifully embroidered with biblical scenes. There was Christ, preaching to the crowd near the sea of Galilee – probably the Sermon on the Mount. Jesus riding on a very realistic donkey, surrounded by enthusiastic disciples waving branches, represented Palm Sunday. Josiah thought one scene particularly appropriate, John the Baptist preaching by the Jordan; like John, Elijah Bradshawe attracted all manner of people.

His white hair was blown about by the up-draft from the cliff. He was carrying a carved ash staff.

'Peace be with you!' he roared and the congregation replied instinctively.

'And also with you!'

'Was this what you expected, Josiah?' Rachael seated herself next to him. Their service done, all the inner group, except Peter, had joined the congregation at the foot of the rock.

'He takes his Christian name more seriously than I had thought,' said Josiah.

'Oh you mean Elijah. Not really, if he had to pick a name in that way it would be Moses.'

'Does that mean that he's about to bring us the Law from the top of Mount Sinai?'

'You will have to judge for yourself, Josiah.'

Again Elijah's voice rang out. 'My children!' Then he raised his hands above his head and looking up to heaven, shaking them violently in exultation. 'God's children! For though a few of you have joined me as Children of Fire, all of us are children of God, for we are made in God's image and likeness.'

Slowly and dramatically, he brought his hands down and placed both of them on the top of his staff. Leaning forward he spoke in a clear but gentle voice to the congregation. 'How do we know that we are God's children?

An ecstatic voice from a woman to Josiah's left cried out. 'Tell us, Brother! Tell us!'

'Fear not, Sister, I will. We know this because at the very beginning of His Holy Bible, God tells us that he created us to be his children. Remember what it says in the twenty-sixth verse of the first chapter of the book of Genesis: "God said, let us make man in our image, after our likeness".

'But how many of you have taken false solace in that verse? How many of you have clung to it when guilt comes over you for things you have done that you know in your hearts God would not approve, things that are against his will?

'Those things affront God and refute the fact that we are all made in God's image. They divide us from God and from our neighbours. Worst of all they divide us from the divine likeness within ourselves.'

He started to walk up and down on the edge of the rock looking directly at the congregation, first to left and then to the right. Wherever his gaze fell, Josiah saw that those caught by it became uneasy. When Josiah himself fell under that gaze, it was as if Elijah could see exactly the sort of sinner he was. Josiah had never heard any preacher with Elijah Bradshawe's charisma.

'If you have come today in the hope of hearing me say that God does not count against you what you are ashamed of, then you have come in vain. For already you know in your hearts what you have done against the image of God within you.'

Elijah's hand clutched at the clothes over his heart. 'You cannot escape responsibility for those choices.'

He stooped down with his right hand held over the edge of the rock as if he were reaching down into water to pull out a drowning man.

'If you will be honest with yourselves, you already know what true sin is and so there is only one answer to your dilemma. That answer is the one John the Baptist offered to the vipers of his generation, repentance.

'With God's help repent! Prove to yourself that your repentance is true, by making choices you know are just, righteous and Godly. And do it each and every day for the rest of your lives. As for the past, ask God's forgiveness for that too and prove your sincerity to him and your neighbours by endeavouring to put right what you have done wrong.'

Elijah's head now bent forward as if in prayer. From somewhere to Josiah's right a male voice cried out, 'Alleluia! Alleluia!' The cry was taken up by many others so that the word rolled round the space below the rock as if made by waves on a seashore. Slowly, Elijah looked up.

'But that verse from Genesis does not finish there, it continues. Do you remember how it continues? I will tell you. "Let them have dominion over the fish of the sea, and over the fowl of the air, and over the cattle, and over all the earth, and over every creeping thing that creepeth upon the earth".

'So much of our sin comes about when we mistake what this part of the verse really means, for it is not about a God-given right for us to plunder and lord it over His creation. It is not about putting our selfish purposes first.'

He raised his hand and wagged his forefinger at the congregation. 'No, children, it is about our responsibility to love and care for that creation.

'Too many in our day have taken this verse as a justification for doing whatever they wanted, both to their fellow human beings and to God's precious, natural world.

'Children, many of you will have heard me cry out against the few who oppress the many in the hellish cotton mills of Manchester.' He pointed across the vale in the direction of the great city. 'They deny to those they persecute their Godly birth-right of life in all its abundance. They defile the image of God within those folk for the sake of selfish profit.

'Of all the aspects of the slavery of the mills, the sin that God finds most offensive, is the denial of happy lives to children. I have named one guilty of this sin here in this valley, Arlon by name. I name him in the hope that he may change his ways and repent. I challenge him to run his mill in a more just and Christian manner.

'But there is a lesser serpent near at hand and his name is Hailsworth. Abram Hailsworth is polluting the river Goyt with filth from his powder mill. Only last week there was a whole host of dead fish found just downstream.'

'Shame!' shouted the woman on Josiah's left.

'Some may see the hand of God in the explosion that stopped the production at the mill three months ago.'

'That's true enough,' she shouted. Elijah looked at her.

'You think so, Sister? You really think so? I do not like to think that. The God I know is not a vengeful God but one who is gentle and forgiving. Only when all hope of redemption is at an end does God bring down His judgement in fire and anger.

'But such wickedness may so affront others here on earth, that they may anger and take violent action in defence of God's gift of his creation. I hear the mill will be in operation again soon. I greatly fear there may be another outbreak of human anger against it.'

Elijah turned to face the cross, in a final prayer, his arms stretch out wide. As a result Josiah could see the scene embroidered on the back of the cloak. It illustrated the passage from the end of the book of Revelation; God's eternal city, the New Jerusalem, coming down from heaven, illuminated by golden rays of hope and mercy from an eternal sun.

Here he comes, climbing the path towards your hiding place, his lantern swinging as he strides forward. You laugh inside yourself as you consider how appropriate darkness is for treachery and how easily this trap has been sprung. All it took was a simply worded note:

> *Information about Powder Mill.*
> *Come to Pulpit Rock two hours after sunset.*

You step out in front of him and level your pistol at his head. He sees your face in the lamplight and gasps before he is struck down from behind.

You drag him to the base of the cross. There is a large wooden beam waiting on the ground. You lay him on it and bind his wrists so that he is stretched, open armed, along its length.

Slowly, he wakes up as you are finishing. You step back and watch as he becomes conscious. He looks around in a daze and tries to get up but the weight of the beam pins him to the earth. He wrenches at the ropes on his arms, twisting and struggling. He sees you and stops.

'Do you remember me?' you ask.

'It cannot be you. You are dead.'

'It is simply by chance that I bear a likeness of a face of someone you destroyed. Oh, I'm sorry, not chance, you don't believe in that? Do you? Providence would, in any case, be a more appropriate term.'

'Perhaps you are right,' he says. 'Either way I know who you must be.'

'And by your own creed you are duty bound to do what you

can to confess and prove that confession by trying to put right, the wrong you have done.'

'And I do confess. I did your family a terrible wrong but I cannot amend it. All I can do is ask your forgiveness.'

'Oh I think you can do something more practical than that and it will be a significant confirmation of the depth of your repentance, for it will take you the rest of your life. It's just that the rest of your life is going to be much shorter than you might have thought.'

You cut off his shirt so that he is naked to the waist. You pick up a hammer and a nail and, stooping next to his left hand, you push the nail into the soft flesh of the upturned palm and the hammer it into the wood behind. It takes several blows. One goes astray and breaks two of his fingers but he does not give you the satisfaction of crying out in what must be excruciating pain. Blood wells up round the shaft of the nail and pools in the palm.

You move round to the right hand. You twist the nail repeatedly into the palm until it goes through to the back. Then you take up the hammer. Still he is silent before you.

You stand up and put your foot across his throat. Then gradually you throw your weight forward so that he starts to choke. After a few seconds he is not simply gasping for breath but uttering strange guttural sounds. Only then do you release the pressure; he is wracked by coughing.

Eyebolts have been fixed through the beam and rigged to block and tackle attached to the cross. He is heaved up so that his arms take much of his weight but his feet are still just touching the ground. There is a terrible involuntary groan of exhaled air as his lungs are forced forward and downwards. More fierce, deep coughing.

You take the crown you have prepared from green twigs of sloe gathered in the wood. Its thorns are long and when you ram it down on his head, trickles of blood flow start down his face like red water tracks on a wet window pane, as they merge with beads of sweat on his skin.

His shoes are pulled off and the stockings cut away. You bind his ankles and come up close to him, so your mouth is by his ear. You say something only you and he can hear and when he reacts and convulses his body in rejection, you laugh. You slip a blade in between his ribs and guide it towards his heart. You are careful not to kill him outright.

Around his neck you place a placard on a cord. You dip a finger in blood from his face and write across it. Then he is lifted clear of the ground until the extra crossbeam is at the same height as the original.

There are only two things left to be done. His legs are pulled back and two nails are driven between his tendons and the ankle bones, to pull the feet onto the upright. In a final touch, you take a sledgehammer and break his thighs.

He will die sometime before dawn, drowned slowly in his own blood from the chest wound. When is unimportant.

7

THE DEVIL'S WORK

Josiah was sitting in the courtyard writing notes on what he had found about the Children of Fire and wondering what he would say when he got back to Stockport and reported to Mr Prestbury. His main conclusion had not changed since the conversation with Sister Rachael: the community as a whole was not a threat either to the powder mill or the person of Abram Hailsworth. But, reluctantly, he had conceded he could not rule out that Elijah Bradshawe might pose an individual threat.

He turned over what Elijah had said at the end of the sermon. There was a possibility that he was angry enough to take violent action over the pollution of the river.

By Josiah's side was his pack and walking stick. He was lingering so that he could take proper leave of Rachael. He heard the gate on the far side of the paddock slam. As he put down the notebook and looked up, Rachael came running round the corner of the barn. She had lost her cap and her golden hair had come undone. For a moment, the vision captivated Josiah. He thought that her hair looked like a shower of gold but the vision abruptly vanished when he saw her face. She was running in desperation, tears streaming down her cheeks. She nearly knocked him over as she threw her arms round him.

'Rachael, what is it?'

'Come... Come Josiah... It is terrible... Come with me,

please,' she kissed his hand and pulled at his arm imploring him like a child. '… Peter needs your help… Please come… It is the Devil's work.'

'Rachael, has there been an accident?'

'This is no accident… it is the Devil's work.' She broke away and started to run back towards the paddock. Josiah ran after her.

Out onto the road to Pulpit Rock she ran, at a pace that Josiah could only just match. Without slacking she turned onto the path up the cliff that led to the cross. Josiah's longer stride helped him climb the path more quickly than her but he still could not catch up. When he emerged at the foot of the cross he saw a harrowing and obscene tableau before him.

Around the foot was a group of the Children of Fire. Two were on their knees praying. Hanging on the cross was the crucified body of Elijah Bradshawe, covered in congealed rivulets of blood which had run down behind where the legs must have been fixed, pooled at the bottom of the upright and soaked into the earth making a reddened, sticky patch. Around Elijah's neck was a blood-stained placard with some lettering Josiah could not see clearly because of the angle at which it hung.

Peter and another of the brothers were behind the cross tugging at ropes. He ran round to them to help. Peter and James were trying to lower the body to the ground but Peter's rope had snagged. Josiah realised that it was the weight of Elijah's body that was making it difficult. He went back to the front of the cross and, grasping Elijah's feet and calves, he pushed upwards to support the weight. Peter tugged again and the rope became free. Slowly they let Elijah down into the arms of Rachael, Sister Rose and Sister Margaret. Gently they laid the body on the ground and the women wept over it.

'You did this!' Peter seized Josiah round the throat. 'You did this. Elijah knew you were a spy! You did this!'

Josiah struggled to free himself but Peter was stronger than him. Josiah began to find it hard to breathe but in seizing him in rage Peter had not made his grip as firm as he could have done. Josiah managed to twist round and, bring his knee up smartly, winded him. Then he was able to break Peter's grip. Before Peter could charge forward again, Rachael came between them.

'For the sake of Christ, Peter, what are you doing? Josiah came at my bidding and has helped you. How can you quarrel with him when Elijah lies dead on the ground behind you?' She started to cry again.

'Ask him. He is one of Arlon's spies. Even if he didn't do this himself, then he knows who did it.' Again Peter made a dive at Josiah but James had him by the arms.

'Let me beat the truth from him, Rachael!'

'No!' Rachael screamed at Peter. 'That is not the way of this community, Peter, and you know it!' She strode towards him and pushed him with both hands in the chest so hard he would have fallen over if he hadn't been held by James. 'We will take Elijah's body back to Long Clough.' Another push. 'We will put him in the chapel and then we will talk, in a peaceful and prayerful manner, about what you have charged Josiah with as Elijah would have wanted.' Then she returned to weep again over the body.

Peter was still enraged but it was clear that the other members of the community agreed with Rachael. He had the choice of refusing to help with taking Elijah's body to be laid reverently at rest, or be seen to be so undisciplined he could not control his own anger. Gradually he relaxed.

A cart was fetched from the farm. While it was coming, they removed the nails from Elijah's hands and the bindings from his wrists. The thorns from his head and the placard from round his neck were also removed. At last Josiah was able to read the word written in blood: BLASPHEMER.

With his arms folded across his chest, Elijah was laid on

a board from the cart. Someone with presence of mind, had included a clean sheet with the board to cover the body. Before it was moved, Rachael took Josiah to one side. Her face was still tear-streaked and she was on the brink of more weeping but she had summoned up a reserve of calm that in the circumstances amazed Josiah.

'I do not think it would be wise for you to come with Elijah's body back to the farmhouse.' She choked back a sob. 'But if you do not follow the body now, I need your word that you will come to the chapel this evening to answer the charges Peter has laid against you. Do I have your word?'

'You do, Sister Rachael. I would not be parted from you or the community on bad terms even if this was not the day of such a terrible murder.' She winced at the word, a reaction with which he empathised.

'Thank you, Josiah.' She smiled bleakly at him. 'I did not think that you would give me any other answer. We will meet again this evening. Pray for us as we take him home.' She turned from Josiah and joined the others.

Peter, James and two other brothers lifted Elijah onto their shoulders and took him down the path to the track. Josiah watched as they disappeared over the lip of the cliff. From the foot of the cross he saw them put Elijah in the cart. The small cortège started back to Long Clough.

8

CONFESSION

At seven o'clock that evening, Josiah, with a heavy heart, walked towards the chapel of the Children of Fire. He did not really have any concerns about telling the community the truth about who he was or what he was doing at Long Clough. He had resolved to be open with them the instant that Rachael had asked him to give his word that he would come to answer Peter's accusation. What really concerned him was the effect it might have on how Rachael would feel about him. He was hopelessly morally compromised in his own eyes, unfit to woo anyone. Even so in the last few days a glimmer of hope of a future relationship with Rachael, impossible as it might be, had grown within him.

He got to the chapel and waited at the door. The community were praying. He could not hear the words, the heavy wood of the door muffled them, but he could hear their tone and pace. It was most likely they were praying for God's guidance at the beginning of what must be an unprecedented meeting. He waited until they had finished, then he opened the iron latch as quietly as he could and went in.

All the community were there, seated in the pews. They turned their heads as he entered. Elijah's body was laid out in front of the small communion table, below the raised central pulpit. It was covered by a white sheet. Candles, in long brass sticks, burned at his head and feet.

Josiah walked slowly forward. Rachael stood up and pointed him to a chair which faced the community. Josiah sat down. There was a pause. Rachael looked at Peter.

'I believed you have something to say to Josiah,' she prompted. Peter rose reluctantly to his feet.

'Earlier today, when Josiah came to help us take down Elijah's body from the cross I... attacked him. I should not have done it. I am ashamed of my actions now and I ask Josiah's forgiveness.'

'Granted, Brother Peter,' replied Josiah.

'Thank you,' said Peter softly though his tone of voice stiffened as he went on; much happier in the role of accuser than apologist, thought Josiah.

'But those who were at the cross this morning heard me accuse Josiah of being here to spy on us for Caleb Arlon. I restate that accusation now and say that if he was spying on us he must be considered the most likely perpetrator of Elijah's murder.'

'That is a very serious accusation, Brother Peter,' said Rachael. 'What evidence do you have that Josiah is even a spy, let alone involved in Elijah's death?'

'As to his being a spy, I pass on Elijah's opinion. He was suspicious of the way Josiah turned up and of some of the questions he asked.'

'If Elijah held such opinions why did he let Josiah stay?' asked Brother James.

'He was confident that any report Josiah might make to Arlon would not be detrimental to us.'

'What say you to this accusation, Josiah?' asked Rachael.

'That it is both true and false,' he replied. There was a gasp from the congregation. Josiah continued, 'True in that I was sent here to find out what I could about the community...'

Peter could not contain himself '... There, I told you so,' he burst out. Josiah held up his hand, appealing to be allowed to finish. He raised his voice as he continued, '... But I was not sent here to spy on you by Caleb Arlon or anyone else living here in the Furness Vale. You should know that I am a constable of the Stockport Police Force and was lawfully ordered here by my superior to gather intelligence about the Children of Fire, and especially Elijah Bradshawe.'

There was another gasp followed this time by a murmur of questions whispered to neighbours. 'Why would anyone in Stockport be worried about what goes on here?' said an incredulous Rachael.

'A question had been asked if the community was a threat to the reopening of the powder mill.'

'And what did you conclude, spy?' growled Peter.

'If you have my pack and notebook then you can read what I was writing this morning when Rachael came to fetch me.' Rachael pulled out the pack from under her pew, found the notebook and offered it to Josiah. He found the relevant place and gave it back to her.

'Sister Rachael, please pass it round the community. All may read what I put this morning. It is not a secret. What I wrote was to be the basis of my report when I got back to Stockport.'

'And it says what?' sneered Peter.

'That I had concluded that the community formed no threat to the powder mill; you are essentially peaceful. But you will also see that I could not entirely clear my mind of doubts about Elijah. I wondered if he might take personal, violent steps to stop the mill opening again.' A surprised silence met this last observation. Rachael put into words what everyone was thinking.

'Why would you believe that?'

'It was the last thing he said himself in his sermon that persuaded me that it was a possibility.'

'Oh really,' said Peter, 'There was nothing in his sermon like that.'

'I'm sure I'm not alone in remembering the words I have in mind,' said Josiah. 'Wasn't it: "But such wickedness may so affront others that they may anger so that they take violent action themselves in defence of God's good earth". That remark, on the tongue of a man of action like Elijah, might easily mean he felt like that.'

'Constable,' asked Brother James, 'did the person who thought we might be a threat to the mill reopening think that we'd been involved in the original explosion?'

'That is a logical conclusion, Brother,' replied Josiah.

'But now Elijah is dead,' said Rachael.

'Yes, I know that changes things. Now it seems impossible that he was planning any violent action on his own and logically that he was not involved in the previous explosion if it was not an accident. But it does not mean that his death is separate from what he said. Someone who heard the sermon, who was already suspicious he had a hand in the previous explosion at the mill, might have thought he was intending more harm. They might have decided to take drastic action of their own to prevent whatever Elijah might do.'

'Ridiculous,' said Peter looking round at the other community members for support.

'Hardly ridiculous, Brother Peter, when one looks at the savagery and care that went in to Elijah's murder.'

'Savagery there was,' said Brother James. 'I've rarely seen anything crueller or more savage anywhere I've sailed and that includes a couple of public executions I witnessed. But what do you mean by care, Constable.'

'Perhaps planning would be a better word. The murder of Elijah Bradshawe was carefully planned and prepared.'

'If you know that, then that's as good as a confession you did it,' said Peter.

'You may think that, but I can prove that I could not have done it alone. In which case how could I have met with anyone to plan the murder in the time I've been here with the community, unless, of course my accomplice was one of the Children of Fire? I know that this crime took two men to perform.'

'How do you know?' scoffed Peter.

'I think I see how he knows,' said Brother James. 'It took two of us on the ropes to let him down, so it must have taken two pulling on the ropes to put him up there.'

Rachael had gone pale. 'And the crossbeam to which he was fastened had to be brought from somewhere, and it would have been too heavy for one person to carry.'

'And there must have been a way of getting the ropes and pulley's in place so there must have been a ladder as well,' added Brother James.

'How could anyone have done that?' said Peter.

'I don't know,' said Josiah, 'I can only think that ladder, the beam, the ropes, everything used, was brought up using the Long Clough track or had been hidden close by.'

'There's nowhere to hide what would be needed near the cross,' said Peter.

'And anyone carrying the beam up the path would be in grave danger of being seen by one of us,' said James.

'I must ask,' said Josiah, 'have any of you seen anyone unfamiliar near the cross in the last few weeks.' There was a murmur of 'no' and a shaking of heads. 'Or anywhere else, near the edge of the wood across the moor perhaps?' As he said this he was surprised to see Rachael look hard at Peter who stared back.

That morning, after the small cortège had left for Long Clough, Josiah had sat on the edge of the cliff and tried to compose himself.

He had felt completely useless. Here he was, a policeman, charged with enforcing the law and bringing wrong doers to book, faced with the worst possible of crimes and he had no real idea of anything useful he might do. Surely there was something that would make a contribution to catching Elijah's murderers. He got up and started to pace up, down and around the cross, just as he had seen Mr Cooksley do when in debate with Josiah's adopted mother Martha.

Those debates, went on for days. They ranged over all sorts of subjects science, morals, ethics but the best were always about interpretation of bible passages. It would have been understandable that anyone who witnessed one of these debates would wonder how the Cooksleys' marriage survived. But Josiah and his stepbrother John knew better, the debates kept the Cooksley's marriage alive and the brothers looked forward to them, trying as best they could to keep up, sometimes daring to chip in views of their own.

In his present predicament one debate came into Josiah's mind. It was about something he needed a good measure of right then, wisdom. The debate raged around the story of Solomon's judgement between two women claiming to be the mother of a single baby. Solomon had said that he could not decide between them and as a fair settlement, he would cut the baby into two and give the women one half each. This immediately meant, to save her baby's life, that the real mother withdrew her claim. Josiah could remember the climax of the argument

'Surely Martha,' Thomas had said, 'you must see that it is God who gives him the discernment to see the truth in the moment of crisis?'

'I see nothing of the sort,' she had retorted. 'I accept God gave to Solomon the gift of wisdom to help him rule justly, but to apply it well, as he does in the passage, he has to combine it with his own common sense to see what is in front of his face.'

Josiah had smiled to himself as he rolled those words round in his mind common sense to see what is in front of his face. That was what he needed to do. Look, observe, see, examine. There might be nothing to see but if there was it might lead to a murderer. There was only one way to find out.

'It might not be you,' said Peter grudgingly, 'but it does not rule out that Arlon could be using you.'

'I leave it to you all to decide whether I am lying when I say I was not sent here at the behest of Mr Arlon even indirectly,' said Josiah. 'Brother Peter, if I am at some future time able to divulge who instigated my presence here, then I think you may owe me a second apology.'

'Even if there were two men involved how did they get Brother Bradshawe onto the cross?' Sister Rose asked.

'That puzzles me as well,' said Brother James. 'He was a powerful man. Whoever killed him, even if there were two of them, they would never have been able to strap him to that crossbeam if he put up a fight.'

'Who was the last person in the evening to see Brother Elijah?' asked Josiah.

'I must have been me,' said Rachael. 'After the evening meal I talked to him about a part of the Bible I had been reading.' She paused and Josiah saw her eyes start to fill with tears. 'I went to bed when we finished. He said he would be doing the same but he wanted to take a breath of air before turning in. It was dark by that time and the last thing I saw him do was to light the candle lamp that hangs near the door to the courtyard.'

She put her head down and Sister Rose put her arm round her shoulders.

The beam was lying where it had fallen as Elijah was taken down. The wood was square, stout and rough-cut, just like timber used for a thousand and one purposes anywhere in town or country. With it were the nails that had been used to fasten him to the cross. They were long, with bulbous, offset heads to which smears of blood still clung. The nails were stout and well made, so that even though they had been drawn from the wood in haste they were bent but still intact. He collected them up from the ground and put them in his pocket. Somehow it seemed sacrilegious to leave them to be lost.

Close to the cross, what grass and heather there was, had been trampled flat by the feet of the brothers and sisters.

He had to walk a few yards away before he found untouched undergrowth of ling, rooted into thin layers of peat. It grew in thick clumps between which sheep had worn grazing paths but there was no indication that the materials need for the murder, like the crossbeam had been brought that way.

A pair of magpies flew over him going away from the valley towards the margin of the wood. Their flight drew his attention to a small cottage. It looked deserted, except for a thin column of smoke rising from its chimney. It was a candidate for storing the materials. He would have to visit that cottage when he had the chance.

It had been then that he had realised what Brother James had just pointed out to the community meeting, that Elijah must have been caught unawares and incapacitated. That suggested he had been lured into a trap in the dark. Josiah had gone straight to the path that came up to the cross. He found nothing unusual until he got to where it passed through the narrow space between two large boulders.

On the low side of these rocks there was a single set of tracks that came round from the side of one boulder before disappearing on the surface of the footpath. On the rock itself, there were splashes of wax, which might have come from a lantern held by someone negotiating the path.

On the high side of the gap, there were more wax stains, this time heavier and very near the ground. Loosely, covered by the path's sand and gravel were two small shards of broken glass.

'Where is the lantern now?' asked Josiah.

'It's missing,' said Sister Margaret. 'I noticed that its hook was empty when I went to the pump this morning.'

9

STEVEN HAILSWORTH

At breakfast the following morning Rachael came and sat by Josiah. She still looked sad and very shaken. Her eyes were red, as though she had spent most of a sleepless night weeping but she still maintained the calm and self-control she had exhibited in public ever since they had taken Elijah's body back to Long Clough.

'What happened after I left last night's meeting?' he asked her.

'We went on 'til well after midnight,' she said. 'We were much divided about what we should do next. Peter was all for burying Elijah in our own way right now.'

Josiah was surprised. 'The law will not let you do that,' he said quietly, 'there has to be an inquest.'

'Yes, I realise that but you must understand that there is a great temptation for us to close ranks.'

'I sympathise. What did you decide?'

'That we would do what the law requires. Elijah's legacy, the standing of this community and our future, depends on our reputation. In this vale, being seen as above the law, would give easy ammunition to those who hate the truth Elijah cherished. It was a difficult decision but we will send word to the local magistrate, Mr Hailsworth, to notify him of Elijah's death.'

'And me?'

'You may remain here until you have done your duty in whatever way the authorities require. Personally, I shall be happy to have you stay. It occurs to me that whoever murdered Elijah may have hoped that the Children of Fire would then disintegrate. If we show signs of withstanding the blow then they could attack us again.'

Josiah said nothing in reply. Rachael had made a very good, if grim, point. Whether she was aware of it or not, her stoicism was drawing her into filling part of the gap left by Elijah's death. In which case, if there was another attack, she might be the target.

When Rachael had finished her breakfast and left, Josiah took a few moments to collect his thoughts before going about his tasks for the day.

He would have to disobey Mr Prestbury's instructions not to tell Prestbury's friend Steven Hailsworth that he was in the Furness Vale because he was duty bound to tell Steven Hailsworth the local magistrate, in which case he should put his findings and thoughts about the murder on paper. A verbal report should not satisfy Mr Hailsworth and would not help Josiah to explain himself to Mr Prestbury when he got back to Stockport.

A written report would have the added advantage that whenever Mr Hailsworth came to see Elijah's body, Josiah would be able quickly to give him a detailed account of what he had found by his examination of the ground around the cross. After that, he supposed it would no longer be his duty to stay.

The prospect of passing on a responsibility, which was way beyond his experience and capacities, should have made him feel relieved but instead all he felt was a mood of disappointment. His days with Rachael were numbered and the thought she could become a target for a killer, when he was not at Long Clough to protect her, was horrifying.

Mr Steven Hailsworth was a tall man, about sixty years old. He had a gaunt face with a firm chin. He did not wear a hat and his hair was thin, white and swept back from his forehead. He must have been a handsome man in his prime but the painful manner of his walking, with his weight on a stick, undermined his natural bearing. It was clear that what Mr Prestbury had said about his friend was right: Hailsworth was a man in ill health at least in his joints. Discretely, Josiah followed him up the steps to the chapel and took up station at the threshold, waiting an opportunity to speak to the magistrate when appropriate. Hailsworth went straight over to Elijah's body. His coachman brought up a chair for him to sit in before going back to the coach.

Josiah watched as Hailsworth lifted the sheet and took his time to look carefully and sadly at the dead face. Then he replaced the sheet, sat down and sighed.

'This is a sad day,' he said to Peter and Rachael who had waited for him in the chapel. 'It may seem strange to you but I will mourn his passing. He was not my friend and I do not see the world in the way he did but none the less he was a great man in his own way.'

'What has to be done now?' asked a subdued Peter.

'I will call in the coroner and he will convene an inquest. If you would be able to hold it here at Long Clough, then that would greatly facilitate matters. A jury will hear any evidence, agree how Elijah died and give their verdict. Then you will be able to bury him.' There was a pause as if no one wished to break the moment's mood.

Finally, Hailsworth spoke. 'Unless you have anything else to ask me I think I should leave you to mourn. Could you call my coachman back to help me?'

'I am afraid there is someone else here who needs to speak with you, Mr Hailsworth,' said Rachael.

'Not by any chance the attentive young man by the door?' said Hailsworth.

'Yes, his name is Constable Josiah Ainscough of the Stockport Police. He wishes to explain his presence and pass on what information he can about the murder.'

Mr Hailsworth's expression changed to one of interested surprise. 'A policeman from Stockport? That I had not expected. Ask him to come in.'

Josiah marched in, stood to attention and saluted. 'Constable Josiah Ainscough, Sir.'

'Brother Peter and Sister Rachael, I do not wish to be ungracious but could you leave me alone with the constable.' When they had the chapel to themselves Hailsworth indicated Josiah should sit in one of the front pews.

'Do I infer you were sent by my old friend Prestbury?'

'Yes Sir. He said you had asked him for advice as what to do about the Children of Fire.'

'That is true but the worries of an over anxious father for a son in a controversial and dangerous new business venture did not warrant sending a constable, however welcome it is having you here. I would thank him for his care.'

'To explain what I have done I have written a report. Perhaps your own police force will find it helpful.' Josiah handed Mr Hailsworth a sheaf of pages. The old man started to read. When he had finished, he looked up at Josiah.

'A first-rate report, Constable. I am sure another officer taking over the case would find it very useful, if we had anyone.'

'But I thought Derbyshire had a police force Sir?'

'It is based in Derby and Matlock. It will be weeks before they can send anyone here. If I read between the lines correctly, you think there is a danger of further violence.'

'I cannot rule it out. The manner of this murder was so extreme. At the very least there is a violent mood festering somewhere in this valley.'

'I hope you are wrong, Constable, but let us be practical. You have made a very good start which makes me think that the best thing would be for you to continue your investigations, at least until the county police can get here.'

'Sir, that is very flattering, but I should say to you that I am the newest and least experienced officer on Mr Prestbury's force.'

Hailsworth chuckled. 'I suppose that was why you were sent. Well, Constable, if you wanted to leave early you shouldn't have done quite such a good job. I will send a message to Mr Prestbury immediately requesting you stay. In the meantime, is there any way I can assist you? I can offer you accommodation at the Hall.'

'Thank you, Sir, but I think I should stay here. There are still things to look in to but there are only two people I really need to meet. Perhaps you could help me with that?'

'Who would they be?'

'Mr Arlon and your son Abram.'

Mr Hailsworth rubbed his chin. He was clearly somewhat shocked by the request. 'I cannot say I like the implications of that request, but it is logical. They should be eliminated from the investigation as soon as possible.' Hailsworth thought for a moment more. 'We are holding a small soirée a week today for a few friends. It is by way of a pre-birthday celebration for Mr Arlon's daughter who comes of age in a month's time, so Mr Arlon and my son Abram will be present. You seem very well educated for a police constable, if I can be so rude. If I get you some suitable evening clothes, do you think you could carry off a whole evening of foppery and meaningless chitchat?'

This method of getting to know the two men would not have been Josiah's first choice but it was an offer with possible advantages, a more formal approach might not allow. He swallowed hard.

'My guardian prepared me to move in all circles with all manner of people, Sir. I think I can do it.'

'Good man. Then next Tuesday it will be.'

10

INQUEST

Over the next few days Josiah went back to work on the farm. The haymaking was completed just in time, as low cloud and drizzle started to cling to the hilltops and obscure the view across the vale.

At first there was suspicion of him among the Children of Fire but gradually, as he worked alongside them again, feelings eased and relationships started to return to their former condition.

The coroner, a local draper, came on Wednesday. Josiah with Rachael and Peter showed him to the chapel. He hardly looked at Elijah's body and seemed far more concerned with preening himself than being business-like. After putting the sheet back over Elijah's head, he took a small silver box from his waistcoat pocket, along with a large, yellow-stained handkerchief, the sure sign of a habitual snuff taker.

'Mr 'ailsworth says you're a police constable from Stockport?' he said to Josiah. He raised the lid of the box and spread a little powder on the back of his left hand. Then he sniffed it with each nostril in turn.

Josiah was about to reply when the coroner gave a succession of short gasps as the powder irritated the back of his nose. He took a mighty indrawn breath and sneezed so hard that it rattled all the brass candle fittings around the chapel. As the echo died away Josiah finally had enough quite to reply to the original question.

'Yes I am.'

'Well you being 'ere to give evidence will attract quite a crowd. Plenty of young ladies to admire you eh, Constable,' the coroner winked at him, 'So we'll not fit it into this poky little church. 'Ave you got anywhere bigger so we can make a better show o'r it?'

'There is the barn,' said Rachael.

'Let dog see rabbit then!' said the enthused coroner. 'Where is it?'

They took him to see the barn, which he walked up and down. 'It'll make a champion setting for such an important matter. You'll be able to bury Brother Elijah the following day. My clerk will come by with instructions how to set things out.' Then he swaggered off, no doubt savouring his part in the drama to come. On Thursday, not only did the coroner's clerk come, with a detailed set of instructions as to how the barn should be arranged but a carter's wagon turned up with a bundle for Josiah.

In it was his police uniform, accompanied by a tetchy letter from Mr Prestbury which gave him grudging leave to help the Derbyshire authorities as best he could. The tone of the letter made it clear that Mr Prestbury had no regard for Constable Ainscough's abilities to help, even if Steven Hailsworth was impressed with what he had done thus far. Prestbury made it clear that Josiah's uniform had been sent so that he could be properly attired when he gave evidence to the inquest and thereby enhance the reputation of the Stockport force. Josiah thought that at least the coroner would be pleased about the uniform, since it would add an extra note of drama to the proceedings.

The arrival of the carter reminded Josiah to do something he had been intending to do for few days. He asked the carter to wait while he wrote a short note to Michael which he wrapped round one of the nails he had taken from the cross. The carter had come from Stockport and knew Michael. Josiah tipped him a farthing to make sure he took the note directly to Michael as soon as he got back.

The barn looked rather strange on Friday. A long table had been brought over from the house and set opposite the main door, behind which, for the coroner's use, was placed the biggest armed chair available at Long Clough. Off at a side, was arranged a smaller chair where the clerk would sit.

On Friday, the coroner was proved right about the interest the inquest would create. From soon after breakfast, people started turning up in small groups; some had brought food and were happily having picnics in the fields. Before putting on his uniform Josiah went into the barn to familiarise himself with the layout, especially where he would stand to give his evidence. Some people had hauled themselves up into the lofts to get a good view down in the court. They were dangling their legs over the side. They stared at him until he felt rather self-conscious.

From one part of the loft he heard giggling, though he could see no one. Then there was the sound of a loud slap and the head of a young woman with bits of hay in her hair poked up, followed by a young man who was rubbing his cheek.

'What did you do that for Elsie?'

'Just 'cause I'm up in a hay loft with thee don't mean your hands can wander were they like, Joe Gibbins. You remember that.' The heads disappeared and the giggling restarted. Josiah thought it was as if a courtroom had somehow become mixed up with the end of a local fair.

The jury arrived at about two o'clock in the afternoon and the clerk swore them in. The coroner arrived soon after and everyone stood up as he made his way ceremoniously to the chair.

'All those having business or information as to the

circumstances of the death of Mr Elijah Bradshawe of Long Clough farm should draw near and prepare to give their evidence,' he boomed in a baritone voice, before sitting down.

'Please be seated,' added the clerk for the benefit of the bystanders. From there on the inquest proceeded quickly.

Peter told how he had found Elijah early that morning when checking on some sheep he was worried about near the cross. Then Josiah, resplendent in his uniform was called. He recounted his proof that two people had been involved in what was clearly a murder. As a result, the jurymen had no difficulty in agreeing a verdict of murder by persons unknown.

II

A WALK IN THE WOODS

After the inquest, the Children of Fire were free to think about Elijah's funeral. There had been only a handful of deaths of members in the ten years since Elijah founded the community but the bodies of those members had always been claimed by relatives and given family burials in their home villages. No one central to the life of the Children of Fire had died, so they had no precedent on which to base a funeral service. All they were certain of was that the ceremony should reflect their beliefs and Elijah's character.

In the end, they decided to cremate his body on a pyre on Pulpit Rock. As a symbol of his soul's oneness with nature, his remains would be allowed to return to God's good earth by the natural processes of fire, wind and rain. The cremation would be at sunset on Sunday.

The women of the community volunteered to wash Elijah's body and dress him. This troubled Josiah. Perhaps a thorough examination of Elijah's body would yield useful evidence, in the same way as the examination of the area around the cross. He went to find Rachael.

'What is it, Josiah?'

'I would like to examine Elijah's body before the cremation. I would not ask if I didn't feel it might be helpful in finding his killers.'

She sighed. 'I had hoped the worst of things was over. An examination is not a very pleasant thought. I don't know what to feel or how other members of the community would react? Would you mind doing it secretly?'

'No, if that is your wish.'

'Then we will keep this between ourselves. Sunday morning the community will pray in the house for at least an hour before we go to prepare him. Will that give you enough time?'

'I think so.'

On Saturday morning, Josiah joined with the rest of the men of the community to gather wood for the pyre. Peter divided them into two groups. He sent one to cut brushwood from along the farm hedgerows. The rest of the men, including Josiah, he took with himself and the cart, following a track to the north. It went gently uphill, came out onto the plateau above the valley and then went towards a building unfamiliar to Josiah.

'Where is that?' he asked Brother James, who was walking beside him.

'It's the old sawmill. We can collect some lumber from there for the pyre.'

'I'm surprised it looks so deserted,' remarked Josiah.

'We never use it, along with the cottage over there,' James pointed south to the cottage Josiah had seen from the cross. 'They used to be for forestry work.'

'I'm surprised the community isn't interested in forestry.'

'Never have been in my time,' James called up to Peter. 'Peter why don't we use the sawmill anymore?'

'Because when the Children of Fire inherited Long Clough from Farmer Tremlet, Elijah wanted the woods to be left as God intended so he stopped the forestry, that and the disagreement about the boundary with Caleb Arlon.'

Josiah pricked up his ears. 'What do you mean, a disagreement about a boundary?'

'It's a long story. The deeds of the farm show its northern boundary as the one with the Hailsworth estate which is well defined by a wall inside the wood.'

'Mr Arlon presumably begs to differ?' said Josiah.

'Yes he maintains that that the correct boundary is marked by the line of an old stream. That line is this side of those buildings. It goes all the way along the boarder of the forest out to the road on the east. Arlon's claim has never been legally upheld but we try not to come here to avoid trouble with him.'

'Why would there be trouble if the courts have never upheld his claim?'

'Every so often Arlon has another go. The man's a fool about it if you ask me. Even if his claim was upheld it would only give him a tongue of land no more than six hundred yards deep between the farm and the Hailsworth estate. I think it just rankles that we got the farm when he expected to be able to add it to his estate when Tremlet passed on.'

So you've got a boundary with the Arlon estate as well as the Hailsworth estate.'

'How very observant of you, Constable,' sneered Peter. 'No more than half a mile to our left and running pretty much in parallel with this track.'

They reached the sawmill and quickly loaded up the lumber.

'Three of you come with me and the cart, the rest can make your way over to the cross through the heather,' said Peter.

Josiah watched as the cart left. 'How are they going to get to Pulpit Rock from here?' he asked Brother James.

'If you know where to look, there's an old path that goes that way which you can get the cart down. We used it to take the material for the cross to the top of the rocks last year but it doesn't go all the way; there's a ridge of stone that stops it short. When Peter arrives, we need to be there to offload the wood.'

The brothers set a good pace through the tussocks. Josiah let them go on ahead. He wanted to know why a deserted Forester's cottage had smoke coming out of its chimney only a few days before. As soon as he could, he doubled back and skirted the boundary of the wood in its direction.

When he got there, it did indeed look deserted. The door was unlocked and he went in. There was some ash in the hearth that looked fresh but when he felt the bricks of the fireplace, they were cold. If there had been a fire when he had first seen the cottage from the cross, it had not been relit. There was some stale bread on the table but how long it had been there was impossible to say. The house was dry and the roof in very much better repair than might be expected of a disused building. Maybe the smoke he had seen was the result of a wandering vagrant spending a few nights in the dry.

He went outside again. At the back, a footpath went directly into the wood. Curiously, about three yards in, just off the path, there was a recently dug earth privy that had been in use up to a few days ago and there was evidence that there had been other privies dug in the same area over some time.

The footpath continued deeper into the woods. He found a stream and not much further on there was a wall which looked as if it marked the Hailworth estate. There was no stile but the path continued on the other side into the deepest and quietest part of the wood. Another hundred yards and the ground fell away sharply into a dell dominated by larch trees where all noise was deadened by the thick layers of needles the trees had shed over many autumns. At the bottom of the dell, hidden under a thick covering of bracken, was a pile of long rough-cut bolts of timber.

Josiah searched around the base of the pile and found an entrance, big enough to crawl through, leading to a hollow centre high enough for him to crouch. There was a candle lamp, which he lit. It had a broken glass. On the floor were some tools: a small hammer with blood on its head, a bag of nails identical to those he had found at the cross, a ladder and some rope.

Taken with the wood, which was pretty much identical to that which had been used to crucify Elijah, he must be looking at all the equipment the murderers had used. More searching revealed the most macabre piece of evidence of all. Thrown in a corner were Elijah's blood-stained boots and stockings.

The tools for the murder had come from this store and the murderers had been confident enough to return them afterwards. Whoever had done this crime was both cool and arrogant. They had not believed that this store would be found.

It was satisfying to have discovered it. Even Mr Presbury's might think more of him if he knew. But those bloody clothes were proof that he had failed to observe at the cross that some of what Elijah's had been wearing was missing. Then it occurred to him that he still couldn't account for Elijah's shirt. He searched but was nowhere in the store. Had the murderers taken it in some sort of imitation of the shirt of Christ taken by the soldiers on the first Good Friday and over which they had played dice? Well he would deny them the satisfaction of keeping the boots and stockings.

He picked them up and started to leave. Then he realised that removing them would be a mistake, betraying to the murderers that their hiding place was known. He put the clothing back where he had found it and was careful to obscure any footprints or other marks he might have left on the ground under and around the pile of wood as he left.

Then he carefully followed the path back to the boundary wall but rather than go back to the Forester's cottage he followed the wall further and came out of the wood to the south. As he emerged, he looked back towards the cottage. There was a figure on the path going into the wood.

The figure was a long way off and most people would not be able to recognise who it was but the way the person moved, their way of walking was instantly recognisable to him. It was Rachael.

12

FIRE AT SUNSET

On Sunday morning, as Rachael had said, the community gathered to pray. Josiah went across to the barn, picked up his notebook and returned to the courtyard. As soon as he could hear the sound of prayers coming from the farmhouse, he went over to the chapel. To make sure he was not surprised, he pegged the catch on the door from the inside.

He pulled the sheet off Elijah's body and folded it neatly. What had been toned muscle, livid with strength and vigour only a few short days ago, was now flaccid and moist. Generally, it looked pale as if made of alabaster or carved from marble but in some places blue-green patches were showing through the skin. Josiah swallowed hard. Though the chapel was the coolest building at Long Clough, he thought that those blue-green areas were likely to be places where decay had already begun. At least, even if the corpse had started to decay, it did not yet smell corrupt. He shuddered.

There was a wound near the heart which was certainly decaying but was still well-defined: a dagger rather than a single-edged blade had been used.

He looked at the back of Elijah's head and quickly found an area where the skin had been broken by a hard blow. Hit from behind as he had passed the boulders on the path? The broad bruise across his throat, which looked as if it might have been inflicted by a boot or shoe, had no easy explanation. All Josiah could do was note it and do a quick sketch.

All over Elijah's chest and arms there were scares from old injuries. They formed a mass of thin white-lines some broader than others, some suggesting no more than scratches, some caused by much deeper wounds. Two stood out as having been caused by serious injuries.

On Elijah's left shoulder, from above the collarbone towards the nipple, there was a white scar that had been inflicted by something very sharp which had cut deeply. Under the scar, Josiah could feel the thickening where the collarbone had been broken but then healed.

The second scar was on the right side near Elijah's waistline over his right hip. It was grotesque. Round, depressed and about an inch across, the skin and tissue around it were puckered. Something had torn the flesh into this strange shape.

Josiah moved on. He examined the marks left by the binding of the wrists to the beam. The bonds had dug deeply into the flesh and some of the bones of the wrists were visible. Elijah must have been incapacitated before being strapped to the beam but these injuries suggested he had awakened and fought against the bindings.

Worried about the time his examination was taking he moved on to where the nails had been. Two fingers on the right hand had been broken. It was while examining this, he noticed a curious tattoo on the inside of Elijah's arm. It was old and faded but on the white skin it was clearer than it would have been in life.

It showed a Celtic harp with a winged male figure carved on the front post and a snake on the soundboard. Above the harp there was a single word: *Equality.* There were some faded words he could not entirely decipher below the harp. *It is… and shall be…* Josiah sketched it into his notebook as best he could. Having finished his notes, he paused before he again covered

Elijah. He looked steadily at body and tried to connect the things he had observed here and at the cross.

The placard with the word BLASPHEMER written on it in blood might suggest a religious motive for the murder; the false prophet of Furness Vale had been crucified by someone who found Elijah's beliefs abhorrent. But a religious motive would also be a good thing to pretend if you wanted use religious imagery to cover up a more prosaic motive such as greed.

Then there were the touches of unrestrained rage in the murder: the stabbing in the chest, the use of the nails, the broken fingers, the possible stamp on the throat. This murder might be motivated by revenge.

At about six o'clock the calling bell near the cross began tolling. Everyone, including Josiah, filed into the chapel. Elijah's body, dressed in his beautiful embroidered preaching cloak, was at peace. The were no signs of blood left on his face or forehead. His white hair had been combed out and arranged to frame his face. His hands held a Bible. His staff lay next to him.

It was a simple service. Bible passages were read and prayers offered in thanks for his life and leadership. In turn, each of the Children of Fire came forward and offered a single personal memory about him. These reminiscences made a fitting eulogy.

Rachael's was the most moving memoir. She recounted how she had been found by Elijah as a little girl living on the streets in Liverpool. Elijah had rescued her and brought her to Long Clough where she had grown up before the Children of Fire were formed.

She spoke of his strength and inspiration, how he had always spoken up for children all the time she had known him. As she spoke of how Elijah had transformed the hell of her life in Liverpool into the peace they had found in Long Clough. The resolve and self-control that had sustained her since the murder, started to weaken and she gave way in grief, slowly collapsing onto Elijah's body. Sobbing, she buried her head in his lifeless chest and tried to hold him in her arms.

As Peter and others comforted Rachael a final hymn was sung. The words were hopeful and brave but Rachael's grief had touched everyone. Whilst the hymn was one of praise and hope, it had taken on a fearfully sombre overtone.

When the hymn was over, before moving outside to form a guard of honour, all present, except those who were to carry the body, picked up a torch and lit it from one of the candles in the chapel. As Elijah's body was carried out, Rachael and Peter lit its way and the rest of the Children of Fire followed behind. Josiah brought up the rear.

The sun was setting over the western edge of the Furness Vale and Long Clough was already in deep shadow. The torches shone brightly and the embroidery on Elijah's preaching cloak reflected the flames.

As the bell tolled, they walked slowly along the path to Pulpit Rock. Up the path to the cross the community carried their leader, then out onto the rock itself and into the last sunlight of the day.

Elijah was laid gently on the pyre they had built near the edge. Peter and Rachael stepped forward and plunged their torches into the wood. The fire seemed to dim and then it took hold as the brushwood and lumber started to burn. One by one the community threw on their torches on to the pyre, Josiah last.

The flames grew in strength and Elijah's cloak started to burn. Suddenly, the fire exploded in intensity and it became impossible to see the body behind sheets of living flame.

Josiah looked out from the rock to the west. The sun was just setting. He imagined what the scene must look like from the other side of the vale. Elijah Bradshawe, Prophet of Furness Vale, Leader and Founder of the Children of Fire was passing from this world. In the morning, there would be no bones to bury, except perhaps the skull, no tissue left, except perhaps the heart. Like the prophets of old, a legend would spring up that he had been taken up bodily into heaven on a column of smoke or by a miraculous whirlwind. No one, not even Josiah, would wish to interfere with that part of Elijah's legacy.

13

HUNTED

'Brother James, where is everyone?' said Josiah as he came into breakfast.

'Some have been and taken some food and then gone to their own private places. Some just haven't yet stirred yet; they don't have the heart.' James finished his meal and got up. 'I'll go and get on with a few chores,' he said.

'Do you want company?' said Josiah.

'Thanks for asking but no.'

Josiah realised that he should have foreseen something like this effect on the members of the community. He had seen others grieve and had his own memory of the feeling. It was inevitable that the stoic solemnity of Elijah's funeral, which had sustained the day before, would turn into a more personal and sadder mood. Elijah's chair was empty in its place. A sense of "so he really is gone" hung almost tangibly in the air and given the uncertainty of the future of the community it had an edge of anxiety as well as grief.

Josiah ate his breakfast alone and in a silence, punctuated only by the ticking of the clock on the dresser. By the time, he had finished he felt trapped and oppressed by the mood. He had not known Elijah long enough to feel the intensity of personal grief of Rachael, Peter and the other Brothers and Sisters. As a result, he felt he was intruding on their grieving.

He should take a walk so as to leave the others in peace and privacy but where?

It occurred to him that he had not had time on Saturday to search the area around the hidden store as carefully as he would have liked. He also wanted to see if there was any evidence that anyone had been back since he'd discovered it. He would approach it from the sawmill which would mean he would cover new ground in getting to it.

Beyond the sawmill he found an overgrown but serviceable footpath going into the wood in roughly the right direction. The wood was thicker here than near the Forester's cottage. Soon he was having to push aside saplings and duck under low branches to make progress. The ground was rough, stony and dry, with rocky outcrops which had to be climbed over. It was relief to find the marker wall for the Hailsworth's estate. After a few more yards beyond the wall, he was struck by the quietness of the wood. A few birds were calling from the treetops, but except for a brilliant Jay he disturbed in a tree which flew close over his head in a flash of blue, russet and white, it was as if there was not a living thing around him.

The path lead through a succession of dells each deeper than the last but none showed sign of ever being visited by people let alone hiding anything illicit. Then, unexpectedly, he was standing on the lip of the final dell looking down at the pile of wood that hid the store. Irrationally, he crouched down, hiding as if the silence had eyes that were watching him. He shuffled forward on his haunches, using the bracken as cover and worked his way round to the entrance to woodpile. There were no new tracks in the earth. It was exactly as he had left it. Ridiculous, he thought, what are you frightened of? With an act of will he stood up and stepped towards the entrance. He bent down his hand on the woodpile ready to enter.

70

You have been watching the store for three days in case the intruder comes back. When you came on Friday morning at first you had not noticed that anything was out of the ordinary. There were no unusual tracks and everything seemed in its place. It was only after a little while that you began to see that some things in the store had been moved. Searching outside you found the branch that had been used to cover the tracks. Whoever your visitor was, they had been thorough. But you can be thorough as well. They had not revealed the store otherwise that idiot of policeman from the inquest would have been here by now. Perhaps they were unaware on what they had stumbled? They could just be ordinary thieves but either way they were likely to come back and you should make sure that it would be their last visit.

You picked your spot, about 400 yards from the hollow. You have a clear view of the entrance to the store, though you are not as high as you would like. You have waited and at last, your patience is rewarded.

There is a figure on the lip of the hollow, a blurred outline against the sky. He stoops, hiding in the bracken. You lose sight of him but you know where he is going. You ensure everything is ready for the moment he tries to get through the entrance; rifle loaded, stabilised and target area clear. Perhaps he is a government agent but if he is, why hasn't he already arrested or assassinated you. Now, you have the initiative.

He stands before stooping to get through the opening. His back is towards you. You cock the rifle, hold your breath and fire.

There was a fierce buzzing and no more than three inches to the right of Josiah's temple, simultaneously something splintered the piece wood on which his hand rested. Dumfounded, he was still looking at the place, when the musket report broke the silence of the wood, echoing off every tree round the dell.

In panic Josiah threw himself flat and dragged himself on his elbows into the thickest part of the bracken he could reach. Then he lay still as he could, hardly daring to breath, trying to cope with the jumble of thoughts that were pouring through his mind.

Did you get him? You think not. Dead men, the others you have shot before, do not fall as he fell. They collapse, they crumple like a doll dropped to a floor. You missed and he threw himself down. Where is he? Where there can be no breeze, the bracken is moving. There is time for a second shot: reload... aim... fire...

Would his assailant think him dead and leave? Josiah realised that if he had fired the shot even if he was in no doubt that he had found his target he would not leave it to chance. He would come to check and finish his quarry off if necessary. He needed to get away from the woodpile and do it before the gun could be reloaded or the marksman got to the dell from wherever he had taken the shot.

Josiah started to crawl forward again. There was another buzzing over his head and another report. That attempt had been less accurate than the first. He might be more difficult to see than he had been by the woodpile but that second shot was still very close. He crawled forward again only then realising that there was blood running from his hand. Sticking out of two fingers were long splinters. The first shot had been close enough to draw blood even though it had missed him. His hands started to shake uncontrollably and he wanted to vomit but there was no time for fear. He had to move as far as he could before the next shot. He was being hunted like an animal, but without any of an animal's instincts. His only hope was to think as clearly as he could.

The third shot was two feet in front of him. He saw it tatter some of the bracken leaves. Josiah started to count as he struggled on. The ground was rising; he was getting towards the edge of the dell. Very soon the bracken cover would be too thin to hide him. He would have to break cover and run for it but which way?

You know that you are being lax. Three shots and there has been no sign of a hit, let alone a kill. What on earth? You see his head clearly, he has worked out how long it takes you to reload. He will make a break for it. The next shot must pay.

As Josiah tried to think, another shot buzzed over him. The shots were getting closer but he had counted thirty; reload time was about thirty seconds. He looked up over the bracken, saw a fallen tree and ran for it.

On the move. Ram home... prime... steady... aim... fire!

It was just over a count of thirty when he threw himself behind its trunk as the fourth shot hit the tree. This time Josiah emptied the contents of his stomach and gasped for air, shaking from head to toe. Any idea of counting was forgotten.

But as he recovered he realised that provided he survived the next shot, the advantage would pass to him. He knew the general direction of his adversary's position: the shot had come from the western side of the dell, the opposite side to the path towards the Forester's Cottage. He waited. A ball buzzed into the top edge of the log, and he was lucky not to get some splinters in the face, but now the race was on.

So it is to be a race, a race for his life. Rifle over the shoulder pistols in the belt, run. You are 400 yards behind him. Don't reload just run. They'll be another chance. Keep him on his toes with the pistols. Make him work hard for escape.

Josiah ran flat out over the lip of the dell and off along the path weaving in and out of the trees to make the marksman's aim harder. It was nearly forty seconds before the next shot came, this time well off target but the time between hearing the ball and the report was reduced. The marksman was after him.

Two more shots were fired before Josiah reached the boundary wall but both were well wide. The sound of the report was different; was the marksman was using a different gun, something smaller perhaps? If so the marksman might not be having to reload and would be catching him.

The trees are thinning out. You are no more than 100 yards behind. You move to your left and line up the end of the path near the building beyond the wood. You reload and kneel on one leg. As you cock the rifle, the man comes into the view. You fire, he falls. It is over... no, damn it, no! He is up again holding his arm but still running. This man has the devil's own luck but you have one more chance.

There had been no more shots and the end of the race was near. Josiah spotted the earth privies and glimpsed the Forester's cottage between the trees. He was just coming out of the wood when a shot clipped his shoulder and he fell. He rolled forward but got back to his feet. There was more blood dripping over his hand. He ran towards the Forester's cottage and put it between himself and the place where the path came out. He paused, took several deep breaths and started to run again, keeping as well as he could, in the safe shadow of the cottage.

You come out at the boundary of the wood. You cannot see him but he could not have gone far enough to evade you. The cottage. He must be behind the cottage. You move to your left there he is running for safety, relying on the building it to protect his back. This will be an easy shot.

You reload, pull the hammer back and aim. For the first time you see his face properly, the policeman Ainscough. He is now well in the open and though you could kill him, retrieving the body and burying it secretly is now dangerous. More policemen will come if his body just lies where you kill him. You uncock the hammer and shoulder the rifle.

Josiah ran as far as he could, expecting every step to be his last, but there were no more shots. Before he joined the track down to Long Clough he indulged in the luxury of looking back. There was no one behind him.

14

HAILSWORTH HALL

Tuesday evening a coachman from Hailsworth Hall brought a smart brougham to take Josiah to the soirée. Its livery was black, the only touches of colour being painted red coach-lining on the wheels, red piping on the external leatherwork and the gold of the polished brass lamps. Even the horse was a fine, black, Welsh Cob.

Inside, the brougham was very comfortable. Padded with leather it was quiet and the seats firm. As they drove along, Josiah relaxed and started to reflect on what the coach said about its owner. It was a quality coach, owned by a man of discernment. Other men of discernment would recognise in it a kindred spirit. That would be enough for its owner. The more he knew of Mr Steven Hailsworth's way of doing things the more he was inclined to respect and trust him.

They joined a main road at the end of the track from Long Clough, and turned north, rounding the end of a gap in the escarpment. After climbing for a few minutes, they turned through two wrought iron gates onto an estate road. This wound on for a mile or so through moor and wood. Eventually the road settled to follow a stream. Then, after a small group of trees, the track pulled upwards and they came out on a dam at the head of an ornamental lake with a fine view of Hailsworth Hall.

The six giant pillars of the Palladian front were astonishing.

Josiah had never expected anything so grand. Everyone he had asked had said that at heart the Hailsworths were farmers whose estate and lands had been founded well before George III but had flourished during the Regency. He had expected a fine building but not such as massive an Italianate house.

After a suitably grand view, reflected in the water of the lake, the road ran round and stopped below the main portico. A footman opened the coach door and Josiah got down. He walked through a short archway into a courtyard, set around a fountain. Mr Hailsworth sat at the top of a double stone staircase at the end of the courtyard. A dazzled Josiah walked up the steps and shook his host's hand.

Mr Hailsworth smiled. 'Do you like the house, Mr Ainscough?'

'Yes Sir.'

'Good. It is rather vainglorious of me but I have to say that I am always pleased when I see it cast its spell on people. It is a beautiful thing.' Josiah nodded and smiled in agreement.

Beyond the doors through which he was ushered was a space that was elegant as well as serviceable. Three wooden pillars divided the entrance hall proper from a sort of open corridor that went off on both sides. A plain wooden floor, brilliantly polished, reflected the light from the silver-gilt candelabra above. Opposite the entrance door was a wood and marble fireplace over which hung a landscape of the estate featuring the hall.

Several guests were already there. An elegantly dressed lady was moving between them, followed by a maid who was carrying fluted glasses on a silver tray. The lady saw Josiah and came over.

'You must be Mr Ainscough. I am Barbara Hailsworth, Steven's wife,' she said. She was younger than her husband by about ten years. Her hair, in a bun under a lace cap tracery, was pewter grey with streaks of pure white. Her dress was gathered at the waist but was not excessively full. The material was shot-silk in pale green and blue.

Josiah held out his hand but Mrs Hailsworth did not take it. Instead, she looked at him waiting to see what he did next. Her lips were smiling but her eyes remained passive. A test, thought Josiah. He hesitated then put his hand on his heart and bowed. Possibly approvingly Mrs Hailsworth nodded in response.

'I am very glad to meet you. Now, can I interest you in a glass of wine?'

After Santiago, he had renewed his commitment to his pledge of abstinence. The wine that night had been no friend to him and he was resolved never to repeat the mistake. As result he had devised a socially polite excuse for the soirée which traded on presenting himself as a traveller, a ruse he had agreed with Mr Hailsworth.

'Thank you, Mrs Hailsworth, but I acquired a liver complaint on my last visit to Italy and I am afraid that, though I am getting better, wine still disagrees with me.'

'I am sorry to hear that, Mr Ainscough. Would you like some of my rosehip cordial with iced mineral water instead?'

'That would be very pleasant, thank you.'

Mrs Hailsworth turned to the maid with the tray. 'Agnes, please could you get some cordial for Mr Ainscough?' The maid curtsied, without even rattling the glasses.

'Yes, ma'am.'

'Now, Mr Ainscough, I will introduce you to some of the other guests.'

She drew Josiah over to a small group of two gentlemen: one was in his early forties the other his late-twenties. With them was a younger lady.

They broke off their conversation as Mrs Hailsworth approached. 'Let me introduce Mr Josiah Ainscough. Josiah, this young lady and gentleman are Miss Aideen Hayes and her brother Phelan. They are from Ireland. Mr Hayes is a painter and he is touring England, gathering enough material for a series of landscape paintings when he returns home. They are staying here while he paints the Derbyshire peaks.' Phelan bowed and Aideen curtsied gracefully.

Phelan had an open face with a sharp chin and nose. A thin moustache offset full lips. The brown eyes were hooded, cautious and observant. A handsome if rather feminine face.

'And this, Mr Ainscough, is my son Abram.'

Abram held out his hand and firmly shook Josiah's. 'I am very pleased to make your acquaintance at last,' he said. 'Since my father met you he has not spoken of anyone else.'

Abram was tall and dark. His features were a conglomerate of those of his mother and his father but though each feature was good in itself he was neither as handsome as his father, nor as reflective as his mother.

'I did not know I had made such an impression on him,' said Josiah trying to understand what this rather fulsome remark of Abram's might mean.

'Well you're a soul mate are you not?' said Abram. Josiah frowned.

'Like you he was a traveller,' said Abram. It seemed to Josiah that Mr Hailsworth might well have over-elaborated their simple ruse.

'I see he has not told you. Come over here.' He led Josiah, Phelan and Aideen over to the side of the entrance hall. There was a portrait of a man in Turkish dress, complete with red turban and pantaloons tucked into short bright red riding boots. The figure was leaning casually against a fine black Arab horse, which pawed the ground. It was Steven Hailsworth, younger, in exotic garb but recognisable.

'This was painted after Father came back from his travels in the Levant around the Dead Sea. He adopted native dress when he was there because, he says, it was more practical in the desert and meant he was less conspicuous in the towns and villages. But I believe that it was just a case of impressing the ladies. You have to admit, Phelan, that he looks very dashing.'

'Indeed, he does,' said Phelan softly. His accent reminded Josiah of Michael O'Carroll's though harsher and sharper than Michael's.

Aideen moved close to Abram. She reached up and stroked his cheek in an astonishingly forward manner.

'Don't worry, Abram,' she said. 'You're the most impressive Hailsworth around.'

With his attention drawn to her, Josiah observed Aideen with more care. In facial features, she looked very like her brother. Her hair was drawn back in a bun except for three or four small curls hanging at her temples framing her face. Her velvet dress was dark claret, which complimented her red hair. Though a much plainer dress than Mrs Hailsworth, it suited Aideen Hayes perfectly. The waist was narrow but the skirt full. The neckline was far lower and the dress more off the shoulder than any Josiah had seen before in polite society. The last touch was the amethyst pendant she wore, which had the effect of drawing any eye to the neckline.

There was a commotion at the door. Steven Hailsworth was being helped across the entrance hall on the arm of a stout man in his sixties. The man was bustling along far too fast for Mr Hailsworth.

'For pity's sake, Caleb, please slow down. I can manage to walk across my own entrance hall safely, but not at this pace!'

Before any harm could befall Mr Hailsworth, Mrs Hailsworth intervened. 'Please forgive him, Caleb,' she said as she released her husband's arm from the grip of Mr Arlon. 'You know how cantankerous Steven can be.'

Deftly, she steered her husband towards the group round the painting. A quick nod to Agnes, who had returned with Josiah's cordial, and a glass of wine was produced for Mr Arlon. As he downed this first glass and reached for another, his wife and daughter Sarah caught him up and joined the group.

Aideen whispered to Abram. 'Oh bad luck for me,' she said.

'With Sarah, here it seems that I will have to do without your dazzling conversation this evening.' Abram scowled at her but her voice had been a little too loud to keep the remark between themselves. Mrs Hailsworth had heard.

'You're right, Aideen,' she said. 'But I am sure that you will find Mr Ainscough interesting company in substitute. I have paired you with him this evening.'

A small bell rang and the butler appeared in a doorway to the left of the fireplace. 'Ladies and gentlemen, dinner is served.'

Mr Hailsworth took Mrs Arlon's arm and symmetrically Mr Arlon took Barbara Hailsworth's. The rest of the guests followed in turn: Abram and Sarah, followed by the unpaired Phelan. Aideen turned to Josiah. 'I think it must be our turn,' she said.

'I hope I am not a disappointment as a dinner companion to you, Miss Hayes.'

'I do not think you will be,' said Aideen, patting his arm comfortingly. 'I believe you have been travelling on the continent recently. I am bound to find that interesting.'

'But I cannot guarantee to be as charming and polished as Mr Abram Hailsworth.'

'Do not worry on that count. Despite what he or his mother may think, Master Abram is not a very entertaining companion. I will hazard a guess that you will be much more interesting.'

15

DUETS

Mr Hailsworth took the head of the table with Barbara on his right, opposite Mrs Arlon. Josiah was at the foot of the table facing Abram. When they were assembled round the dining table with its lavish silver decorations, Mr Hailworth proposed the Royal Toast. Then Josiah held Aideen's chair as she sat down to his left.

Josiah wondered what the kitchens of a great hall like this might offer but he found that in front of him between an impressive array of forks knives and spoons was a had written menu. If this was an informal soirée, what would a grand dinner be like?

The first course offered pea soup or trout in a Dutch sauce, presumably from one of the estate's streams.

'So where did you travel in Europe?' asked Aideen. Josiah looked at her. Her expression was determined and expectant.

'France, Spain and a little in Italy.'

'Which country did you prefer?'

He thought for a moment. 'The food is excellent in France and the countryside, away from the large cities, is varied and pleasant. Plenty of comfortable hedgerows to sleep in if there are no friendly farmers or unlocked barns. Spain is more exotic but if you insist I choose one, then I will choose Italy: the great art of Florence, the majestic Tiber, the mountains and the lakes of the Alps.'

'I am spellbound, Mr Ainscough. I apologies that I dared to expect you to be merely interesting, astonishing would have been more appropriate.'

The next course, pigeon pie with potato croquettes and French beans, was about to come up from the kitchens and the servants were clearing the debris from the soup and the fish.

Aideen continued. 'Would you say it is people or landscape that is most important to the traveller?'

You didn't dodge a question from Aideen Hayes easily, thought Josiah. Every question she asked assumed a succinct and informative answer.

'Landscape is impressive and picturesque but people are always more significant.' Even though she was direct, in some way, he couldn't identify, he found Aideen Hayes an easy person to talk to.

Aideen continued, 'I have often thought that if I was able to travel widely then it is the people I would find the most interesting. But the most important question is not where but why. Why did you decide to travel?'

'Well I could say it was because I wanted to perfect my foreign languages, or it was because I wanted to see what being independent would feel like.' Again she was looking at him with her complete attention. He was convinced that if he lied she would see through him so he told her the truth. 'I travelled because I wanted to find out what sort of man I was.'

'And did you succeed in your quest?

'Yes. Perhaps I found out far too much about myself,' he said quietly and then ridiculously laughed nervously. 'I suppose I felt the call to find a new point of view from which to see my home country and my own life, as well as to see if there were different virtues to understand in the way people live in other countries.'

'Virtue in other countries boy. What arrant nonsense.' It was Arlon, pugnaciously leaning forward. 'I am disgusted that any native-born Englishman would admit to being able to learn anything from the goings on in any heathen country across the channel.'

'It seems the old bull has good hearing,' whispered Aideen. 'So Mr Arlon, you would no doubt apply the same reservation to my native land across the Irish sea.'

'I would make something of an exception Miss in the case of Ireland, after all, your home and mine are joined at the hip, so to speak. Your country is not independent of us. In any case, Ireland is about as far as I would be prepared to travel.'

'Well I suppose I should be grateful for your endorsement of my country's exceptional status,' reposted Phelan. 'But, Mr Arlon, not everything one encounters in foreign countries is valueless. Like Mr Ainscough when I have travelled, I have always hoped to see my own country in a new light and profit by that experience. I have rarely been disappointed.'

'I would endorse that as well, Caleb,' added Mr Hailsworth.

'So did you find this new point of view, Mr Ainscough?' said Arlon in a rude, mocking tone.

'Yes, I think I did.'

Arlon laughed. 'What everywhere!'

'Wherever I went I invariably found out something about myself from getting to know the native people.'

'So you had no regrets about leaving your home and family?' said Mrs Arlon.

'Regrets? Perhaps some. Times when I missed them? Certainly. But there were only one or two occasions when I wished I had never ventured from home.'

'You will pardon me for saying, Mr Ainscough but as a mother, I think that sounds too much like the voice of a wilful, disobedient child,' said Barbara Hailsworth.

'Let Mr Ainscough be, Barbara,' said Mr Hailsworth looking at his wife and stroking her hand. 'I agree with Mr Ainscough. I have been a better man most of my life because of what I learned in the Levant. Barbara, when you met me, I am vain enough to think that you fell in love with me, in some part, because of the romance and mystique that travelling leant me.'

'Poppycock,' snorted Arlon. 'You would have been as much of a man, even if you had never gone travelling. If it was adventure you wanted why didn't you just stay home and take up the challenge of manufacturing. That is what your son has done. That is what will make him a fitting husband for my Sarah more than all Mr Ainscough's experience of parts foreign.'

Abram stirred in his seat, as if declarations about his possible marriage by his potential father-in-law had made him uncomfortable. 'Oaf,' muttered Aideen. 'Why does he assume that if he says jump, Abram will jump.'

'But Sarah and Abram are betrothed are they not?' Josiah whispered.

'As far as I can see that is a bargain not yet confirmed by either party,' replied Aideen under her breath. She smiled at Arlon. 'Mr Arlon, you give the impression that trade and the profit of your mill is all that you prize.'

'If I am honest, there is not much else more important to me.'

'So, if you found a bunch of foreigners in another country making better and cheaper cloth than you, are we to believe you wouldn't try to find out what they were doing, to the benefit of your own production methods?' said Abram.

Arlon paused. 'If it was a new and better form of weaving, which would make my mill more profitable, then I'd adopt it even if I had to learn it from the most primitive of Hottentots or even, God forbid it, the French! But in manners, religion and way of life then I am an Englishman through and through and will not give ground to the views of any other nation.'

'Have any new technologies or developments come to your attention recently?' said Abram.

'You think I would tell you that? If you knew what I know, you would become my rival. You only get access to my business brain when you marry my daughter. But I'll tell you this, sometimes a return to the past and older trades could be more forward looking than any new-fangled idea. Now can we get on with the serious matter of eating our hostess's fine food?'

Food dominated until well into the course following the pigeon, a saddle of hare vigneronne with pomme l'Anglais. There was an alternative, a rabbit curry and rice. The private conversations that had dominated before the general discussion returned, including the details of Josiah, which still seemed to fascinate Aideen.

'Did I hear you say that you slept in hedges when there was no better accommodation?'

'On occasions, but mostly I bought my bed with work of various sorts.'

'Sorts? What sorts?'

'Farm work, acting as a servant, working my passage as a deck hand on a ship. That sort of thing.'

Aideen started to laugh. 'Mr Ainscough you are either the most remarkable person I have ever met or you are the biggest spinner of tales I have ever heard.' She looked up at him and he was aware she'd seen the rather hurt expression in his eyes.

'Oh, Mr Aiscough do not be offended. In Ireland, to be thought of as a great storyteller, is more of a complement than being thought a great traveller.'

The last course was a choice of a port wine jelly with a garnish of cherries, a strawberry and cream vol-au-vent or, as a savoury, crayfish. After that had been dispatched, the ladies withdrew to the library and the men were left at the table. Mr Hailsworth's butler brought in a tray on which was a decanter of brandy, a box of cigars and a pot of coffee.

The gentlemen took their ease, Abram stretched and walked over to the window. Phelan moved towards the coffee pot. Mr Hailsworth poured himself a glass of brandy and lit a cigar, offering a second to Mr Arlon.

'Can I help anyone to coffee?' said Phelan. 'Mr Hailsworth?'

'Thank you my boy but not for me. Coffee keeps me awake at night. I will content myself with the brandy.'

'Mr Arlon?'

'Same with me I'm afraid.'

'Mr Ainscough you surely will not let me down.'

'No, Mr Hayes, you can count on me. One of the things I learned to appreciate in France was coffee.'

Mr Arlon snorted. 'Back to the domination of the foreign, eh, Mr Ainscough?'

'May I be bold, Mr Arlon?' said Josiah as Phelan passed him his coffee, 'Is it foreign ideas of fashion, politics or religion that you dislike or any ideas that are new or unusual even if they come from our own land?'

'I fancy you threw down a small gauntlet just then, Mr Ainscough,' said Arlon. 'Are you asking if I reject new ideas on principle, even if they come from this country?'

'I hope I put the matter politely but yes that was my question, Sir.'

'Did you have something specific in mind?'

'I do not wish to be discourteous to Mr Hailsworth as my host or cause an argument, but I wondered what you would say if you knew where I was staying.' He looked over to Mr Hailsworth.

'Tell him, Josiah, I take responsibility for getting everyone to sit on him if he explodes like a badly made steam engine.'

Arlon looked uncertain. 'I had assumed, Mr Ainscough, you were staying here at the Hall?'

'No but I am staying in the Furness Vale not far away from your mill. I am staying with the Children of Fire. I am gathering information for my writings and having heard of them, I went to see them because of reports of their interesting religious ideas.'

'And you will have discovered that I am no friend of them nor they of me. The fact is they get in my way and that I do not tolerate.'

'And what of their leader?'

'Elijah Bradshawe? He was the sharpest thorn in my side. Not only did he persuade the old fool Tremlet to give his land to his cult, which even now thwarts my plans, but he also roundly attacked me for how I treat the children I pay. Then to add insult to injury, when he attacked me in his sermons, it fermented disruption and bad feeling among my workers.

'It also encourages ne'er-do-well apprentices to run off from my mill, causing me all the expense of paying parish Beadles for finding them or the cost and inconvenience of retrieving them from the Liverpool or Chester magistrates. Over the last four years, I have lost twenty apprentices outright, that never returned.

'I will not be a hypocrite, Mr Ainscough, I am glad he is dead. Without him, the so called Children of Fire will collapse. I will bide my time, offer a low price for their land and then I will be shot of them for good.'

When the cigars were finished the gentlemen rejoined the ladies. Sarah was playing the piano. As soon as he saw this, Arlon had a quiet word with Abram, who seemed to Josiah to look somewhat irked by whatever Arlon had suggested.

When Sarah finished the piece, to polite applause from the company, Abram strolled over and placed some music on the piano stand for her to play. It was a simple folk tune, which Abram joined her in singing. They were reasonable singers: she with a passable soprano, supplemented by his rather more uncertain baritone.

Mr Hailsworth was in conversation with Mr Arlon and Josiah did not relish joining Mrs Hailsworth, so he followed Aideen's lead and sat with her and Phelan.

Aideen began muttering to herself again. 'What a cat's chorus. I hope her father gains satisfaction from this display for I doubt the rest of us will.' Suddenly she looked hard at Josiah.

'Mr Ainscough, do you have singing on the long list of your accomplishments?'

At that moment, Josiah was rather distracted by the wound in his arm. He had been able to dress it himself but as the evening wore on it was beginning to ache as he became tired by the strain of politely dodging the questions. The result was, guilelessly he said, 'Yes.'

'And read music?'

'Be careful, my friend,' whispered Phelan but it was too late. Josiah had already nodded.

'Good,' said Aideen.'

When the duet was done she got up and strolled over to the piano. 'Mr Ainscough and I would like to offer a contribution for your entertainment,' she announced. Josiah gulped. He could sing, it was almost a requirement of being a Methodist, and he did read music but doing both together in company was not something he did outside his immediate family, except when singing hymns in chapel. But the polite applause in anticipation, gave him no choice he had to follow her lead or suffer public embarrassment.

To his relief he found that Aideen had placed something he knew on the piano: an arrangement of the Scots song, "Will ye go, lassie, go?" Aideen started to play and sing the first verse.

Where Sarah Arlon had been competent, Aideen was brilliant. Where Sarah had been a reliable, unadventurous soprano, Aideen was a deep full-blooded metzo: a voice that quivered with emotion.

Josiah joined in the chorus feeling his way into his voice in preparation for the next verse which was traditionally sung by the man, at least in duet.

After a slightly uncertain start the beautiful simplicity of the tune took him and he sang without self-consciousness. By the time the chorus came round again everyone in the room was singing or humming.

In the final verse Josiah and Aideen's voices blended and wove in and out of each other. At the end, the applause was more than polite. Josiah saw Aideen flash a glance at Abram: half challenge, half triumph.

16

SURVEYING THE POSSIBILITIES

It was the following morning and Josiah was sitting in the courtyard at Long Clough writing up his notes on the previous night.

After other guests had offered their musical contributions to the evening, people had drifted into small groups and the conversation, though it ranged over many topics, none were of much use to him. He has mixed feelings about the success of the gambit. Caleb Arlon was no longer an unknown quantity. What Josiah had seen of his character and obsessions, especially his violently hostile opinions of Elijah Bradshawe and the Children of Fire, had convinced Josiah he was capable of murder. A reason for killing Elijah was a different matter.

Arlon might be vicious but he wasn't subtle. He had freely admitted that he looked forward to the collapse of the Children of Fire and that he would then buy their land but, to Josiah, Arlon was an unlikely collector of land for its own sake. The gain he would value would have to be connected with his business. He had already showed he wanted to get his hands on the tongue of land near the woods. Maybe it wasn't the land of the Children of Fire in general but that smaller piece of land in particular he craved?

In contrast Josiah had not been able to observe Abram in anything like the detail he had hoped. In fact, the younger

Hailsworth had been rather adept at avoiding getting into anything other than the lightest of conversation. It was only at the end of the evening that Josiah had been able to create an opportunity to get to know Abram Hailsworth better.

The Arlons had gone and Mrs Hailsworth had ushered a tired Mr Hailsworth to bed. Abram was politely standing with Josiah at the exit from the courtyard, waiting for the coach to take him back to Long Clough.

'Well, Constable, having seen all the "bears in the menagerie" at once you'll be wanting to talk to me.'

'I would hardly term your family and guests bears.'

'What not even Mr Arlon?'

'Perhaps, but bull more than bear might be more appropriate.'

'Well put, Constable,' said Abram with a chuckle.

'But you are right, Sir. I had been thinking I should like to see round your powder mill. When I have done that then my questions for you might be more pertinent.'

'Be my guest. I will not be available tomorrow. How about if we meet the day after?'

As Josiah closed his notebook he heard a voice calling from the front of the house. Then a man with a bundle came into the courtyard.

'Can I help you?' said Josiah.

'You can if you 'appen to be Constable Josiah Ainscough,' he replied. 'This bundle's for 'im and it's 'eavier than it looks.'

'Well you don't need to carry it any further. I am Constable Ainscough.'

'That's good,' said the man. 'It's from the Navigation in Marple. It were left by Sergeant Smith's brother. 'E said you'd know.'

Josiah unwrapped the bundle when he got it into the barn. Inside were some spare clothes, including a jacket, some extra shirts, trousers and a cravat. At least he could go to the mill dressed reasonable smartly. There was also a letter from Michael.

Constable Josiah Ainscough,
c/o The Children of Fire
Long Clough

Dear Josiah,

Well, lad, you might be interested to know, that thanks to your evidence at the inquest, you're the talk of the whole of Stockport. The Advertiser described the murder of Elijah Bradshawe in gory detail and they also ran an editorial which praised Mr Prestbury and the new police force. It said that if the new force was capable of recruiting men of your capability and stature then the town would be well served and a safer place in future.

Privately, Sergeant Smith tells me that Mr Prestbury is spitting feathers about not being able to get you back under his wing, but he is trapped. He cannot recall you without undermining the plaudits he is receiving for his perspicacity, especially since those plaudits are coming from all sides, including the mayor and corporation.

In short, until the Derbyshire force relieves you, you are going to remain where you are no matter what Mr Prestbury wants. More than half the populace of Stockport are hoping you find the perpetrator before the Derbyshires arrive. That would be a very satisfactory one-up for the town

But to business, you sent me a nail to see if I could identify it as specific to a particular trade. Well I can, it's a farrier's nail for fixing horseshoes but there are two things peculiar to your example.

First, it had a very large head that would be proud of the slot round the bottom side of the shoe. Nails like this give the horse more grip so they are fitted to dray horses working in wet or slippery conditions.

Second, they are wrought not cut nails. Most nails

these days are cut from sheets of iron and filed sharp but these have been hammered from hot metal, probably from thin iron bar. That takes skill and a forge. Farriers have to have small forges to make the horseshoes fit when shoeing but the person who made these nails is using much more than a portable forge and it is evident from their quality that he takes pride in his work. I would guess he has regular access to a full blacksmith's works and can make harnesses, the shoes themselves and much more.

Mary and I will pray for you as, we are sure, will the good folk at Tiviot Dale. Take care, lad.

Michael

Josiah could not help but feel pleasure at being prominent in the thoughts of his neighbours in Stockport and rather pleased that his actions were being a source of annoyance to Mr Prestbury.

That the nails were unusual would make them easier to recognise but they sounded, from what Michael had said, to be old fashioned and therefore might merely have been lying about. It might lead to a connection to a place but a connection to a person seemed very unlikely. He tucked Michael's letter away with his notebook.

Until tomorrow, he hadn't anything to do directly connected to the investigation. He ought to be helping on the farm but after a late night and the stress of an unfamiliar social situation he felt rather jaded. A walk seemed in order. Perhaps he should take a look at the boundary between the Children of Fire's land and the Arlon estate, to see whether anything made it clearer to him concerning Mr Arlon's obsession with the exact line of Long Clough's boundary.

He climbed up the track onto the top of Pulpit Rock and looked out across the vale. The clouds were scattered and fast moving. As the brisk wind took them, staircases of light came down to illuminate the valley in golden patches. He found the end of the track they had used to bring the wood to the funeral pyre and walked along it until he got to the deserted sawmill.

Beyond, the wood was just as still and quiet as ever. A cloud passed over the sun and the bright sunlight gave way to sudden shade. The wood seemed more threatening in shadow. He wondered if the marksman was still there, perhaps watching him. It would take time for him to get back his nerve for going far into the wood. He was relieved when the sunshine returned. The wound on his arm seemed to ache in sympathy.

He struck out again, keeping the border of the wood on his right. After about two hundred yards, the short grass gave way to a path marked by horse prints. Then the fringe of the wood cut away to the right and there, completely unexpectedly, with his back to Josiah, was Caleb Arlon. Arlon had another man with him. Josiah carefully backed off and hid behind a tree.

As he watched, the man with Arlon held up a red and white banded pole. After a few minutes of holding it vertical, he put it down and picked up something from the ground. It was a long cloth tape measure, which he started to wind into its case. Beyond them, the ground fell away. As he watched a third man came up the hill carrying a sturdy folding tripod with a theodolite on the top. They were surveying.

'What was the overall gradient, Governor?' said the man who had been holding the pole to the newcomer.

'From here to halfway down about one in fifty. From there down to the river, it's a bit steeper, then there's a steady climb from there to the boundary of the estate.'

'So what does all that claptrap mean Jimmy?' interjected Arlon. 'Can we get a loaded wagon along here to my land without needing a team of four?'

If we prepare a good roadway then it should be possible. In fact it would be quite easy if we use the McAdam surfacing.'

'Better than the packhorse route?' said Arlon.

'Oh very much better than that, Sir,' said Jimmy, 'Better than most turnpikes.'

'And you are certain it is possible to build a road from here all the way through to join the canal north of the Marple aqueduct?'

'Yes Sir, I think so.'

'Then you can pack up now. That is all I wanted to know. I bid you good day.'

From his hiding place, Josiah watched as Arlon mounted his horse, which had been tied to a tree a little way off, and cantered down the hill towards his own land. After he had gone, the men packed up their instruments into a dogcart, which they brought up from lower down the hill. Then they climbed aboard and trotted past him, intent on the direct route to the main road.

So the reason that Arlon coveted the tongue of land was he wished to build a new road to the canal. That made no sense. Arlon owned Mellor Mill which was no more than a mile and a half from the basin at the Marple limekilns. Why go to all the cost of a circuitous new road and, presumably, the expense of a new basin north of Marple?

17

FALLING DOWN

He emerged from the wood and watched the dogcart pass the Forester's cottage and disappear into the distance.

There it was again, the thin column of smoke rising from the chimney of the allegedly abandoned cottage. Was this another passing vagrant lighting a fire? This time he would catch whoever it was red-handed. There might be useful information to be gleaned from such a person about those who had hidden the tools and the paraphernalia of Elijah's murder in the woodpile.

There were no sounds to be heard and no movement as he approached the cottage. If it hadn't been for the smoke nothing would have indicated anything was or could be happening inside. The side of the cottage facing him did not have windows only one simple wooden door. He stopped outside it and listened.

Ringing all the roses,
Smelling all the posies,
Attachop! Attachop!
They'all tumble down.

The rhyme was followed by laughter. Then it started again; strange thing for a bunch of vagrants to be singing. He opened the door and stepped in. There was a group of small children facing two older teenagers who were organising the game. They had just got to the "tumble down" bit and the leaders had started to throw their arms in the air when they saw Josiah. The arms stopped half way and looks of horror came across their faces. The children turned, screamed and scattered to every corner of the small building and into every small crevice or place of shelter.

From the kitchen Brother James emerged. 'Heavens above! What's happened!' Two of the littlest girls threw themselves at his legs and clung on screaming for him to save them from the monster who had just appeared. He looked at Josiah in astonishment.

'Calm down, children,' he said. 'Josiah is a friend, just not one you've met before. One of the children attached to James shot a glance at Josiah and clearly though escape was a more reliable option than getting to know the newcomer. She tore herself away from James' knees and ran at Josiah, dodged him with remarkable agility and shot through the door behind him.

'Help me, Rachael! Mary's on the loose!' shouted James.

Josiah turned in pursuit. The girl was very quick and, once outside ran straight for the wood. She used all her ability to get under low branches and big bushes to evade him. He managed to keep her in sight, but when well inside a dense stand of larches she simply disappeared.

He looked to left, then right and finally turned all the way round in a clueless sort of way until he heard laughter from behind him. He turned to see Mary hugging Rachael.

'It's all right, Mary, Josiah doesn't bite and it's time for some food now. Would you like to help me invite him to dinner? He's usually hungry this time of day just like you.'

Tentatively, while still holding on to Rachael's hand, the girl came over and offered her spare hand to him. They walked back to cottage, Mary happily swinging between him and Rachael.

There was a substantial pot of stew on the fire and James had already started to put spoonsful into an assortment of bowls the children held up to be filled. Josiah stood in line with Mary and got his own spoonful in a spare bowl. Then along with everyone else he found a space to sit on the floor to eat. Rachael came over and sat by him.

'So this is the real reason there were so many children's clothes to hang up to dry the day I came.'

'Yes,' she was obviously not going to give him many hints to help him work out what was really happening.

'Is it one of the main reasons Mr Arlon has lost so many apprentices?'

'Yes.'

'And why there are so many earth privies just inside the wood?'

'Yes.'

'And I suppose they've been here under my nose for days.'

'Yes,' she started to laugh again at his discomfort until tears came into her eyes in amusement. She blew her nose and composed herself. 'But to be serious, I need to ask, will you have to report what you've seen here?'

'As far as I know runaway apprentices are not a police matter. It's the parish Beadles that have to catch them. I suppose it might be my duty to tell Mr Hailsworth?

She started to laugh again. 'Oh you can tell Mr Hailsworth as much as you like. In fact I would encourage it, he's not in much of a position to see for himself how our little joint enterprise works on the ground.'

Josiah would not have said anything about the matter, even if Mr Hailsworth had not been Rachael's accomplice. He was amused at the thought of the sense of irony Steven Hailsworth must enjoy listening to Caleb Arlon rant about the loss of his apprentices, at the same time being a conspirator in one of the main reasons for their loss.

'How does the system work?' he said to Rachael.

'They usually come to us in ones and twos. They hear a

rumour about us and just arrive, usually badly fed and sore footed. Sometimes people who are in the know see them and bring them to us. Sometimes it happens we have a large party like this one, then we house them in the cottage while we try to make arrangements for them.

'Some are running away not because they do not like working in a mill as such, but they have been badly treated in a particular mill. For them we find mill owners that offer better conditions for their apprentices. For instance, the Gregs at Quarry Bank have found places for such children in the past. They issue new indentures and after a while, the authorities give up looking.

'Some need other sorts of employment. Some take to working on the land. Steven Hailsworth is one landowner who has found decent employment for some of them. Mr Hailsworth thinks one of them will be his next head groom because of his natural affinity for horses.

'Another, Frederick, was taken on as an office boy by Abram Hailsworth. He was unusual in that he could already read, write and add up when he came to us. Mr Abram was just setting up the powder mill and needed a reliable office boy. Frederick lodges near Hayfield.

'We had placed most of this group by the time you arrived but when Elijah was killed I realised we had to move them on quickly.

'They will all be gone by this evening. One group are going home to their families in Liverpool, accompanied by a local man who has done that work for us for several years. The others are going north to a settlement of the Moravian Church near Sheffield. They have a community of families where all children are cared for as a single group. A few extra are easy to fit in. We only send orphans to them and they receive a wonderful education as well as practical skills.'

For the rest of the afternoon Josiah played games from his own childhood with them, teaching his favourites marbles and fives to a couple of the boys. The man for the Liverpool group came at about four o'clock and were waved off on the path into the woods to be set well on the road by carts from the Hailsworth estate.

Led by the two older girls who had been doing the nursery rhyme when he arrived, a second group of younger children went off in the direction of Sheffield following the packhorse route.

The fire was damped down and the cottage left with no trace of its visitors. Then Josiah, Rachael and James walked back to Long Clough. Josiah was greatly relieved that, in reality, Rachael new nothing about the woodpile store. He now knew that when he had seen her on the day he had found the weapons she had a secret but it was an honourable one.

18

THE MYSTERIES OF THE ART

The following day Josiah found it an easy walk to the powder mill. Almost as soon as he had got through the gates he was approached by a broad-shouldered man, aged about thirty-five, in a good quality frockcoat and black cravat. He must have been keeping an eye open for Josiah.

'Mr Ainscough? I'm the mill manager, Matthew Bridges. Welcome to Furness Vale Powder Mill.'

'Pleased to meet you, Mr Bridges.'

'Come over to my office and we can talk for a bit before I show you round.'

He led Josiah over to a large wooden building set back from the gates. There was an outer office manned by a clerk and an office boy who must be Frederick. It had a counter with a flap that Bridges lifted.

'Come into my inner sanctum,' he said. Then he led the way through to a second office, with a carpet, a substantial desk, and a comfortable visitor's chair.

'Would you like some tea? I usually have a pot at about this time after I have done my morning rounds.'

'Tea would be excellent,' replied Josiah.

'Please sit down.' Bridges stuck his head out of the door into the outer office. 'Can you make me enough tea for my visitor as well me this morning, lads?' Then he came back to join Josiah.

'Let me start with a question, Mr Ainscough. How much do you know about gunpowder?'

'Not much. Invented by the Chinese; made of saltpetre, sulphur and charcoal. That's all I know.'

'Not many people know that much. If I gave you a mix of those materials in the right proportions and we set fire to them outside, they would burn fiercely with a satisfying flash.'

'They wouldn't explode?'

'No. Loose gunpowder, what we call blackpowder, does not explode but burns very rapidly. If you want a bang you have to pack it into a confined space, such as in the barrel of a gun or in a hole drilled into rock. It's the gases given off in the burning that cause the bang. The faster the powder burns the bigger the bang.'

Josiah warmed to Bridges. He was an expert in his field and like all experts, an enthusiast and evangelist. To Bridges, Josiah was a potential convert to the church of explosives. In Josiah's experience, listening to people like Bridges was never a waste of time. They might leave you lost in the detail but you always came away from conversations with them with new facts or perspectives. He nodded and smiled, all the encouragement an enthusiast like Bridges needed to tell him the accumulated knowledge of a lifetime in half an hour, not to show off, but simply so that by the end of it you too would share his wonder and pleasure in what he knew.

'So the trick is to make powder that burns very fast. There are nine separate processes in making blackpowder. Most are about making powder that burns as quickly and evenly as possible.'

There was a knock on the door and Fredrick brought in a tray with two cups, a milk jug and a china pot. He put the tray carefully on the desk in front of them. He was a lad of about twelve or thirteen with a tousled mop of curly black hair. He reminded Josiah of himself at that age but this boy was working for his living whereas at the same age Josiah was receiving an education. He wondered if there would ever be a world where all children got the sort of education he had been given.

'Thank you,' Bridges waited until the boy, had closed the door behind him. 'Very good lad that. He's an orphan who was recommended to us. He'll have my job one day.'

Bridges poured the tea. After sipping in silence for a moment, Josiah put down his cup and took out his notebook.

'Nine processes all very dangerous.'

'Not really. Blackpowder doesn't burn when wet so by keeping things damp we reduce the possibility of accidents. The dangerous processes are those where the powder is dry and being squeezed in some way inside machinery. There are three processes like that. The least dangerous is the one unique to our main product.'

'Sorry to interrupt you isn't your main product simply blackpowder?'

'Of course you won't have seen the product.' Bridges went over to a safe in the corner and opened it with an impressive key. Then he brought out what looked like a short stick, six inches long and about an inch in diameter wrapped in paper. He gave it to Josiah. Along the paper was printed "The Furness Patent Blasting Charge – Easy as lighting a candle". The wrapping formed a tube open at both ends. One end was solid, charcoal black, with a texture rather like a block of salt. The other end of the candle was similar except that there was a small hole at the centre that disappeared into the core. Josiah weighed in his hand. It was surprisingly heavy, probably a pound to a pound and a half.

'What is this?'

'It's blackpowder. All that has happened to it is that we have taken it, dampened it a bit and compressed it into these rods. We don't know why but because it's solid it burns better than the lose powder it's made from and gives a better bang. It doesn't even need sulphur in the mix?'

'I'm sorry I thought sulphur was essential in gun powder?' interrupted Josiah. Did I hear you correctly?'

'Nothing wrong with you hearing Mr Ainscough. We have no sulphur anywhere on the site. We don't use it.

'But it's in the original Chinese formulae.'

'It is true it is commonly used but it's not essential. The Chinese didn't know, but all the sulphur does is reduce the temperature at which the powder ignites. In powder for muskets and canon sulphur is used because reduces misfiring during battles. We don't make military grade blackpowder. Our product is for use in mines and quarries, so no sulphur.'

And not having to import sulphur from abroad makes the product more economical, thought Josiah. He continued to his next question.

'Was the explosion in March due to one of the dangerous processes?'

'Yes it started in the corning-mill where up to a thousand pounds of dry gunpowder is ground up by toothed metal rollers. With the rotating rollers there's always the possibility of something extraneous, like a small stone or piece of metal getting into the process and causing an explosion.'

'Is that what happened?'

'Almost certainly. There was not much left to examine to be sure but it's the most likely cause.' There was another knock on the door. 'Come in,' shouted Bridges. It was Fredrick again.

'Please, Sir, shall I tidy up the tea things?

'Please do,' said Bridges. 'Mr Ainscough, if you want to know about the explosions in the spring then I think you see where they happened.'

They left the office and walked down a steep hill towards the river. The mill was made up of a series of small buildings spaced 400 to 500 yards apart. Between them ran a small railway track, which linked them together. As they walked wagons, some being pulled uphill by ponies and some going downhill under their own weight passed them. As they walked Bridges pointed out and named the various sheds none of which Josiah could distinguish from another. They were close to the river when they came to a high, solid stonewall.

'Here's the corning mill,' said Bridges, as they walked round the wall revealing a large but insubstantial lean-to. 'The wall we have just come round is a blast wall and as you can see there are two others, one behind the building and another opposite the first. The only place we can't build a blast wall, due to the trackway, is protected by that earth bank over there. The purpose of the bank and walls is to contain flames and debris to the vicinity of the corning mill in the event of an explosion.'

'So why did they not contain the explosion in the spring?'

'Pure bad luck. It was a still day with only a light breeze. That meant that the fireball from the explosion here could form quite slowly without being dispersed. But once it got above the level of the blast walls, what breeze there was pushed it down the hill, to the press house.

'What happens in the press house?'

'That is where most of the water in wet powder is pressed out in machines rather in the way you squeeze juice out of apples for cider. It a tossup if the press house or the corning mill are the most dangerous. A press house went up on its own in one of the Cumbrian powder mills and devastated pretty much the whole of that factory. In our case it was even worse. Two other buildings went up.'

'From the flames?'

'No. I think the blast from the press house brought down the roofs on them and set them off. Then we only had blast walls round the watch house and the corning mill. When the most dangerous processes are running, the men stay in the watch house.'

'So why weren't the men from the corning mill safe in the watch house?'

'Because the explosion occurred very soon after they started the corning mill running. They hadn't time to get to the watch house. The others who died ran from the watch house to try to help their mates. They were caught in the open by the second blast. Two were killed outright. The third, who got to the river to snuff out his burning clothes, initially survived but died two days later.'

'Of burns?' said a horrified Josiah.

'Of a smashed chest. He was badly burned but his blast injuries killed him.'

Frederick came running down the path. 'Sorry to disturb you Mr Bridges, but the cart from Poynton Mines is here. The driver needs you to sign out the consignment before he can take it.'

'Tell him I'll be right there.' Bridges turned to Ainscough. 'I'm sorry I will have to go back and sign it out. The regulations involving transporting blackpowder are strict and it is my responsibility to see that the load is secure before it leaves the mill. You are welcome to have a look round on your own but don't go into any of the sheds unless someone can provide you with the correct safety clothes and shoes.'

'One last question before you go,' said Josiah. 'Could one of the workers in the corning mill have made a mistake that caused the explosion?'

'I think that is what I have to assume, though they were both very reliable lads.'

'Could it have been deliberate?'

Bridges looked very pensive. 'I would not want to think that, but there is no way of distinguishing between an accident and a deliberate attack. All it would have taken was some one to drop a bit metal into the rollers.' At that Bridges went back up the hill towards the office.

Josiah pondered what he had learned. The issue of motivation for such an attack came to his mind. He remembered from his latin classes at school that the great Roman lawyer Cicero had coined the phrase cui bono – to whose benefit? – as a principle that helped find guilt. But who could possibly have benefited from blowing up the powder mill? The powder mill had no commercial rivals for miles around. But if the explosions earlier in the year was the result of a deliberate attack, the corning mill was the target and that suggested some sort of expertise. Though, because of its blast walls, of all the buildings Josiah had seen that morning, it would have been the easiest to recognise, even by someone as ignorant as himself.

He walked over to the corning mill and looked in. It was dim, cool and quiet inside. He called. His voice sounded muffled in the dusty interior. In the half-light all he could make out were the massive shapes of the machinery. He pictured them as sleeping dragons, ready to belch searing fire and death at a moment's notice.

But since there was no one about to show him round, he started to follow Bridges and stroll back to the site office. Beyond the blast wall, outside a nearby building, a gang of men was unloading charcoal. Idly he walked towards them.

One of the men came over to him. He touched his forehead respectfully.

'Can I do anything to 'elp'e, Sir,' he said. 'Mr Bridges said to 'elp 'e if you needed anything.'

'Is there anyone who can show me the corning mill?' Josiah asked.

'Sorry Sir. The grinder's as we calls 'em have gone to the press house. You'll find them down there.'

As he had talked to the man, Josiah had become aware of the revolting smell emanating from the store next to the one for charcoal, a miasma of urine and excrement seeped out of it.

'Thank you for your help,' he said to the man and turned to go. Then in curiosity he looked into the store to see just what was causing such a stench. He was somewhat taken aback that the source were no more than piles of a rather innocuous looking grey powder. He covered his mouth with a handkerchief but it still made him retch.

'What is this awful substance,' he said to the man.

'Saltpetre, Sir.'

'What a sickening smell.'

'Tis that, Sir. But if you think the store smells bad 'e should niff the beds where we meks it. Me sel I wonders 'ow somet made from 'orse shit, piss 'n limestone smells as good as it do.'

'Are the beds by the river by any chance?'

'Aye, beds need water.'

It sounded as if it was the saltpetre beds that had polluted the river and killed the fish. The thing Elijah had condemned Abram Hailsworth for in his last sermon.

The men were still off-loading the charcoal. Over to his left there was another shed half hidden by a bank. He strolled up to the building. It looked unused, its windows opaque with dirt. It was the first locked building he had seen on the site. It was on a spur of the trackway but the rails were polished by use, not rusty as one might expect if this store was deserted.

Then he noted a splash of bright yellow on its step. He bent down, licked the end of his finger and picked up a small sample to taste. The flavour was intensely evocative. As a small boy he had had a bad case of colic and was prescribed a mixture of flowers of sulphur and treacle as a laxative. Even mixed in with the sweet treacle the bitter taste of sulphur was plain. On this step were flowers of sulphur; so much for Mr Bridges protestation that there was no sulphur anywhere on the site.

19

DEFLAGRATION

When Josiah got back to the site office and went in, he was greeted by Fredrick.

'Please Sir, Mr Bridges sends his compliments but he has been further called away and will be some time. He says if you have any more questions for him, would you be kind enough to write them down and he will send you a reply or come to see you at Long Clough. I am also to say that Mr Abram is here and is ready to answer any questions you may have. He is in the inner office. Do you want me to show you in?'

'Please do,' said Josiah.

Abram Hailsworth was sitting at the desk. 'Ah, Mr Ainscough. Has your visit been rewarding?'

'I think so Sir.' Josiah sat down and took out his notebook and pencil. 'I'll take notes if I may but they will be confidential between us.' Abram nodded.

Where to start. During the walk back to the office, two questions had concerned Josiah: why had sulphur been on the step of that storeroom and why did Abram Hailsworth feel the need to make saltpetre on site? Concentrate on the saltpetre first, he thought.

'Mr Bridges has shown me your patent blasting candles, most ingenious if I may say so.'

'Thank you. I like to think they are.'

'When I was walking here, I came across a store of what the men said was saltpetre. Disgusting stuff. I understand you make it on site in beds near the river?'

'True.'

'Was Elijah right? Was it effluent from those beds that killed the fish in the river?'

'A very unfortunate accident which I regret. The beds require water from the river but we built them inside clay banks to prevent any run off getting out of them but after several days of steady rain and they overflowed. We've taken steps to see that it can't happen again.'

'Do all powder mills make their own saltpetre?'

'It used to be made in this country.'

'Used to but not now?'

'No it's normally imported from overseas.'

'Why don't you do the same?'

'I didn't see the need. As Mr Arlon implied the other evening, the old ways can sometimes be just as good.'

Not my experience, thought Josiah. People don't go to the expense and trouble of importing vital commodities they need in their factories if there is a good way of making them near to home. If others import saltpetre it will be for a good reasons like quality or reliability of supply.

'Where abroad would you get it from if you had to?'

'India. It's not the nearest source but it's the most reliable and the East India Company already brings it into Whitehaven for the Cumbrian mills.'

'Isn't this just about cutting cost?'

'I have to admit that there is an element of that. This powder mill is an unusual sort of business in this area and the blasting candle an unusual product.'

Josiah thought that to an outside observer Abram Hailsworth would have looked calm and in control as they talked but he also wondered whether that was really the case. Compared to the witty Abram at diner, this Abram was perhaps a little tense, even defensive.

Why he should he be? This was his domain, his fiefdom. Arlon would have never confessed to being regretful about polluting the river. He would have dismissed Josiah's suggestion of cutting cost as well by being bullish about that being good business.

'Why did you branch out into this line of trade? It seems a long way from the farming background of your family.'

'Simple, I thought it a good business opportunity. There are plenty of mines in the Poynton area and quarries in Derbyshire. It seemed time for a local supplier.'

'With due respect, Mr Hailsworth, that does not really explain why you were motivated to start up such a radically different sort of venture. There must be many business opportunity for someone with your contacts and drive.'

Abram pursed his lips. 'Truth is, rather like you and your travels on the continent, I wanted to be my own man and that quickly. Don't misunderstand me, I love my father dearly and I respect him, even for the things lesser men like Arlon sneer at him for behind his back: his honesty, his taste, his integrity, his kindness. But a day came when I realised that I needed to be free of his guiding hand.' Abram got up and started to pace up and down. 'It was just after I met, how shall I put it, a particular friend of mine.'

'Do I take it this friend is female?'

'You can. I met her near the time that Mr Arlon started to indicate he favoured a marriage between me and Sarah. Her name is Elizabeth. She is a young widow with a small son and she quickly became my mistress and then more than a mistress. We found that our temperaments were well matched and I realised I loved her. We are an unexpected partnership of passion and friendship. But to marry her I need to be financially independent. Then I can stand clear of Arlon's assumptions and can afford to follow the lead my heart gives.

'Please don't think that I'm being ungallant to Sarah. Sarah and I have been friends since we were children and I am very fond of her but I look on her as a sister.'

Before he could stop himself, Josiah chuckled, to which Abram immediately responded. 'Mr Ainscough I can't help but ask what you find amusing in that story?'

'Oh nothing intended to offend I assure you. It's just that if someone had asked me who might be your mistress before this conversation I would have picked someone entirely different.'

Abram laughed and for the first time in the interview relaxed. 'Oh you can't say that and expect me to let it rest there. Come on Josiah, one man to another who would you have named?'

Josiah swallowed hard and blushed. 'Well since you insist, Miss Hayes.'

Abram frowned not in anger but in curiosity. 'What made you think of her?'

'Well I thought she seemed rather attached and familiar with you at the soirée.'

'Yes, she has that sort of manner,' Abram sighed. 'But witty and alluring as Miss Hayes can be, she could never be that sort of particular friend of mine.

'Josiah the powder mill is a risky business but not in manufacturing terms. At the moment the blasters themselves buy the powder they need from approved apothecaries. That is convenient for the mine owners since the men pay for the powder but the quality of the powder varies and that leads to inconsistent results.

'We sell the candles to the mines, not the men. That is more expensive for the mine owners but by using our candles there are fewer failed firings.'

'Can't you just put in a new fuse or repack the gunpowder if it doesn't go off?'

'Not unless you want to risk blowing your own head off. A new blast hole has to be made and a new charge set. Our "candles" offer another advantage, they are quicker and easier to use so you don't need to pay as many experienced blasters. But don't take my word for it, the charges have been perfected with the help of the men at my father's coal mine on our estate. You are welcome to go and talk to them.'

Josiah recalled Charlie Jones on the market, an example of why new sorts of customers need to be convinced that a new product is worth extra cost. Charlie got hold of some Indian Shawls well before they were the fashion. He paid a good price on the basis that the ladies of Stockport would clamour to get them and he'd make enough money to cover the extra cost. He was right but the trade was slow to take off because no one had seen an Indian Shawl before. He nearly went bust before he made a profit.

'But it's not just about who buys them,' Josiah said. 'There's the novelty of being sulphur free. Doesn't that count against the candles?'

'As Mr Bridges will have told you we are stuck with the candles being sulphur free. We can't manufacture them with it.'

Crisis point, thought Josiah. He could believe that a combination of financial risk and the pressures of love could explain Abram's cutting corners on the saltpetre. Josiah's own experience of love had revealed to him how it can drive someone to do things they wouldn't normally think appropriate.

His intuition told him that he should now press Abram about the sulphur but being rude to Mr Hailsworth's son and heir by effectively calling him a liar about the mill's use of sulphur, might mean Josiah would be back in Stockport double quick.

'Thank you, Mr Hailsworth,' he said and he closed his notebook. They both stood and shook hands. But Josiah's heart was not in the gesture. The handshake slowed and they were left holding hands across the desk in a ridiculous posture.

'I believe the blasting candles do contain sulphur,' Josiah said without force or passion. 'I found a store of sulphur this morning. Why are you lying about it?' The words hung in the air of the office.

Abram shook himself free of Josiah's grip. 'You are a guest here and that is a terrible insult. If you were anything other than an officer of the law I would knock you down. Goodbye Mr Ainscough. See yourself out.'

Josiah did not by nature swear but as he retreated in disarray from the powder mill he repeatedly levelled, at himself, words like blast, damn and some even more profane and colourful ones learned from Stockport market. What had possessed him to utter that bald statement accusing Abram Hailsworth of lying about the sulphur? Josiah was so engrossed with these thoughts that, near to the turning to Long Clough, he was almost knocked down by a horse. A voice spoke out of the heavens.

'Really, Mr Ainscough, you must pay more attention to where you are going, if you are to survive to a ripe old age. It beats me how you ever managed to navigate safely all that way across Europe.' He looked up to see Aideen Hayes, mounted side-saddle on a fine grey.

'I am terribly sorry. You are quite right. I should look where I am going,' adding silently and bitterly to himself: In more ways than one.

'Don't worry,' she laughed. 'Help me down and I'll walk with you. I was getting a bit stiff and my mount could do with a rest before I take him back to his stable at the Hall.'

Josiah took the horse's reins and stood at Aideen's stirrups ready to help her down. She put her hands on his shoulders. As he reached up to steady her, she jumped towards him and he caught her round the waist. Embarrassed, he let go and stepped back. She looked at him and laughed. Advancing on him, she stroked his cheek as she had done to Abram before the dinner at the Hall.

'I promise not to eat you alive, Constable.' To his surprise he wasn't shocked either by Aideen's familiarity nor that she knew who he was.

On the first count he remembered what Abram had said about Aideen only a few minutes before and judged it was not an indication of real affection. On the second count, he realised that, deep down, his mind had already accepted the inevitability of someone other than the Hailsworths finding out his identity. After all, he had appeared at the inquest. Whether she expected a reaction he couldn't say. All he did was grin and shrug in response. 'How did you find out?'

'I suspected and once the idea had come into my brain I simply wheedled it out of Abram. The stories you told about your travels in Europe, were they true, or as I said, are you just a very good spinner of tales?'

'All true. Until towards the end of last year I was travelling in Europe but I came home because my guardian was sick. The tales were all real and all mine, as were the motives for travelling.'

'Good. I enjoyed them and hope to hear more.'

'Where is your brother?'

'Out painting a picture of a rock somewhere,' she waved a dismissive arm at the countryside in general. 'He set off early this morning saying he was going to something called the Staffordshire Roaches. I suppose I should be getting back. He could be returning quite soon.'

She offered her hand to Josiah who shook it gently. 'I hope we run into each other again soon,' she said. 'Can you hold my horse's head steady while I remount?'

'Of course.' Josiah held the bridle and reins, wondering how, politely, he was supposed to help Aideen to get back into her saddle. He need not have worried she swung herself up without difficulty or hesitation. He gave her back the reins.

'Thank you,' she said. 'Even though I have deciphered your official disguise, may I call you Josiah? I think we make good enough friends to allow ourselves that liberty?'

'If you think that would be appropriate, Miss,' Josiah replied.

'Then I shall call you Josiah and you must call me Aideen. Our relationship must always be one of equals.'

She turned the horse's head and trotted off back towards the main road. Josiah watched her go. Then he continued walking towards Long Clough, disconcertingly unable to get out of his head how it had felt to have Aideen Hayes in his arms.

20

FIRELIGHT AND MEMORIES

After Josiah had returned to Long Clough he went to help in the fields. All the time, he was expecting to see a coach appear, rapidly followed by his dismissal from the case by Mr Hailsworth. But nothing happened.

By evening he was feeling a bit more optimistic. The labour had been a tonic to his spirit. As he had worked his mind had turned to the loose ends of the investigation, particularly the scars and tattoo he had found on Elijah's body. Even if he was about to be discharged he would like to find out about them for his own satisfaction and only Rachael would be able to shed any light on them.

As usual after the evening meal he found her in the kitchen tidying up. As they worked Rachael talked about her day. She had been doing some sewing and in the afternoon had gone to see neighbours who had an ailing child. Happily, the child was the first person to answer the door when she knocked. Clearly well, and renewed in energy and naughtiness, he had raced round the garden as Rachael and the wife of the house caught up on family news.

'It was a very good time,' she said to Josiah. 'I found that I forgot about Elijah for a little. That was good. I suppose that is the first sign of healing.' She finished wiping the table. 'Well I will bid you goodnight.' She turned to go but he stopped her.

'Rachael I need to talk to you about Elijah. We can do it some other time if you don't feel strong enough now but there are some things I found when I examined him before the funeral that puzzle me. I wondered if you might be able to help me?'

She sighed. 'Would this help in catching his killers?'

'There was much about how he died that was very brutal. It has made me wonder if he was killed in anger, even revenge.'

'Mr Arlon hated Elijah for attacking the way he treated the children in his mill.'

'I have talked to Mr Arlon. He considered Elijah his enemy but I do not think he was angry enough to have killed Elijah in such a brutal way.'

'What about Abram Hailsworth? He must have seen Elijah as an obstacle to his pursuit of a fortune from that horrible business in explosions.'

'Abram Hailsworth might have had some suspicion that Elijah might have made more trouble for the mill when it reopened but kill him, unlikely.'

Rachael sat down next to the fire and put her hands in her lap. Superficially, she looked relaxed and attentive but below the surface Josiah detected the tension his request had aroused.

'Ask me whatever you want. I will do my best to answer.'

Josiah sat opposite her. The sun was going down and the light was fading from the kitchen windows. Where they sat the firelight illuminated her face and gave her hair a flattering pink tinge.

'Thank you. I will be as quick as I can. I may have asked this before, did Elijah have any enemies in his past? You were with him a long time. You are the only person who might know. '

She looked wistful. 'Yes I was only eight or so when I met him. A long time ago as you say. Many happy times.'

'You said, when you gave your eulogy, that he had found you living on the streets in Liverpool?'

'Yes. I never knew my father, and my mother drank herself

to death. I lived with a woman who said she was my Aunty but I'm sure she wasn't. She was very cruel. She sent me and some other children out to beg for her.' Her voice was expressionless as if she was talking about someone else not herself.

'Is that how you got to know Elijah, while you were begging on the streets?'

'No. Would that it had been,' a desperate, haunted look passed over her face. She paused. 'Organised begging wasn't the only business Aunty ran,' again the haunted look, before the expressionlessness returned. 'I may as well tell you the truth. In her house she sold oblivion by the smoke of a pipe.' Josiah didn't immediately understand what she meant and she read it in his face.

'She was an opium queen. Lots of men and some women came to her for that sort of relief. Elijah was one.'

Josiah was shocked. He found it hard to believe that the upright Elijah Bradshawe he had briefly known could be brought so low. 'How did he get in such a state?'

'I do not know. He was always a physically strong man and he was in much demand on the docks because of that strength, loading or unloading the ships. But in all other ways he was a wreck. When he had money he spent it on the drink and the smoke. Every so often he'd spend a day or a night in Aunty's house instead of the public houses. When the money ran out he'd get up, sober up and go back to work until he had enough money for another binge. But unless he was entirely drunk or drugged he was kind to me.'

'So how on earth did he come to look after you?'

Rachael squeezed her right hand with her left. Josiah noticed that the skin whitened under the force of her nails. She looked up at him and then quickly down.

'I don't remember all the details. If I did not bring Aunty back what she expected from my day's work, she would fly into a rage. If she had been drinking, she would beat me with a broom stave, shouting that I had stolen the money.' Josiah flinched.

'One day Elijah was recovering from the smoke and getting ready to go back to work when she started on me. She went to hit me and he pulled the stick out of her hands and broke it in two.

'He told her that if he caught her beating me again he'd take me away from her even if he had to knock her down to do it.'

'How did she react?'

'She laughed. Surprising really, as a threat like that from a man the size of Elijah was no laughing matter. She started screaming that I was not worth the food she gave me. If I were going to be so much trouble, he could have me for a sovereign and she'd be done with the trouble.'

'What did he do?'

'He didn't say a word, he just put his hands down the front of his filthy trousers and pulled out a small bag rather like a purse on a sting. He emptied it onto the kitchen table. There was a sovereign, two shillings and a penny. It must have been his emergency supply of money, hidden down a leg of his trousers so that it was less likely to be stolen if he passed out when drunk. He gave her the sovereign and when he asked for my clothes she charged him the shilling for them. He got the clothes out of the cupboard where they were kept, took me by the hand and out we went into the night.'

Rachael got up and moved over to the dresser. She poured two beakers of water from a jug left there in case anyone wanted water in the night. She gave one to Josiah and sat down with hers.

'How did you manage to live?'

'The first few days I begged while Elijah worked on the docks. After a week we had enough money to rent a dingy, dirty cellar in a backhouse near the river. For me it was heaven, there were no more beatings and Elijah refused to let me beg anymore.

'But looking after me changed him. He wasn't the leader of

the Children of Fire then. He was sad and downtrodden. He never really told me properly but he had come to Liverpool from Ireland. I think he had an Irish accent then. I used to ask him questions about what it was like in Ireland but he would just go quiet. If I asked too many questions it provoked him to go on a binge.'

'It doesn't sound as though you were doing anything more than surviving.'

'You're right, that was what it was like,' then she smiled slightly, 'but two things changed him and threw us in the path of a good providence.' She sipped the water.

'When Elijah drank he was always careful to make sure I was safe before he got drunk. In one house where we lodged, the landlady lived on the ground floor above us. She looked after me when he was away or working at night. She taught me my letters and read to me from the Bible. She was a churchgoer and she persuaded Elijah to let me go to church with her. Gradually he took to coming along as well if he wasn't working. Slowly he became less unhappy.'

'What was the other thing that changed him?'

She looked at Josiah, tears in her eyes. 'That was very tragic and yet hope came from it.' She sipped at the water again.

'There was an outbreak of smallpox which the old lady caught. Elijah once had the disease so he nursed her but she did not have the strength to fight the sickness and died. Elijah grieved for her as if she had been his own mother. After the church folk and us had buried her, I thought he would despair again but he didn't. He talked to me very seriously and said he thought I would be less likely to catch a disease if we left the city and tried to live in the country. I remember he said that he had been brought up on a farm. So that's what we did.

'The more he worked in the fields, in the clean air, under the sky, the healthier he looked and the happier he felt. He stopped drinking. We followed the cycle of the year through spring, summer and autumn: sowing, reaping, harvest. In winter we'd find a room in a cottage to rent while Elijah did some ditch digging if we hadn't got enough money saved to get us through. Then we came here and he met Farmer Tremlet. It was Farmer Tremlet and Long Clough which properly saved him.'

She got up again and started to pace up and down.

'Tremlet was a good man. He had never married and had no children. The farm was prosperous and he had a workforce of twenty. They were his family. He provided them with work and food to care for their bodies. He provided schooling for their children to feed the minds of the next generations. Last, but to him the most important, he built the chapel, the bethel he called it, so that they would have somewhere to praise God.

'In Elijah he found a soul mate, and he loved him like the son he never had. Elijah reciprocated and loved Tremlet like a father. They would talk for hours. They dreamed of a holy community, free from the greed and filth of the cities. Under Farmer Tremlet's care Elijah and I were baptised. We went down into the river Goyt hand in hand. That day I took Elijah,' she swallowed hard, 'as my father.'

She stopped pacing, sat down and started to cry softly. Then she took another sip of the water. Josiah leaned forward and took her free hand in his to caress it.

'Do you want to stop?'

'No just pass me a cloth. These are tears of joy as well as tears of grief. I want to remember that day.' He passed her the cloth and she wiped her face.

'Farmer Tremlet died soon after we were baptised. When the will was read we were amazed: he left us the farm. There was a condition in his will. Elijah could only inherit after giving a solemn undertaking to create the community he and Tremlet had talked about so often. That was the Children of Fire and here we are. That is all I know. I never found out what his life was really like before he came to Liverpool.'

She sat up straight and took a deep breath. 'Now you had some questions about things you found on Elijah's body.'

Josiah tried to steady his own nerves and concentrate on the facts. His desire to hold and comfort her was near overwhelming but duty was duty.

'Yes. In fact, you and the other women may have noticed them. There were many old scars over his chest. With a life of manual labour, that was not surprising, but there were two that suggested he might have been wounded in battle. Did he ever say that he had served in an army?'

'You mean the sword cut on the left shoulder and the scar from a musket ball above his right hip. Yes, we noticed them. I knew they were there already. It is difficult for any child to get through life without seeing their father without his shirt. They too were things I asked about when little but he never told me anything about them.'

'What about the tattoo?'

'What tattoo?'

'It was on the underside of his right arm very near the armpit.'

'No I didn't see that. I remember someone who was washing his arms remarked that there was a strange mark on one of them but I didn't think much about it. It must have been very faint.'

'Yes it was.'

'What was it like?'

Josiah handed her his notebook open at the sketch he had made. Rachael looked at it with interest. Then she handed the notebook back. 'I don't recognise it at all.'

Josiah shut the notebook. 'Thank you, that is all I have to ask. I hope I have not upset you too much. I wouldn't do that for the world as I think you know.'

Rather abruptly, he stood up to go, fearful his emotions would break and he would embarrass both of them. She remained sitting and showed no sign of stirring. He was nearly through the door when she called him back. He turned to look at her. She had stood up and looked very determined.

'I have not told you all the truth Josiah.' Outside it was now completely dark and the firelight complemented her beauty even more.

'I told you, Aunty organised begging and ran an opium den. That was true but, occasionally, she offered another service for some clients. A business in which she forced me to participate.'

Josiah's mouth went dry and his heart began to pound.

'What I am going to tell you now only one other living person knows. I am telling you because I return the feelings I think you have for me but if those feelings are to grow then you must know the whole truth so that it cannot come between us in the future.

'Aunty was a dame de maison. In her house she not only sold oblivion in the smoke but oblivion of the flesh as well. She sold young women.' Josiah started to move towards her. She held up her right hand.

'Stop! You should know Josiah that she sold me to her clients as young as I was.' Josiah felt tears on his own cheeks. 'One of those clients was Elijah. She put me in his bed when he was in opium fuddled dreams.'

He stepped forward and embraced her holding her close to him to comfort and protect her but she screamed and pushed him away.

'No, Josiah, I cannot bear to be close to any man, not even you... not yet. I may never be able to. That is the real horror of all this. It seems the sins of this child are being visited on her without waiting for the next or any other generation.'

21

RESERVE CRU

He was unclear how he had left the kitchen. He had a vague impression of having stumbled out leaving Rachael standing by the fire: immobile, passive, bereft. In cowardice he had run away, being unable to comfort her or simply remain. He went back to the barn and tried to hide in the darkness, vainly hoping for some sort of rest. But he could neither sleep nor think. He was trapped by compassion, love and guilt.

Pictures wracked him of Rachael with Elijah at the first meal he had attended at Long Clough, as well as fevered nightmare images of Rachael as a young girl in a dirty, degrading bed. Nothing made any sense to him.

In the end, he got up and went out into the clear night where a full moon hung on the horizon. An owl hooted from a tree and was answered by another near the chapel. The scream of a vixen ripped at the stillness. She called again and then a third time. Was she calling for her mate or lost cubs? It was an unearthly sound, a soul in torment, mirroring his own.

He wandered about the fields until the moon set. Then, exhausted, near the paddock, he found a comfortable tree to lean against. The next thing he remembered he was surrounded by the grey light of dawn and being gently shaken awake. It was Rachael. She put down a tray of bread, butter and water next to him.

'I saw you from the kitchen door,' she said. 'You need to eat no matter what happens.' Then she left him.

He ate the food and walked back to the farm, leaving the tray by the wash house rather than risk seeing her by going inside. Then he went to the barn and came back with soap, towel and shaving gear. He stripped off his shirt and pumped cold water onto himself until he was fully awake. Then he rubbed the wet soap hard into his skin until it tingled; finally he shaved.

On returning to the barn he dressed in his uniform. There would be no more evading his position and authority, no more hiding under the camouflage of ordinary clothes. He would find Elijah's murderers, no matter who they were. He would be a pure and implacable avenging angel. He would do his duty.

He had recognised one thing during the night: the abuse of Rachael provided a motive for murder. She might not be directly involved in the crime but the abuse could still have given someone in love with her reason enough. She had said one other person knew. If that person was Peter he was hot-headed enough to kill in some distorted demonstration of loyalty to her. The implication of Elijah in the abuse of Rachael would account for the savagery of the murder and even the wording of the placard that had been hung around Elijah's neck, BLASPHEMER.

Peter would have to be confronted but that might be dangerous and before Josiah attempted it, careful preparation would be required. In the meantime, it would be best for him to be away from the community. A visit to Mr Hailsworth's coalmine would take care of that for a day.

He walked to Hailsworth Hall across country. Whilst a carriage had to go round by the road, on foot Josiah could reduce the distance from Long Clough by following the track from the Forester's cottage to the main road. It was only a short, if steep walk from there.

Josiah rang the bell at the servant's entrance and waited. If he applied for an introductory note for permission to visit the mine, he could avoid seeing Mr Hailsworth and therefore running the gauntlet of the dismissal he was expecting because of his confrontation with Abram.

The butler opened the door. He saw Josiah's uniform but betrayed no surprise. 'Mr Ainscough, a pleasure to see you, Sir. Mr Hailsworth told me that if you call you are to be admitted at all times. This way. I will take you up to the library. Mr and Mrs Hailsworth are taking coffee there as is their custom in the morning.' They climbed the servants stairs. 'My appologies for the dust and clutter,' the butler said. 'It would probably better when you call again to use the main entrance. The footman on that level will let you in.'

'I don't really need to disturb Mr Hailsworth. If you could give him a message then I'm sure he can just give me a note.'

'Mr Hailsworth was quite explicit, Sir. If you came you were to be shown up to him. He was very firm in his instruction.' It was clear to Josiah that no matter how desperately he tried he was not going to be able to avoid encountering Mr Hailsworth.

'Shall I take your hat?' asked the butler. Josiah handed it to the butler and followed up the stairs him with the air of a man going to his execution.

The library was warm and quiet, its acoustics tempered by its marvellous collection of books. In one corner, there was a circular alcove with bench seats of plush crimson whose windows gave a beautiful view across the lake. On the walls were two plaster reliefs, one clearly Greek and the other most likely Roman.

In this comfortable space sat Mr and Mrs Hailsworth; a small table held a Turkish coffee pot which simmered over a brass spirit burner. Above the table hung a filigree Turkish lamp. An ormolu clock on a bracket just to the right of the alcove chimed ten, as if conscious of its duty to tell accurate time with as much reserve and style as possible.

'Josiah, a pleasant surprise,' said Mr Hailsworth. Josiah was surprised by the friendliness of the greeting. Mr Hailsworth's voice gave no indication of an imminent reprimand. Perhaps Abram had not told him of their argument?

'Pardon me if I don't get up. Legs particularly painful this morning. Do I take it that your uniform indicates a more formal approach to your investigations?'

'In short, yes Sir. I thought it was proper.'

'Quite right, Josiah. Quite right.'

Barbara Hailsworth looked up from her sewing and stiffened but she nodded politely enough to Josiah. 'Mr Ainscough.'

'Mrs Hailsworth,' he said as he bowed, remembering not to repeat his mistake at the dinner.

'No need to bow, Constable. You're now clearly no more than a tradesman.' Mr Hailsworth shot his wife a hard glance.

'Steady on, Barbara. Whether Mr Ainscough is in uniform or not makes no difference. He has been our guest.'

'I would say that it makes a very material difference,' she said through tight lips. 'Many of our friends would be horrified to see you treat this,' she searched for an appropriately cutting word, 'mere servant with such cordiality.'

Josiah was becoming more and more embarrassed at the interchange between the Hailsworths. He had extended his respect for Mr Hailsworth to Mrs Hailsworth even though she was clearly not well disposed to him. The fact was he was unused to seeing married couples disagree in this way and it troubled him.

The Cooksleys were a well-matched couple and their mutual love and respect meant that he could hardly remember any cross words between them, except in the throes of their vigorous intellectual debates.

Mr Hailsworth reached over and held his wife's hand. He spoke softly. 'I understand how disturbed you are by all this, my dear. How close it has all come to the family and how you wish it could be gone; I feel the same. But you were no more than a farmer's daughter before we married and I have always been proud to be known as a farmer as was your father. We may have a grand house because our ancestors prospered but that is our good fortune not proof of our moral superiority. Mr Ainscough's chosen profession is a worthy one and we should honour his choice with our friendship regardless of how hard the world laughs at our folly.' He turned to the butler. 'James, can you arrange some more cups for us?'

'Yes Sir,' James replied, and left.

'Well, Josiah, you did well on the coffee the other night so I am curious to know how you do with my reserve cru, so to speak.' He bent his head forward and whispered behind his hand. 'There's a secret ingredient,' then he relaxed. 'But sit down first. Unless your sense of smell is supernaturally sensitive, you have not come to drink my coffee. I would warrant you'll either want advice or be seeking permission for something you intend to do. Am I correct?'

Josiah was sitting facing the Hailsworths, his back to the library proper. 'Correct as ever, Mr Hailsworth. It is the latter. I need to speak with the foreman powder-man at your mine.'

As he spoke he became conscious that the butler's footsteps had been replaced by a sound not unlike quiet waves on shingle: a lady's dress dragging slightly on carpet. Then there was a smell of rose water and a gentle hand was placed on his shoulder.

'You were saying, Constable?' It was Aideen. Josiah looked round, straight into the steady gaze of dark eyes framed by red hair, which was brushed out and hung down her shoulders as if she were a young girl, not the fashionable beauty who had sat next to him at dinner. Josiah rose. Aideen moved past him and sat between him and Mrs Hailsworth.

'Please sit down again, Constable. I did not intend to disturb you.'

'Merriman? Why do you want to speak to him?' said Mr Hailsworth.

'I am simply following up on the visit I had to the powder mill and what Abram told me about the new type of blasting cartridge he is making. He said that they were being tested at your mine and I was welcome to ask there about them. I thought it was only polite to ask your permission before visiting.'

Mrs Hailsworth smiled. 'It is a short walk. Steven, give him a note of introduction and the constable will be able to get on his way,' she said.

Agnes, the maid who had served on the night of the dinner, came in and set two fresh coffee cups and replenished the cream jug on the table.

'I think I can do better than that, Barbara. I could do with visiting myself.'

'Are you sure, Steven? You have been very stiff this morning.'

'Perhaps a drive will relieve that a bit,' said Mr Hailsworth. 'Agnes, ask them to send round the coach for Mr Ainscough and me. Not the landau mind, we'll be comfortable enough in the brougham.'

'Very good, Sir.' She curtsied and left. Aideen got up and poured two cups, one of which she passed to Josiah.

The coffee was similar to what he had drunk at the dinner party but it was deeper and more bitter. Cardamom was present but there was something else, something not as usual in Turkish coffee. Josiah inhaled the steam and then sipped. 'Mr Hailsworth, I would say that the secret ingredient in your reserve cru is liquorice.'

'Very close, Constable, but not quite right. Have you ever come across anise? The fresh beans are sent to me from an old friend in Constantinople and have seeds of both cardamon and anise added. Roasting is done in the kitchens here and they are ground only when the coffee is to be made.

'Well it is excellent, at least to my taste.'

Mr Hailsworth sipped from his cup. 'You are right, Josiah. The older I get the more I appreciate the small things of life, like excellent coffee. But you were saying you wanted to go to the mine.'

'Yes Sir.'

'So does this mean you have got a new lead, Constable?' asked Aideen.

'No not really. It is more about making sure I understand fully the nature of Mr Abram's business.'

'You are commendably thorough, Mr Ainscough,' Aideen said. Josiah thought he could detect in her voice a slight sense of amusement at his expense.

Agnes came back into the room. 'Pardon Sir but your carriage is on its way round. It will take a few minutes and I was asked to say there is no need to rush. '

'Good, I shall have time for another coffee. Thank you Agnes.' Mr Hailsworth turned to Josiah. 'Can I interest you in another, Josiah?'

'It would be rude of me to refuse.'

They chatted on. The farm was prospering, the game had been good this year, the lambs were growing and the harvest of both wool and mutton was set fair. Finally, the coffee was drunk and Agnes returned to announce that the carriage was ready.

'If you can offer me your arm, Constable, we can be on our way?'

'My pleasure, Mr Hailsworth.' Josiah stood and held out a hand. With the aid of his stick, the older man eased forward on his seat before Josiah pulled him up gently and steadily. Then he took Mr Hailsworth's free arm.

'Let me help,' offered Aideen. She got up and went round to Mr Hailsworth's other side.

'Thank you, my dear. If you could take my arm I'm sure Josiah will be able to handle my cane as well as stabilising me. I get set in one position sitting down but once I get going I am usually all right. We will go down the back stairs to the courtyard, it is quicker and easier.'

When they got down the stairs the coachman took over helping Mr Hailsworth into the carriage. Aideen waited with Josiah until Mr Hailsworth was settled.

'This is opportune, Mr Ainscough. I had resolved to ask you, the next time I saw you, if you ride?'

'A little,' said a puzzled Josiah.

'You see that I am again deserted by Phelan. He is away for several days on a trip to Matlock. I wondered if you would care to ride out with me one day this week. You could regale me again with some more of your excellent stories.'

Josiah hesitated. An extra day sheltered from the grief of Long Clough would be welcome. To be in the company of one as easy and charming as Aideen Hayes would be a double relief. What would be the harm?

'Yes I would like that. Could I suggest tomorrow or the day after?'

'Tomorrow then, if the weather is good. I will bring a horse for you at nine.'

'I will look forward to it,' he said. As he pulled himself up into the carriage for the first time that morning his thoughts turned from Rachael or the investigation to the prospect of a fine day on the high hills away from all his troubles.

22

MERRIMAN

It only took the first few hundred yards of the coach journey, for Josiah's feeling of relative peace, to be blown away by a remark from Mr Hailsworth.

'Have you concluded anything about Abram being in danger?'

Was this the moment, Josiah wondered? Was this it? Was Mr Hailsworth about to broach the question of the sulphur and then make clear his disgust at Josiah's suggestion that Mr Hailsworth son could be lying. Was that his main reason in taking this a trip to the mine, of which his wife so clearly disapproved?

Josiah tried to detect anything in Mr Hailsworth manner that might guide him but there was nothing he could discern. There was tension but Mr Hailsworth spoke with all the assumed casualness of a man trying to make a topic of vital interest seem of little importance. The tension concerned his worries for Abram.

'Not entirely, Sir.'

'Do I take it that you think he is holding something back?'

'Not exactly,' Josiah stuttered, 'More that the conversation left some loose ends,' he steeled himself for the blow.

'If it helps, I know about Elizabeth.'

'Pardon?'

'Elizabeth, Abram's mistress.' A smile of satisfaction came across Mr Hailsworth's face. 'Oh Josiah don't tell me you don't know about his mistress.' Josiah was taken aback. This was not what he was expecting and it surprised him.

'... And your attitude is, Sir?'

'In general, I approve of her. She is sensible and intelligent. She is an experienced woman of the world. In many respects she is exactly what he needs. For all the veneer of sophistication and self-assurance, Abram is not as mature as he might appear. She will make him a good wife.'

'Thank you for being so frank, Sir.' Josiah swallowed and tried as best he could to appear to be in control of his feelings but failed. Seeing his discomfort Mr Hailsworth laughed. 'I had got used for you to be well ahead of me in this investigation, I am pleased to be one up on you, my boy.'

'But...'

'You did not think I would approve of Elizabeth, did you?'

'No.'

'Josiah don't look so shocked.' Mr Hailsworth sighed. 'Methodism is a fine institution but it can be a very harsh task master when it comes to moral weakness. Shall I shock you further?' Josiah could not reply.

'My reserve cru that comes from Constantinople. I said it is supplied by a friend. Not quite true. It is supplied by my other son.'

'Your son?'

'Yes my illegitimate, much-loved, firstborn. I was a young man when I went to the Levant, I had a young man's appetites. I fell in love with an Arab lady in Jerusalem and Ishmael, as we named him, was the result. I was fortunate to be able to see that he and his mother were well proved for in material things and to pay a suitable debt of honour to her family. I helped set up his business in Constantinople and he prospers. What I could not provide for him was myself, though I wished most sincerely to do just that. My duty lay here. As Elijah Bradshawe would have said I have tried to make amends for my sin, though I regret that I will never be able to hold my eastern grandchildren in my arms. If someone knowing this were to ask what even on my travels most influenced my character, then it was Ishmael's birth. It prevented me from becoming a selfish wastrel.'

Finally, Josiah found his voice. 'Does your wife know?'

'I never confessed to her but it would not surprise me if she has guessed.'

The carriage was rolling over rougher ground now. Mr Hailsworth looked out of the window. 'Not far, now,' he said.

The carriage slowed and pulled up. A man, wearing a rather dirty frock coat, was making his way hurriedly towards them. He opened the door of the brougham.

'To what do I owe the pleasure, Sir?' he said in a cautious tone.

'Don't worry, Johnstone, it is just a social call. Let me introduce Constable Ainscough of the Stockport Police Force. He is assisting the Derbyshire authorities in investigating the death of Elijah Bradshawe. He wants to talk to Merriman about the new cartridges.' Josiah shook hands with Johnstone.

'Constable, I'll leave you in Mr Johnstone's capable hands. Since I am here, Johnstone, I will have a look round but I would be obliged, if I have to go before Mr Ainscough has finished, if you could arrange to get him back to either the Hall or Long Clough where he is staying.'

The mine looked more like a quarry than anything Josiah had seen before. There was a flat area with a scattering of buildings. This was criss-crossed by a trackway very similar to the one in the powder mill. At places at the ends of tracks there were sidings on raised frameworks where coal was emptied from wagons onto conical piles.

'Ever been to a mine before?' said Johnstone.

'No,' replied Josiah.

'In this mine, coal seams come to the surface. They can be followed using tunnels, dug from ground level, called drifts. We were surveying for a new limestone quarry a few years ago when we came across a shallow seam of coal in the rock face over there,' Johnstone pointed to a cliff, towards which several trackways ran. 'We dug out a test tunnel and followed it for about twenty yards before it opened out to a height of fifteen feet or so. We still haven't got to the end of it though the main drift now goes in near enough half a mile.'

They reached the tunnel entrance. After a couple of yards, there was a small room cut into the wall. Inside was a rack of brass lamps, a row of numbered disks on strings and a large lighted candle.

'Take a disk, Constable, and a lamp,' said Johnstone, who did the same himself. 'Anyone who needs to know how many people are in the mine just counts the numbers of missing disks. Your Davey lamp is all the light you'll have while you're in there. It is probably a good idea to leave your hat here as well; the roof can be low.'

They lit their lamps from the candle and turned down the main tunnel. It sloped slowly but its ceiling got lower the deeper they went. Soon it was no more than a foot or so above Josiah's head. To complete his discomfort, the floor was wet and slippery.

A few yards further and the daylight faded completely. Josiah became dependant on his lamp. As his eyes adjusted, he could make out details of the stout wooden props to the roof; even shadows began to appear. He followed, the light from Johnstone's lamp, which extended back to him like a lifeline. The air started to taste stale. It was unexpectedly quite, except for occasional muffled sounds which seemed strangely distant. Then without warning Johnstone turned right and ducked. Josiah followed.

The quiet was broken as the ringing of hammers on metal. Two men were chiselling holes into a vertical stone face. A third was holding a lamp and examining their work.

'Got a visitor for you, Merriman,' called Johnstone above the din.

'What sort of madman visits down 'ere?'

'A policeman brought by the Master. He's interested in how well the new cartridges work.'

'Then if 'e 'angs on for a few minutes I'll give 'im a practical demonstration. That'll do, lads.' The hammering stopped. 'You two clear out while I shows this visitor 'ow we set the charges. You can check the drift's clear for me as yo' go.'

'I'll go with your lads, Merriman,' said Johnstone. 'Just make sure the constable gets back to the surface in one piece.'

Merriman held out a dirty hand. 'Solomon Merriman a' yo'r service.'

'Josiah Ainscough, Mr Merrimam. Pleased to meet you.'

'Right, pleasantries over. Come up here, lad. You'll get a better view.' Josiah stumbled forward. There was a mysterious regular pattern of holes cut into the rock face. Very near the ceiling was an arc of seven. Below that a second arc of six and then one very deep one right in the middle of the face.

'If you look down you'll see there's been a slot cut into the face at floor level; all this rock is hanging from the ceiling. The 'ole at the centre we call the cut shot, it takes double the charge of the others and it's fired first. Next are the easers,' he pointed to the arc of six, 'last the trimmers next to the ceiling.'

'So the main part of the rock comes out first, then the bit above it and then the very last so there's a new roof,' said Josiah.

'That's the theory.'

'How do you get them to fire in the right order?'

'That's the beauty of the new cartridges. It used to take three goes but now we can do it in one. The fuses are reliable enough for us to set sequential charges from a single point. Will ye give me an hand to place the charges?'

Merriman showed him a box near the foot of one of the nearby ceiling props and Josiah passed cartridges from it as Merriman requested them. The Foreman Blaster pushed them into the drill holes leaving ends where the fuses would, go poking out. A second box contained the fuse cord wound on a large wooden bobbin. It was a cross between very stiff sewing thread and thin rope.

Merriman cut the fuse cord and connected it to each of the cartridges. Then he used a piece of wooden dowel to push the cartridges down to the bottom of their respective holes and sealed them in with clay. Finally, he tied all the fuses together and ran out a long length for several yards back down the tunnel.

'That should be long enough,' he said. Then he double-checked everything. 'Now all we 'ave to do is light the long 'un and wait for the bang. Would you mind carryin' the cartridge box for me? I'll take you and it out the drift. When you're clear I'll come back and light the fuse.'

'Where will you take cover?'

'I'll run back to the main drift and take cover in one of the alcoves cut in the wall next to the trackway to give room for wagons to pass. They give enough protection.'

'Don't you have to leave the mine entirely?'

'Provided ye don't stand close to a gallery entrance, there is not much danger in getting' 'urt.'

Josiah felt an impulse. The mixture of emotions he was feeling in the aftermath of what Rachael had told him, made being near to danger appealing. He wanted to be near the explosion, to feel the thrill of its power.

'Then, if I may, I will stand with you. I want to see for myself everything these cartridges do.'

'Are you quite sure, lad?' said Merriman. 'Mr Johnstone said I was to get you back in one piece. It would be more than my job's worth not to.'

'Quite sure. I want to stand with you Mr Merriman and share your risk. I've spent far too much time in my life watching and not participating.'

'There's a feeling I understand, lad. I'll take the risk but you'll have to do exactly what I tell ye.'

They went back up the drift and Merriman found Josiah a safe alcove in the main tunnel and left him there. Josiah waited in the silence. There were no sounds at all, except water dripping on the muddy floor. He imagined that he and Merriman were the only ones underground everyone else safely on the surface.

Merriman was back surprisingly quickly. 'Crouch down and turn yo'r back to the gallery. This will be a quick 'un.'

Involuntarily Josiah started to count. Then the ground shook and bits of roof fell onto his head. He felt the explosion through his feet before he heard it through the fingers stuffed into his ears. Then a fraction later, a wave of dust and smoke engulfed them from the gallery.

Creating foggy halos around their lamps, the dust cleared sufficiently quickly for them to go back to see what the explosion had done in no more than a few minutes. Josiah and Merriman crawled over the pile of rubble that had come down. It wasn't as big or as neat a pile as Josiah had expected but even Josiah could see that the new roof level was good.

'Champion,' Merriman said to himself.

Merriman's drillers had joined them. 'Right, lads, yer can clear the spoil and get the carpenters in to shore up the new roof.'

Josiah and Merriman started to walk back to the surface.

'That was a very effective demonstration. Thank you,' said Josiah. 'I have only one question about the cartridges. Mr Abram Hailsworth makes great play that they are sulphur free. As far as you can tell is that the case?'

'There's definitely no sulphur in the cartridges or the fuses,' said Merriman. 'Normal blackpowder always leaves a smell of sulphurous smoke in the air, especially fuses, but these cartridges don't.'

'You're certain. So as far as you are concerned both are sulphur free?'

'Aye. I were very sceptical that cartridges without sulphur

would be as good as a well-tamped loose powder, but I was wrong. It must be to do with the way they compress 'em but properly ignited, they burn as quick as the best military grade powder. I 'ave tested it myself. When contained in the shot holes I think they're probably five or six times better than loose powder.'

'What about the fuses. Wouldn't they burn hotter and be more reliable at firing the cartridges with sulphur in their mixture?'

'It's logical to think so but I can say while we've been using them, we've 'ad fewer misfires than normal. If 'e press me then maybe I'd rather the fuses were hotter but they are very reliable in terms of timing. You've seen for yourself. We did that rip at one go, all because of them fuses. That's an advantage not to be sniffed at.'

A few minutes later, covered in dust they came out of the drift. Josiah's uniform looked pale grey rather than dark blue. He took off his coat and shook it until most of the dust had gone. Then he ruffled his hair until it had returned to its normal brown and swilled his face in the water trough near the entrance before putting his coat back on. Mr Johnstone came over.

'Did you find out what you needed?' he asked Josiah.

'Yes thank you.' A miner with a pony pulling three wooden coal wagons, passed them.

'Is it alright to go down, Mr Johnstone?' said the miner.

'Should be alright if you're going beyond the first gallery.'

'Yes Sir. Goin' all the way.'

At its own patient pace, the pony walked on, pulling three empty wagons. But just before the tunnel entrance, where the downward gradient started, there was a small gap between the rails. The first wagon rattled smoothly over this step, as did the second but the third stuttered and its wheels got caught. The miner urged the pony forward and the wagons moved but the pony started to lose her footing. The miner tried to steady her by holding her head and but the animal dug in her back legs. The result was that she slid about three yards before coming to a halt.

Josiah and the others went to help but by the time they got there everything was under control and the pony was standing calmly. As Josiah arrived, the miner tapped her back leg and the pony obediently raised her foot so that he could see if the skid had damaged her hoof. Ranged evenly around the horseshoe, Josiah saw four nails with familiar, raised square heads.

23

MCBRINNIE

So the mine could be the source of the nails used on Elijah. 'It must be a big job keeping all the ponies you need shod securely,' Josiah remarked to Johnstone.

'We have our own blacksmith for that job as well as repair of any machinery that's needed,' replied Johnstone.

Josiah's could see Mr Hailsworth talking to some of the women workers near one of the piles of coal.

'Mr Johnstone, will Mr Hailsworth be ready to go soon do you think?' he said.

'Not yet, Mr Ainscough. He'll be talking to the women for a while. He always takes particular care when he comes to see they and the children they bring are well.'

So Josiah might have enough time to get to know the blacksmith if he could think of an excuse. As usual when indecisive he started to bither, as he mother put, with his clothing. He checked the buttoning of his coat, adjusted the stock at his neck and tightened his belt. As he did so his hand brushed the handcuffs that were clipped to the belt.

'Then could I impose on your hospitality a bit more?' he said to Johnstone.

'Of course, Constable.'

'My handcuffs have been damaged and are not as secure as they might be. Would your blacksmith have a look at them for me, while I wait for Mr Hailsworth?'

Merriman chuckled. 'I'm sure he would,' said Johnstone. 'His name is McBrinnie. His forge is over there.' The manager pointed to a building at the far end of the site. 'Mr McBrinnie will help you if you tell him I sent you.'

'Aint ye going to warn 'im, Mr Johnstone?' said Merrimen, clearly amused.

'Yes I suppose I should,' said Johnstone. 'Mr Ainscough when dealing with Mr McBrinnie bear in mind he doesn't like to be called a blacksmith. He insists on calling himself a farrier. He can become rather dour and uncommunicative if you call him a blacksmith.'

Merriman chuckled, 'He do that, lad.'

The smith's workshop was a well-made building and reminded Josiah of many of those he'd seen in villages over the years. It had a slate roof and stonewalls but the front was open, with the roof supported by stout timbers. A man was silhouetted against the dull red light from the forge. As he got closer Josiah could hear the ringing of a hammer on an anvil.

His target was in view. He'd introduce himself, give McBrinnie the handcuffs and while McBrinnie was working on them he would find look for a supply of nails. with which to confront the blacksmith or whatever he wanted to call himself.

On a large anvil, a thickset man, a good six feet tall, with powerful arms and a large but rather unkempt black beard, was hammering what looked like a pickaxe blade. Apparently satisfied with his efforts, he pushed it back into the hot coals. He pulled twice on a chain that operated a pair of bellows. The coals on the hearth glowed fiercely: blue, yellow and red flames danced on their surface.

'Mr McBrinnie?' the man looked up. 'I am Constable Ainscough, Mr Johnstone said you might be able to help me. I think my handcuffs are in need of repair.' Josiah went over and handed McBrinnie the cuffs.

McBrinnie took them and looked carefully at them. 'The ooter links look soond. If there's a problem it's with the middle shackle. Give me a wee second then I'll check the threads for thee.' He returned the handcuffs to Josiah and went back to the pickaxe blade.

So far so good. While McBrinnie's attention was occupied, Josiah took the opportunity to look around. There was a long row of tongs and hammers hung near two other anvils of different sizes. Two different cooling troughs were close by: one plain water, the other a pale yellow, oily looking liquid.

'You seem to have a well-appointed workshop here?' he said.

'Aye, bit more than a farrier's normal workshop that's for shuir.'

He pulled the red-hot pickaxe out of the hearth with some tongs, gave it two more well-chosen blows on the anvil, pushed it back and applied the bellows again.

'I heard you prefer to be called a farrier rather than a blacksmith?'

'By ma ain choice. There's skill in being a farrier that no simple blacksmith cud comprehend. I was apprenticed a farrier and I'm proud of my trade.'

'How long have you worked here?'

'Nearly a year.'

The blade glowed brightly from below the coals, turning from red to white hot. Next time he pulled it out McBrinnie clearly thought it ready. Suddenly he plunged the blade into the yellow liquid. A thin trail of blue-black smoke emerged from its surface. Josiah could hear the Scotsman counting under his breath. When McBrinnie got to twenty he pulled the blade out of the first bath and plunged it into the water. The water sputtered and hissed, and a great cloud of steam billowed up to the rafters. When the ferment was over McBrinnie removed the blade from the trough, tested the residual temperature with his forefinger. Satisfied, he put it with others on a shelf at the back of the workshop. He took off his protective leather apron and wiped his hands on the cloth one underneath.

'Let's see about yer 'cuffs.' After a couple of minutes' work McBrinnie had them apart.

'Anything wrong?' asked Josiah.

In reply the farrier passed the middle shackle to him. 'Look carefully at yon thread. Ye see whaur it's been damaged? Someone chaffed agin 'em in the past when they've been used to restrain some reprobate. Ah'll re-tap it for ye, but ye need to show it to ye ain people. There should be some pegs at the ends of the thread that lock thaim. I'll replace them for ye as well. Without 'em someone cud break them in twain if they waur braw enough.'

Whilst Josiah had looked around carefully as much as he could he had not seen any evidence of the hoped for nails. In fact there seemed to be no evidence of horseshoes or anything needed for what McBrinnie prized as his true calling.

'How many ponies does the mine have, Mr McBrinnie?'

'About twenty.' He paused and looked up at Josiah. 'Constable, I cud get on wi' this job a lot quicker if you wheesht yer haver.'

'Sorry,' said Josiah.

McBrinnie unlocked the cuffs from the vice he had been using and gave them a tug or two. Then he handed them back to Josiah.

'Thank you,' Josiah said. Behind him, there was the noise of someone coming into the workshop. It was Johnstone.

'Mr Ainscough, Mr Hailsworth asks if you're coming with him or do you need more time?'

He looked at McBrinnie but the farrier had gone back to his forge. Time had run out for Josiah. His choice was clear, confront McBrinnie with Johnstone there as witness or bide his time. He had been too quick to accuse Abram of lying about the sulphur at the powder mill and he might still live to regret that. He would be prudent and wait a better opportunity. There might be hundreds of nails within touching but he had found none of them and as a result could do nothing.

'I'll be right with him,' replied Josiah. Frustrated he turned and followed Johnstone.

As he walked back towards the entrance to drift Josiah was glad to see that Merriman was talking to Mr Hailsworth's coachman who had brought the broughman over. Even if he had failed with McBrinnie in Merriman he felt he had found a useful ally.

Josiah shook hands with him. 'Well thank you again.'

'Yer welcome, lad.'

Josiah paused. 'Could I ask you one last question?'

'Ye free to ask lad.'

'A craftsman's view of Mr McBrinnie, does he do his job well?'

'Very well. The only issue I have with 'im is the daft idea that he always has to be called a farrier. He is a good bit more than that. In fact he's much, much more than that, if you tek my meaning.'

'Not really,' said a cautious Josiah.

'Well all he does, is done with ease.'

'Yes he spent ages heating and reheating a pickaxe blade just now and cooled it twice in two different liquids.'

'He were case-hard'n the blade. That's not even done in the foundries. Case-hard'n blades have an outer layer that makes them last longer and cut better. He's one of the best foundry men I've ever worked with and he could earn three or four times what he earns 'ere at any of the larger mills in Stockport or Manchester. He's a craftsman and no mistake. He pays just as much attention to making the nails for the horseshoes as he does to mekin new wheels for trucks. Ye should see the concentration on 'is face when he's at it.'

So McBrinnie did at least make the nails. Josiah felt in his pocket and pulled out one of the nails head collected from bellow the cross. 'Nails like these?' he said.

Merriman took the nail. 'Yer a brave man taking one of these away with ye. He's particularly proud of these. He says they are his own design.'

Josiah looked at the nail in Merriman's hand. It was evidence but he had a few left. If he sent a nail to McBrinnie through Merriman, the farrier would know Josiah had not taken it from the forge. Perhaps he might react in some sort of way that would be helpful. Josiah took the chance.

'Then you'd better prevent any argument and return it to him with my apologies. Thank you again.' Then he turned and joined Mr Hailsworth in the brougham.

At last Josiah had a firm link from the crucifixion to a suspect, even if he did not have enough proof of McBrinnie's involvement to accuse him. He could not show it but Josiah was elated.

24

HAM AND PICKLES

Josiah's excursion to the coalmine had been productive in unexpected ways but it had not lasted the whole day so that he ran the risk of meeting Rachael, something he recoiled from. What could, what would he have to say to her?

To successfully avoid her for the whole day also meant he could not appear at the community evening meal. It occurred to him to ask Mr Hailsworth for some food instead but the frosty reception that Mrs Hailsworth had given him that morning suggested that if he asked then there would be a conflict between Barbara and Steven Hailsworth about where he should eat: with the family or below stairs. He did not care to be the cause of such conflict.

Then it occurred to him that one of the public houses in Marple would be able to feed him and they might have the advantage of offering such exotic fare as ham and pickles. He reflected that though he was happy enough on the plain food at Long Clough he had a craving for something a little sharper to the pallet. So he asked Mr Hailsworth to drop him as near to Marple as was convenient, which of course, to Josiah's embarrassment, meant that after the broughman had delivered Mr Hailsworth back to the Hall, it took Josiah on to Marple.

It was late in the afternoon and the Navigation was the only public house open. He sat down on a bench in the courtyard and tried to write up his notes but he could not concentrate on them, his head was far too full of what Mr Hailsworth had said about his illegitimate son. It had shown Josiah something in his own feelings and thoughts, he had never really understood. Mr Hailsworth had been right, Methodism with it standards and discipline could be a harsh mistress. Forgiveness was, of course, at its centre, he and all, of his fellow adherents were saved sinners. But somehow it was easy to lose any thought of the forgiving nature of God in the middle of so earnestly living a useful, determined, dutiful life for others. Had he ever really understood this? Understood that God did forgive? Was overwhelmingly happy to forgive. Could he be forgiven for his seduction of Maria?

He could not do what Mr Hailsworth had done in making peace with his past. Maria was gone. There was no way to return to Spain find her and ask her forgiveness. So he could not do what Elijah had thought was the central moral duty of reconciliation.

God would forgive him. So perhaps all he could do was trust that God would then in some way make it up to Maria. But that involved a trust of God he did not possess. The fact was that the best Josiah could do was try to do for other Marias something that was not equivalent but still of value, as a symbol of his desire for atonement. But that would mean he would have to forgive himself. With a shock he realised that he could not do that yet.

It was the simple delicious smell of fresh bread, wafting out of a nearby window that brought him back to the here and now, reminding him of his original purpose in coming to Marple. A serving girl passed him.

'Excuse me, Miss, but could I have some ham, pickles and bread to eat?'

'Of course you can, my dear,' she laughed. 'Shall I add a pint of our best ale to that?'

'No beer, Miss, thank you. It doesn't agree with me but could I ask for a cup of tea if that could be arranged?'

She grinned. 'Well I'm not sure our reputation will stand it if a good looking officer like you is seen drinking tea, in preference to our best bitter but I'll see if the missus is prepared to take the risk.'

A few minutes later she popped her head out of the door to the bar. 'Beg pardon but missus said you drinking tea in the yard just won't do. Apart from anything else, she's frightened her china will get chipped. So she's set you up at a table just inside if you don't mind.'

Having eaten one ham sandwich and drunk two welcome cups of tea, Josiah tried to return to his notes. But as he relaxed at the end of his meal and finished the tea, he heard a familiar voice.

'Right you lot! I have not got all day. Have you got the plans finished?'

'Yes Sir.'

The first speaker, Celeb Arlon, was using all his usual politeness and felicity. The other voice was also familiar, Jimmy, the surveyor he had caught on Children of Fire land with Mr Arlon. Josiah pricked his ears up.

There was a pause. All he could hear was a low burble of voices without being able to distinguish individual words. Then he heard Arlon again.

'How much will it cost?'

'Within the sum you originally mentioned,' said a third unfamiliar voice.

'Including the basin?'

'That is my professional opinion, Mr Arlon, backed up by twenty years as an engineer.'

So there was to be a new basin at the aqueduct at the end of the new road. But Marple was Arlon's town, dependent on the work he provided at his mill? Except for the limekilns, there wasn't much work outside Arlon's control.

'In that case, I thank you, gentlemen. Your work is done until I get control of the land.'

Josiah was consumed with curiosity. What was Arlon about? But it didn't sound as though Josiah was going to find out more until the Engineer spoke again.

'Mr Arlon. While you have given enough details to make our measurements and estimates you have not told us of the purpose of this very expensive development.'

'Why should that be any damn business of yours? I pay you.'

'In principle nothing, Sir. But in practice as it says in the proverb, there can be many a slip between the cup and the lip.'

'Meaning?'

'Engineering is a matter of art as well as science. I make judgements, guesses if you like, about what we might or might not find when we put picks and shovels into the ground. It helps reduce the risk of my making an expensive misjudgement if I know more about a proposed constructions general purpose.'

There was a pause before Arlon spoke. 'I take the point. So I'll tell you but the reason must not get outside this room. I need the road and the new basin for the transportation of a new product at my mill. I need to avoid the dirt from the limekilns in Marple. It's the same reason that Macclesfield refused permission for the railways to build a huge junction in their town.'

'I understand,' said the Engineer. 'That eases my mind.'

'Well it don't easy my mind,' said Jimmy. 'If you make a mistake my livelihood's on the line as well.'

'I'm going to change from spinning and weaving cotton to spinning and weaving silk.' said Arlon. 'Silk has to be kept clean. Everyone satisfied now?'

Josiah considered what he should do. The prudent course would be to withdraw and pretend he had not heard Mr Arlon. That was what Mr Prestbury would expect, perhaps also what Mr Hailsworth would advise, but what purpose would it serve? If Arlon got his way, his bullying way, for everything seemed to be a matter of bullying with Arlon, nothing good would come of it. Josiah decided he would shake Arlon's tree to see what fell out.

The serving girl came to clear the plates. 'Is that Mr Arlon's voice I can hear?' Josiah asked.

'Yes, Sir. He is in the room next door to this one.'

'Thank you, I must pay my respects to him before I go. Where is the door to their room?'

'Just to the left over there,' she pointed.

He went through an archway and knocked on the door he found.

'Who the hell is that?' shouted Arlon.

'I'll see', said Jimmy. The door half-opened in front of Josiah, showing the surprised face of the surveyor. Before he could recover Josiah spoke. 'Is Mr Arlon with you?' he asked.

'Get rid of whoever it is,' Arlon blustered. A heavy tread came across the room behind the door and it was flung fully-open.

'What the devil? Ainscough?'

'Yes,' said Josiah. 'Constable Josiah Ainscough of the Stockport Police at your service. I heard your voice, Mr Arlon, and I felt I should apologies for my deception the other evening. Though it was with Mr Hailsworth's permission, I still felt it might look as if I spying on you.'

'Why in blue-blazes did Steven Hailsworth give a policeman permission to attend a private party for my Sarah?'

'Because, at Mr Hailsworth's request, I am investigating the murder of Elijah Bradshawe, at least until the Derbyshire constabulary can get here. I felt it important to meet you and Mr Hailworth concurred. It seemed to be the best and most discreet way.'

'Why?' then the reason occurred to Arlon. 'God's blood, you thought I had something to do with it!'

'Yes, especially when I heard about the disputes you were having with the Children of Fire over the useless piece of land near the wood. What did you suggest at the dinner? Wasn't it that you expected to get the land cheap when the community fell apart after Elijah's death because they would have no leader?'

'So what difference does that make?' reposted Arlon standing full-square with his hands on his hips. 'Police aren't concerned with civil disputes.'

'True but thanks to your loud voice and the rather thin walls in this public house, I know why you want the new road.'

Arlon was white with rage by but controlled himself. 'It's still none of your blasted business, Constable.'

'No it's not but if I witnessed a trespass in the course of my investigations it would be my duty to discuss with the local magistrate whether it warranted further investigation by him.' There was a pause as the implied threat to tell Steven Hailsworth about the meeting and the plans sank in. Jimmy panicked.

'He must have seen us, Mr Arlon.'

'Keep silent!' said the Engineer.

'You are right, Jimmy. I was up by the sawmill when I saw you surveying. Perhaps I should have mentioned it earlier to the Children of Fire but I was busy investigating the murder. However, they still might wish to ask their lawyers about the matter even at this late date. Who knows they might even be prepared to sell you the land you need for the road at a fair price. Good day, gentlemen,' and he turned on his heels.

Josiah paid for his meal and left the Inn and started his walk back to Long Clough. Arlon was a dyed-in-the-wool hypocrite. The only way he could hope to make better profits from silk compared to cotton was to cut his workforce severely. That would bring ruin to Marple. Also, he would have to use the newest form of Jaquard looms available, to ensure he could weave the variety of patterns into the silk, the trade expected. Those new looms would be French – so much for never taking up any idea from France.

But though Arlon was a very unpleasant man, Josiah was now sure that he could rule him out as a suspect for the murder. He neither had the imagination to come up with the details of the methods used to kill Elijah nor the personal viciousness required. In any case a connection of Arlon with McBrinnie seemed rather unlikely.

Perhaps Arlon might order a murder, to eliminate someone who was getting in his way of his plans but his motive would be profit. He wouldn't do it himself or be anywhere nearby when it happened. He would hire a couple of ruffians with pickaxe handles to do the deed in a dark corner.

Arlon's was a mind of money and profit, nothing more. Josiah despised him, pitied his workers and even more his daughter and wife.

25

A Ride in the Country

The following morning, Aideen Hayes was not only punctual but looked magnificent on a pie-balled thoroughbred. With her, on his own horse, a groom led a docile looking mare for Josiah. Today, Josiah was not in uniform; this was his own private time. Aideen was not a suspect, just an acquaintance; he was not investigating and he was going to be himself. So he was dressed in his comfortable, familiar travelling clothes.

His jacket and waterproof were packed into the saddlebag on the mare. Then with girths tightened and stirrups adjusted, came the testing act of mounting up. Much to the amusement of Aideen it took Josiah two attempts but he managed well enough the second time.

'I suppose you will say you are out of practice,' she laughed.

'That may sound a convenient excuse but it's true. I did learn to ride reasonably well when I was a footman in France.'

'I sense another story coming on but let us save that up until we are on our way.' She spoke to the groom. 'Thank you, Paul, I'll bring Meggs back to the Hall myself. You can go now.'

'Yes, Miss.' Paul turned his own horse and started to trot back towards the main road.

Josiah frowned. 'Aideen, is that wise? Wouldn't it be more proper if he stayed as your chaperone?'

'Oh, I can look after myself.'

'But what will your brother say?'

'Well if Phelan wants to defend my honour then he'll have to be here to do it. I've spent most of my life riding alone on the beaches and cliffs of Donegal and I am not going to change now simply because I am in a more straight-laced country. Now to business, Let's see if you can still remember how to go fast.'

She urged the horse forward into the canter, giving Josiah no choice but to do the same, unless he was to be left hopelessly behind. They cantered on briskly for about half a mile until Aideen slowed her horse to trot, then walk and allowed Josiah to catch up.

'Where shall we go?' she asked.

'Well I've never ridden around here. Where is your favourite place?'

She looked thoughtful. 'Let us combine a good ride with peace in the countryside. Follow me.'

They went down the track from Long Clough to the road and turned uphill towards Hailsworth Hall. But before they got to the estate road, Aideen turned onto a green lane which traversed the hill below the mines, eventually coming out above the village of Hayfield which they circled to the north. Turning northeast, they crossed a plank bridge and started to climb a narrow valley next to a stream.

The sky was blue but there was a steady breeze from the southwest. Josiah watched and marvelled at Aideen's skill as a rider. Side-saddle was, in his view, a ridiculous way to attempt to control a horse. Sitting astride, as he was, legs, and therefore knees and ankles, were stable on each flank of the mount giving a symmetry of weight and force. But on a side-saddle with both legs hooked on pommels on only one side, the rider's weight was perpetually off-centre. It looked, if not against nature, then at least against common sense, as well as being, he assumed, terribly uncomfortable.

Again, Aideen reined in her horse and let him catch up. She was breathing easily whereas he was definitely puffed.

'I do not know how you manage to ride in that position in the saddle,' he said, wiping his hand across his brow.

'It's nothing. Watch this.'

There was a flat open space by the stream. Aideen walked her horse out on the left as far as a stonewall. She turned the horse on the spot and faced towards the stream. Throwing her weight forward and giving the horse a quick flick with her crop induced an instant gallop. She only had room for about five strides but it was enough; the horse jumped the stream with room to spare but Aideen did not slow her down. The wall on the other side of the stream was in front of a flat, if tussocky field. She took all of the momentum from leaping the stream towards that wall and though it was a good four feet high jumped it with grace and control.

She walked back through a gap in the wall up stream and allowed the thoroughbred to drink as a reward for the effort. Josiah applauded.

'If I had a hat I would take it off to you,' he said as his horse joined hers 'I could never be that good a rider no matter how much practice I had.'

'I doubt that, Josiah. I doubt if there is very much you could not do well if you set it as your aim.' It sounded to Josiah a flippant comment but when he looked at Aideen's face there was no sign of amusement. In fact, she looked rather serious, so serious that he changed the subject.

'How far do we have to climb?'

She pointed up the valley. 'See where the stream turns right. There is a small cascade round that bend then there is a steady climb up to what I believe is called Ashop Head. Then it is only a few hundred yards onto the Kinder plateau.

They pushed on. Grass overhung the edges of the cascade, where the stream tumbled happily through tufts of coarse grass, round boulders made of a fine-grained, dark rock and between peat banks.

They dismounted before the steep climb onto the ridge and led the horses up the path. They emerged onto a plateau near a jumble of larger brown stones scored by weather and wind so that deep notches ran in straight lines along their sides. Their flat tops had been sanded smooth by wind and frost.

Before he remounted, Josiah looked back along their path. The stream snaked away. The colours of the vegetation changed as it went westwards down into the valley: short orange grass among the rocks at the top, green bracken dominating lower down and heather purpling raised areas away from any water course.

The day was still very clear, though white tousled clouds were beginning to form as the temperature rose. These were moving in on the breeze.

'A clear day on which to see far but is it a day whose clarity may end in rain,' said Aideen. Josiah looked at her. She was looking out to the horizon with another serious and preoccupied expression.

Quietly they rode on towards the downfall where the River Kinder cascaded to the floor of the valley. Here they stopped and gave the horses a proper rest.

A slot had been cut by the river just before it hurled itself over the edge. This slot seemed to collect all the wind available, in a futile effort to blow what little water there was back and prevent it jumping to destruction. But despite the wind's efforts the brown peaty river flowed implacably towards its doom. They sat down.

Josiah had brought a bottle of Long Clough water with him to drink. Aideen came back from checking that the horses were securely tied to a small tree away from the downfall. She held two bottles of her own, one of which she offered one to him.

'I thought you might appreciate this. It is an improvement on plain water.'

He took it and uncorked it. It was Barbara Hailsworth's cordial. He was hot and tired by the unfamiliar exercise, so it was even more refreshing than it had been at the dinner.

'Thank you,' he said after he had taken a good swig. 'Most welcome and thoughtful. Please thank Mrs Hailsworth for me.'

'Mrs Hailsworth! Mrs Hailsworth fiddlesticks!' exploded Aideen. 'I'll have you know I filled these bottles with my own fair hands. I took the trouble to go down to the kitchens and fill those bottles with you specifically in mind and while I did it thought of this moment and how pleased you'd be. Barbara Hailsworth had nothing to do with it!'

'Sorry,' said Josiah in the tone of a reprimanded schoolboy. 'I didn't...'

'... Think! No you're a man and your race never do think. What would you do without women to rule and guide you either as wives or mothers.' Her tone of voice had started light and playful but as she got to the end and said the word "mother" Josiah heard her voice catch. He saw she was crying.

He went over and sat down next to her, confused as what to do. He had the reflex to put his arm round her shoulders in much the same way he would have held Rachael a few days earlier but Rachael's rejection of him had undermined whatever confidence he had in such impulses. In the end he compromised by taking her hand.

'Something has been upsetting you as we rode up here. It would be a privilege to listen to what troubles you if that would help?'

'Yes, perhaps,' she wiped away her tears with her hand. 'The day has reminded me of another when I was much younger. That day the sun was bright with clouds, like these, moving in from a western sea.' She paused.

'In Donegal we lived high on the cliffs, my father, my mother, Phelan and me. It was a beautiful place to live but there was always a shadow over it.'

He waited, trying to say nothing and so allow her to speak in her own time.

'When a young woman, my mother had been a beauty, or so people said. She was about to be married, when there was a fire at her family house. It started early in the morning while everyone was still in bed. By the time the alarm was raised it had already taken firm hold in the part of the house where she, her young sister and brother slept. He was about three.

'She got out of bed, and would have got out safely, but she heard her brother's screams. When she got to his bedroom, smoke and flames were coming up through the floorboards. She pulled him out of bed and started to carry him out but the flames caught up with her on the landing and the floor collapsed.

'After the fire was out, the bodies of her mother and father were found in the ruins. Everyone thought she had been killed and that only her sister had survived. When they searched they found the charred remains of her brother but they could not find her body until someone discovered that she had fallen through the ground floor into the cellars.

'She was badly injured: one arm and both legs broken, as well as being very badly burned, particularly where her hair had caught fire. But she lived. She recovered after many months of pain. Most of her hair grew back but she was left with a terrible scar down her right cheek and neck,' Aideen traced on her own cheek the line of the scar.

'When she was well enough to look in a glass she saw the ruin of her own face. She could not come to terms with it. She broke off her engagement and swore she would never marry.' She sighed and paused.

'But you and Phelan are here so something must have happened to change her mind?' said Josiah. His voice was soft and controlled. 'Did she come to terms with her disfigurement?'

'Never, but she met someone who both loved her and for whom the look of her face was irrelevant. The man who became my father was blind. Even then it took all his persuasive skills to get her to marry him.

'They were happy for a time. Phelan was born and then me. But she never came to terms with what she had lost. She despaired but she hung on for as long as she could to bring me up. When I was nearly five, while my father was away on business, and Phelan and I were out walking with friends, she went up to the headland and threw herself into the sea.'

As she had told the story, she had stared resolutely out towards the west. Only at the end did she look at him 'Oh Josiah, it was a day just like today. I can remember the silence in the house when we came back. I remember running everywhere, calling and looking for her. I had a little posy of flowers I had picked on the walk and I wanted to give them to her.' Tears were running down her cheeks. 'They soon found the note she had left and her body came back to us the next day, on the evening high tide.'

Josiah was aware of the wind in the heather, far away he heard the song of a skylark and nearby the trickling of the water. What words if any was one supposed to put into stillness at times like this? He squeezed Aideen's hand gently in comfort.

'Thank you,' she said. 'It is difficult for me to talk about it, even to Phelan.'

'You are not alone. Other people can understand if you let them.' He knew it was the wrong thing to say as soon as the words had left his mouth.

Her temper flared. 'How can anyone know? How can anyone understand?'

'Those that have been through similar experiences might. My mother and father died of a fever when I was a young child. I cannot feel what you felt but there must be some common ground in our experiences. I was the same age as you when it happened.'

She looked at him steadily. Then she put up her hand to his cheek, stroked it as she had before, but this time, she put her fingers gently at the back of his neck and drew his face towards hers to kiss him fully. Without conscious thought, he pulled her towards him and returned her kiss.

As he did so one part of his mind tried to maintain that his intention was to offer comfort but a more honest part admitted a thrill of desire made possible by that thread of recklessness he seemed to have acquired due to the hopelessness of his feelings for Rachael. It was the same thread of desire, which had so disastrously entangled him with Maria.

26

A Secret Garden

They collected up the bottles and walked back to the horses. Then they rode on, following the edge of the valley. They forded a smaller brook, which fed a lesser downfall and then climbed to a summit passing a line of ten tombstone-shaped rocks. It was as if the hands of some giant troll or ancient earth god had thrust up through the thin soil.

The edge over the valley was now less sharp but the view across the plain was still clear. Far out, haze was beginning to form as well as more cloud. Some were building impressively high and developing heavy triangular tops with a pinkish tinge. Josiah remembered Aideen's remark about a day so clear it could end in rain. If this day ended in rain, it would be a thunderstorm.

After the rocks, Aideen turned down a gulley following the first brook to be flowing east rather than west. A well-defined track went steadily downwards until suddenly they were at the top of a path that zig-zagged down to a deep valley.

Aideen broke their mutual silence. 'It is steep but the horses will be confident if we are. Leading them down is not as safe as riding. Just follow my lead.'

Backwards and forwards they followed the track down the slope. The horses remained surefooted and after the initial mild panic at the illusion of all the time being about to fall forward over his horse's head, Josiah started to feel confident in his mount's ability and even his own horsemanship.

At the bottom there was a stone bridge across the stream, now a reasonable sized river. There was flat pasture in front of them with a few sheep. Without warning Aideen urged her mare into a gallop.

'Oh enough of this solemnity!' she cried. 'Catch me if you can, Josiah.'

The hooves pounded the turf, bringing to Josiah's mind a horror he hoped he had buried long ago. He concentrated on following Aideen, forcing the memory back inside himself.

Aideen seemed to be heading for a building but he didn't have the comfort of time for detailed observation; she was convincingly outpacing him and he soon lost sight of her. All he could do was to rely on following the general direction of her horse's tracks.

At the end of the field, he found her mount tied to a tree. Aideen had removed the saddle and the thoroughbred was happily cropping the grass. Josiah followed suit, taking the saddle off his own mount.

There was low wall and a cracked stone pathway half buried in the grass. Beyond the wall, through the trees, there seemed to be a fine, but dilapidated house. Carrying his bag, he followed the path to a gate, hanging askew in the wall, which led to the house's garden.

There was no glass left in the windows of the house and the roof of one of the outbuildings had fallen in. The garden was overgrown. Self-seeded sycamore and elder choked the frontage; ivy and nightshade were crawling through the broken windows. The only bright challenge to their tyranny was from vigorous wild-roses, which had pushed up high enough to bloom. Their pink and white flowers rambled over the eaves of the house and onto the main roof.

Josiah pushed through the plants. There had once been a wooden portico over the main door but it had collapsed, blocking the entrance. Aideen had clearly not gone that way. There was a stone-wall which extended from the side of the house; this had a pointed gothic-arched door which looked intact. When he pushed, it opened onto a path where there were signs that the undergrowth had been pulled down to make passing easier. A few feet and he was under a lighter canopy of beech trees. In front of him was a generous walled garden. He opened a wrought iron gate and entered.

He could see that the garden had once been magnificent. There had been espaliers of apples on the walls. These had not been pruned for years and had grown into lopsided half-trees, but they had still managed to set some fruit in the spring and this was now swelling. Roses were in bloom and, to his left, a glorious wisteria hung down over a trellis above an alcove in the wall. In front of the alcove Aideen had spread a blanket and was putting out food she had brought. She looked up and smiled.

'I see you have not lost your sense of direction, Josiah. Do you like my forgotten garden?'

'It is beautiful,' he said, 'though perhaps a little sad.'

'Perhaps,' she said looking round. 'Someone once loved this garden. It brought great joy to them and, I sense, to others. Now it is only the cold speculative possession of a cold-hearted man who loves money.'

'It sounds as if you know who that is?'

'I do, but I fell in love with it before I knew to whom it belonged. So I do not covet it out of spite for him; it's Arlon. The people of the village further down the valley believe it is intended as a wedding present for his daughter. They also say that he has refused to do anything about its condition until that wedding is announced. No presents until the contract involving Sarah and Abram is signed and sealed. A very prudent but careless man is Mr Arlon. Because of his neglect we may trespass and enjoy.'

Josiah sat cross-legged on the blanket while Aideen leant against one of the posts that supported the trellis. They passed round slices of game pie and cold chicken. They tore pieces of fresh bread from a loaf baked that morning at Hailsworth Hall and still warm. Last there were some fresh strawberries from the Hall's fruit garden which they washed down with more of Barbara Hailsworth's cordial.

When they had finished their picnic Josiah went over and lay next to Aideen, with his head on his jacket. He watched the clouds run overhead. She looked at him then bent down and kissed him slowly and deeply. Her lips were soft and tasted of rose flowers from the cordial, her skin smelt of lavender water and country air. He embraced her and she settled down close to him with her head on his shoulder and her hand on his chest.

'Have your spirits recovered?' he asked.

'Somewhat,' she said. 'Telling you helped. I have always kept too many things locked up inside myself. This time I was lucky to have you on hand to call me into the light from the dark that was haunting me.'

He sighed. 'I think you and I are similar in that way,' he said.

'Yes. When we first met, I sensed you might have pain in your life by the way you told the stories of your travels. Sorrow makes people self-contained and observant in a specific sort of way. When you told me of the death of your parents, it explained it to me. Thank you.'

Though the death of his parents was a scar in his life, it did not haunt him; Thomas and Martha Cooksley, as well as Michael had seen him safely through that grief. Neither was he thinking of Maria. It was something much more recent, a grief not a guilt. I was the thing that until just a few minutes ago he though had gone, until the sound of hooves had brought it back to his mind. Something in the day had brought it back to him as the day had brought Aideen's memory to life.

'It's not the death of my parents that troubles me. It is something else with which I have not shared with anyone.'

'Can you share it?'

'If you will listen I will try.' She propped herself up on an elbow and affirmed consent with another kiss.

'It was on a day very like today. I was walking in the foothills of the Dolomites. There are several small principalities up there of various degrees of prosperity and I was headed to the main town of one. I hoped for some food, maybe some work to pay for it, but most of all, though I was tired, I was content in the peace and quiet of the mountains.

'I washed my face in the fountain in the main square and only then did I really take in my surroundings. Everywhere was empty and the shops shuttered. I was wondering why it was so quiet when from one side of the square there came an orderly group of about thirty people. There was the local priest in his black robes, a brace of shopkeepers, and a group of poor agricultural worker families, who the French would call the sans-culottes. The group made its way to the imposing bureaux, outside which hung the principality's flag. They knocked and an official answered the door. The priest offered him a document. The official took it, looked at it, then he threw it in the priest's face and slammed the door shut.

'Immediately from behind me there was a jingling of harnesses and half a dozen troopers on horseback came into the square from a side road, sabres in their hands. They charged the crowd. I was caught in the middle and dived for cover behind the fountain. The crowd scattered but as I watched, the soldiers hacked down several people, including the priest.

'Then one spotted me. He spurred his horse towards me and I ran for it. The sound of the hooves of that horse still haunts me. The soldier aimed one stroke at my head but he missed and he didn't have a chance for another as I crammed myself into a passage between two buildings too narrow for his horse. He gave up.

'When it was over, I helped the townspeople carry the dead and the injured from the square. I remember a little boy, his head gashed by a sabre. All he could say was "Maman, Maman,

Maman". He repeated it until he died in my arms. We found his mother's body in the square. I helped to dig the grave where we buried them.

'All they were doing was petitioning the local prince for a rebate in taxes to tide them over because it had been a hard winter. The attack was the prince's way of showing that the people were his possessions, not neighbours who he should serve.'

'Is that why you joined the police?'

'It played a part. It made me realise that rights under law are nothing if the people cannot get unbiased access to justice or have their complaints investigated by people like themselves. But because of that day in that town, I know that police responsible to local citizens are essential to our communities.'

'You have a strong sense of duty do you not, Josiah?'

'Yes.'

'Do you not feel that such a sense of duty is a great burden, even a curse?'

'Sometimes.'

'Then why not put it down. Why not just live to be happy?' Suddenly she stood up. 'Josiah, marry me and we will live in this place.' Her voice was commanding and urgent. 'We will make this garden our own. In play, our children will run free here and the past will not touch them.'

Josiah also stood up. It was true, here he could find peace in the form of a simple life with this woman who he could easily love. He imagined the garden as it must once have been. How many children had been brought up here? Many people said the past had ghosts. Some claimed to see them. If the future had equivalent spirits then those of his and Aideen's children were at that moment invisibly playing round them in the sunshine.

But he would not be at peace unless he found Elijah's killers. If he gave up that commitment his conscience would not rest easy.

'It is a wonderful thought. But I have sworn to uphold the

law and I must find Elijah Bradshawe's murderers before I can put that oath aside. After that, perhaps I can court you here or in Ireland in a proper manner. Then the dream may come true.'

Suddenly she seemed desperate. 'If you will marry me I will give myself to you here and now. We will consummate our covenant in a space that will, by that act, become sacred to us.'

She undid the top of her grey riding habit. Underneath was a dress held with a line of buttons. Her hands moved to release these. Lace was visible at the low neckline.

How would he react? The idea of welcome rest after all he had been though at Long Clough contended with duty. She had got to the last button. Once loosed then she would be able to slip the dress off and he knew desire would overcome him as it had with Maria. He pulled her towards him and contrived an embrace that allowed him to hold her hand. This time he would resist his instincts.

'No Aideen, it would make our relationship precarious. I promise you, when the investigation is over, when we will have time to grow together, I will court you, but now duty is duty.'

She relaxed in his arms and put her finger on his lips.

'Shhh. At least there is no duty at this moment.'

Heavy drops of water started to fall from a darkening sky. A peel of thunder heralded the bank of dark cloud that had built steadily during the day and had now caught them. As the rain fell, they laughed and held each other, hidden from the future by the garden and the valley.

27

A Boxing Match

After careful preparation the trap was set. All Josiah had to do was provide himself as bait. Nonetheless, before he stepped out of the cover of the edge of the wood, he took pleasure in watching a puzzled and confused Peter wait at the sawmill. When he was ready, Josiah shouted to Peter's irresolute figure.

'I had wondered if you would bother to come. I was counting that you would still like to punch me good and hard. Well this is your chance, if you're man enough to take it.'

Peter turned slowly and smiled. 'What do you think Rachael would say if she saw us fighting?' he shouted back.

'Well I rather thought that your dislike of me revolved around her. Maybe if you beat me she will go back to preferring you to me.'

Peter's expression hardened. Josiah saw he was getting through to him and was pleased in a bleak sort of way. After all, in this strategy of confrontation, he was counting on an enraged Peter being indiscrete, capable of saying too much.

'One problem, Constable.'

'What is that? Aren't you confident you can take me when you don't have surprise on your side, like you did at Pulpit Rock?'

Peter grinned. 'No not at all. It's that uniform of yours; it's an obstacle. This is between you and me. I will not be seen as attacking the law.'

In response Josiah took off his hat and placed it on the boundary wall. Then he removed his belt and his coat.

'I would not want my duties and position to intimidate you. Now do I look sufficiently less like the law to remove your scruples?'

Peter took off his own jacket and hung it on a fence post near the sawmill. Then he rolled up his sleeves, turned and charged at Josiah. At the last second Josiah stepped aside and tripped Peter as he went past. Peter stumbled and fell flat on his face in the dust. To his own shame, Josiah felt pleased at the effect.

He let Peter get up. 'Not quite so brisk this time brother. But then I suppose knowing Rachael thinks I am the better man of the two of us does take the edge off one's judgment.' He put up his guard as he had been taught in the few boxing lessons he'd had at grammar school and concentrated on not getting caught in close by Peter's strong arms.

This time Peter was enraged. He came at Josiah, swinging with both hands. Josiah ducked the blows and skipped backwards, hitting Peter on the nose with two crisp jabs. Again Josiah felt the warm glow of success, especially when Peter felt his nose and looked surprised to find a trickle of blood running down from a nostril.

In his mind Josiah allowed himself some preening, imaging mock footwork, shadow jabs and upper cuts, but this daydream was almost his undoing. Peter collected himself and circled in a much more organised way with his own fists in a proper defensive position. Josiah decided more goading was in order.

'Of course I can understand your reluctance to give up hope of her. Her kisses are most sweet, and she is most generous with them.'

Peter moved in, Josiah danced back and avoided being engulfed in Peter's arms but not before Peter had delivered two heavy blows to his ribs, winding him.

'You liar!' Peter screamed. 'She would never kiss you!'

'How sure are you of that?' retorted Josiah. 'Women are women, the source of all human temptation and original disobedience. They know how to stir the blood in a man with their wiles. How can you be so certain that she would not kiss me and perhaps offer even more?'

'Because she would never kiss me!' Peter shouted in tones of heartbreak and fury. 'She will not kiss any man!'

'Come now, she is a red-blooded woman in the prime of life, in need of a mate to give her children. Do not deceive yourself; I have more than enough evidence of those facts.'

There was no avoiding Peter this time. Even though Josiah backed off, ducked and weaved and got in a few good jabs to the head, Peter came after him. He parried Josiah's one attempt at a right cross, ducked inside and hugged Josiah under the armpits lifting him clear off the floor. Josiah hammered his fists down on Peter's shoulders but Peter was intent in squeezing the life out of him. Josiah forced Peter's head back by pushing his fingers into his nostrils and eyes but Peter was immune to all pain. Josiah was starting to feel giddy when Peter's grip slackened.

Michael O'Carroll's soft Irish voice spoke. 'That's right me, boyo. You let go slowly and I won't break your neck. Got it?' Peter nodded as best he could, considering his head was now pulled to the right, in a very painful and awkward position.

'Let the constable down gently onto his feet.' Peter did so. 'Now let go with those braw arms of yours.' Again Peter obeyed. Josiah squatted down, struggling to get his breath back. When he got up Michael had changed his grip. His left arm was across Peter's throat with Peter's right arm twisted up his back.

'Where do you want him put, lad?'

'In the sawmill. There are a few questions I need to ask him.'

'Right you are. Come on, boyo, were going for a little walk. Now you might think I'm old and you could take me easy but you've probably never heard the old proverb that where young men use skill and strength, and lose, old men win by cheating and cunning. At present when I let go your arm it will be limp for only a couple of hours but if I move my grip just a bit it will be lifeless for several days. So come quietly, I don't like hurting people. It's not really in my nature.'

Josiah collected up his own uniform and Peter's coat, while Michael walked Peter over to the building and into what had been the sawmill office. There was a chair in the middle of the floor, into which Michael pushed Peter. Then he sat in a second chair against the entrance door to the office, got out his pipe and started to smoke. Josiah put on his uniform except for the hat. He leant against a dusty old desk, trying to look confident despite the pain in his ribs.

'I have a few more questions I must ask you and explanations I must insist on having about what you said just now. I warn you at this moment I suspect you of being responsible for the murder of Elijah.'

Peter looked incredulous. 'What reason would I have for that?'

'We will come to that.'

'That accusation is ridiculous!'

'I'll be the judge of that.'

'Why should I answer any of your questions?'

'Because as you remarked a few minutes ago I represent the law. It's the law who asks not me.'

Peter was cornered and he knew it. 'Oh very well ask your damned questions.'

'Thank you. I think it is clear to all of us that you love Rachael and would do anything for her.'

'Do you really need me to say that?' said Peter mocking. 'Haven't you humiliated me enough?'

'Please, Brother Peter, I want to hear it from your own lips.'

'Yes, I love her. I love her more than my own life. Satisfied?'

'While we were fighting you said Rachael has never kissed you. Well that I can understand.' Michael coughed in a disapproving way. Perhaps Michael was right and there was no more goading required. 'You also said that she would never kiss any man. Why would you say that?'

'Mind you own business,' Peter snapped.

'I understand that this is a difficult question. As a measure of how seriously I suspect your guilt is I would be prepared, if you cannot give me satisfactory answers to my questions, to turn you over to Mr Hailsworth. Do you understand?' Josiah stood up and paced slowly around Peter trying to look as threatening as he could manage.

'Yes,' said Peter.

'Good. I will repeat my question, why did you say she would never kiss "any man"?'

The expression on Peter's face was one of agony. 'Because I have tried and always she has rebuffed me. She cannot stand to be kissed by me, or even touched by me!'

'You did not say "me" you said "any man". How do you know that is true?'

'Tell me if she has ever kissed you, or was that just hot air to make me fighting mad?'

Josiah paused. He couldn't think of any advantage of continuing the illusion that Rachael had shown him physical affection she had denied Peter. He decided to tell the truth.

'No I have never kissed her. I have tried but she has rebuffed me as well. We have common ground after all.'

Josiah noticed a slight smile appear and as quickly disappear on Peter's lips. Poor fool, he thought. All it takes is one admission from me to rekindle his hope that one day she will turn back to him and away from me. We are all too easily comforted by the discomfort of others. We are all fools in the court of love.

'I want to turn to another issue. What do you know of Rachael's relationship with Elijah before they came to Long Clough?'

'You mean what happened in Liverpool?'

'Yes, about how they met?'

'Not much?'

'Come now, Peter. You and Rachael were an important part of Elijah's inner circle and closest to him. You have admitted that you love her. I find it very hard to believe that you never discussed Rachael's life before she came here.' Josiah circled Peter again.

'Not in detail.'

'Will you swear to that?'

'Yes.'

'Even if I tell you that I know? I know about Aunty and the opium when Rachael was only eight and alone in the world without protection.' Josiah pressed on, pacing up and down a bit more quickly. 'I know about the organised begging.'

Peter shook his head, surprised. 'No you cannot. She would never tell you.'

'I know what else Aunty sold in her house near the docks.' Peter went to get up but Michael had anticipated him and a large hand on his shoulder, returned Peter to his seat.

Josiah stepped forward, bent down and looked Peter in the eye with his face no more than a hand's span from Peter's.

'I know, Peter,' he said quietly.

'No!' Peter wailed. 'No! She swore she would not tell anyone else.'

'If it is any comfort, I do not think she ever envisaged having to tell anyone else.'

'Before she met you!'

'I suppose so.'

Peter hung his head and covered his face with his hands. Josiah watched, feeling sympathy despite their rivalry.

Slowly Peter looked up. 'Is that why you suspect me of Elijah's murder?'

Josiah resumed pacing. 'You must admit that the childhood abuse of the woman you love, by a man you respected, such that she cannot respond to any sort of physical expression of your affection, is a very strong motive for murder. Especially, when today and on Pulpit Rock you showed how jealous, hot-headed and violent you can be in defence of your affections towards Rachael.'

Peter looked stunned as the logic of Josiah's statement sank in.

'But let us move on again,' said Josiah. 'Do you know a man called McBrinnie?'

'Who?'

'The farrier at Mr Hailsworth's mine?'

'Yes. Yes, I do.'

'How?'

'Our horse badly damaged a rear hoof during the winter. We did our best to stop it being infected, with poultices and the like, but it got worse and worse. Eventually the hoof cracked almost in two. A horrible green pus started to ooze out of it and she was so lame she could not bear any weight on that leg. All she could do was lie in her stall. We were frightened she would die.

'I was going to Marple one day when I met Mr Hailsworth's coachman on an errand. We fell to talking and I mentioned the problem with our horse. He suggested I ask McBrinnie if he could do anything.'

'And did he?'

'Yes he was very good about it. He came down here the following Sunday to look at the hoof. He cut out the infected tissue, sealed the wound with a hot iron and then closed up the crack by nailing the halves together. He sealed it with some pitch and secured the lot with a new horseshoe. He said the damage had most likely been done by a slip on a patch of ice. So he put some special nails into the new shoe and into the shoe on the other rear leg. He said they would help her feet grip on slippery ground.'

Josiah glanced at Michael. He had stopped smoking. Josiah felt in his pocket and pulled out a nail from Pulpit Rock.

'Were the nails the same as this one?' He handed it to Peter.

'Yes, it was, how strange that you,' his voice tailed off. 'Where did you get this one?'

'Pulpit Rock. I am surprised you didn't notice them when you took Elijah down. It is one of the ones used in the murder.'

Peter went pale.

'Did McBrinnie leave any spares behind?'

'Yes. He left me six. We don't do much smithying but he showed me how to replace any that broke off before the hoof was completely healed. He wanted the horse to work, when she could, to help encourage the growth of a new hoof.'

'Do you have any left?'

'No I had to use them all. In the spring the old broken part of the hoof fell away and was replaced by new growth. It's not quite grown back yet but it is sound and it doesn't seem to hurt her anymore.'

'And the used nails?'

'They got thrown away when she had new shoes fitted a month or so ago.'

'Was that when the idea of the crucifixion came to you, when you had the old nails in your hands? Maybe it wasn't then but while you were raising the new cross above Pulpit Rock? Perhaps it was just a delusion up to that point, a daydream of revenge but when the cross was there then it gradually dawned on you that murder could be made to look like religious fanaticism as well as providing an opportunity for sweet, violent revenge on the man who had dashed all your hopes of happiness.'

'No I never did anything of the sort! I never would, as God is my witness!'

'It would be better to confess now, if you are lying.'

'No, I will not confess to something I have not done. In any case did you not say at the inquest that Elijah was killed by two people?'

'Yes, I did.'

'Then who do you propose was my accomplice?'

'One other person has as direct a motive for revenge as you.'

'Who?'

'The person that Elijah first abused.'

Again Josiah watched as the logic sunk into Peter's mind. 'You cannot mean Rachael?

You must admit she would have a motive.'

28

WAITING AND WATCHING

Josiah sat in the courtyard and waited. He was tense, but his mind was resolved. This had been necessary, and whilst he recognised that it ruined any sort of future friendship with Rachael, it was his duty and could not be shirked.

She was sitting a few yards to his left with Peter and some other members of the community. She was upset but, like Josiah, in control, hands folded in her lap.

They had been waiting for over an hour; as occasional noises from the house suggested how the search was proceeding. It was clearly an extremely thorough search. Judging by all the clanging, Brother James and Michael had spent a goodly time checking all the pots and pans in the kitchen. At one point a sweep's brush had appeared through the top of one of the chimneys, complete with a puff of soot. The barns, the chapel and even the field-walls near the house and in the paddock had been scrutinised. But now it was quiet and it crossed Josiah's mind that Michael and James were deciding if anywhere else needed attention.

The same idea had struck all those who waited because they were all still and quiet, their eyes fixed on the door from the house into the courtyard.

It seemed a very long time ago, though it was only yesterday afternoon, that Michael and Josiah had watched as Peter walked off back to Long Clough after the questioning at the sawmill. Even from the back, he had looked dejected, and occasionally, as Michael had predicted, he shook his right arm, trying to get some life back into it.

'Do you think I am right to let him go?' Josiah said.

Michael puffed on his pipe. 'He's very jealous of you, there's no doubt about that, and he's a real hot-head. I think you were right to have my help on hand.'

'Thank you for responding so quickly to my note.'

'You're welcome, lad. I was glad I was here. I think he could well have killed you if you'd been alone. You goaded him as well as any Dublin drunk looking for a fight after the pubs have shut.'

Josiah rubbed his ribs. 'I couldn't help thinking you could have been a bit quicker when he had me fixed in that hug.'

Michael grinned. 'Well the way I look at it, you both had something to get out of your systems. But in your case, it might make you a bit more cautious in using a technique like that to get information out of a suspect. When did Josiah Ainscough, the well thought of and reliable Methodist preacher, become so reckless?'

Indeed, though Josiah exactly when. 'About the time Rachael told me about Liverpool.'

'First time is it, lad?'

'Not exactly, but she was my ideal, Michael: a good, practical and faithful girl. A girl to sooth my pains and ease my doubt,' And assuage my feeling of guilt, he thought.

Michael laid his hand on Josiah's shoulder. 'First love is the worst and the best. You have a very bad case of it, as you well brought up sheltered boys often do. I can't do much for you there, except to say time heals.'

'Thank you, my friend.'

'Welcome as ever, lad.' Michael paused and then returned to his practical self. 'Well I can't help your heart but I can do something to improve your fighting skills if you want to take advantage of the experiences of my misspent youth. I could show you some tricks that aren't exactly fair but they are effective and will help keep you safe in a tight corner.'

Josiah smiled. 'I will take you up on the offer when we are back in Stockport.' He looked again at Peter's receding figure. 'At present the question is whether he is guilty?'

'Do I gather that the nails and his knowing the farrier McBrinnie was a surprise?'

'I knew McBrinnie was the source of the nails, though it was good to have Peter's story confirm it. Now we know that Peter had some of those nails, his guilt is more likely.'

Michael took a big thoughtful draw on his pipe. 'What about Sister Rachael?'

'I admit she has motive as well but.'

'Come now, lad, don't let love cloud your judgment.'

'I doubt if she would have the strength required. It took two men one on each block and tackle to get Elijah down.'

'She wouldn't have had to do the heaving, just be strong enough to hold one at a time as Peter went backwards and forwards between them lifting the body gradually.'

'Sounds terribly a clumsy method. Why not use block and tackle you can lock off?' said Josiah.

'Could McBrinnie and Peter have been partners?' asked Michael.

'McBrinnie would have to share Peter's motive which seems very unlikely. Surely Peter would not have told us about having the nails from McBrinnie if they had been partners.'

'What you need lad, is a direct piece of evidence, an object or piece of information that only the murderer could have.'

Josiah had chuckled. 'There is one. At least I think there's one. The shirt Elijah had on the night he was killed is missing. I found all his other clothes in the woodpile store I told you about but the shirt was not with them.'

'Why do you think the murderer has it? Couldn't it just have been destroyed during the murder?'

'Whoever it was kept everything else, they didn't even bother to clean them. Maybe the murderer took it as some sort of macabre trophy.'

'Or as proof for someone else that he had killed Elijah?' mused Michael.

'Who would need such proof? No one local that's for sure; they would know Elijah was dead because of the gossip, the inquest and the reports in the papers, all of which are much better proofs of the death than a torn, bloody shirt that could have come from anywhere. But in someone's hands whose already a suspect it would be enough for a hanging. In the case of Peter and Rachael it's the only thing that can confirm their guilt but without it I would have to follow my instincts and look elsewhere for the murderer.'

'Can you search for it at the farm?'

'I suppose we must. But I think I'll sleep on it before I make a final decision.'

Off and on last night, in the fitful spaces between sleep, Josiah had tried to decide if he could bring himself to search Rachael's clothes and other personal possessions. The idea was repugnant to him. There was a practical problem as well, which he had not thought of initially. Though he had been living in the community for over a fortnight he had no idea if its members had any personal possessions, let alone where they might keep them.

As a result he had been sitting in the courtyard for some time that morning, trying to work out an acceptable plan as how to search for Elijah's shirt, when he heard the determined stride of an angry Rachael coming down the corridor from the kitchen. He had tried to escape but he was not quick enough.

'Stay there, Josiah! I wish to speak with you.'

'Of course, Sister Rachael. It would be a pleasure.' He had tried to smile but thought it had probably been rather forced and unconvincing of his sincerity.

'When you have heard what it is about, I doubt you will find it any sort of pleasure.' She hurried up to him.

'I have only just seen Peter this morning, or more specifically I have just seen the condition of the bruises on his face, especially his nose. He was reluctant at first to say how he had got them, giving me some cock and bull story about falling over when chopping wood out at the sawmill. In the end I forced an explanation out of him. He said he was given them by you when the pair of you were fighting over my affections. Is that true?'

Josiah looked her in the eye. 'I did give him the injuries in a fight and I made him fight me by goading him about my affections for you. That much is true.'

'How dare you! On many occasions in my life I found situations when I have doubted the common sense of men folk, when I have found your race doing or acting in ways that were degrading, pointless or worse. But this is the first time I have been fought over by idiots like you two!'

'Rachael please let me explain.'

'Let you explain! Explain! What possible explanation is there for either your or Peter's actions?'

Rachael paused for breath before launching another salvo of criticism, allowing Josiah time to speak. 'Please, Rachael, I had a very serious reason for my actions.' She paused and he continued. 'I admit it may have been a bad way to proceed but it was only because I could not think anything better.'

'I beg your pardon! Are you trying to tell me that there was some sort of higher motive for you instigating a brawl with Peter?'

'I suppose I am, though I know it must sound a pretty thin sort of excuse.'

'That is a grave understatement.'

'I deliberately goaded him into a fight in the hope that when angry he might let slip evidence to support a suspicion I had come to as a result of my investigation into Elijah's death.'

Rachael frowned. 'A suspicion about Peter?'

'Yes.'

'Are you telling me that you suspect Peter of being involved in Elijah's death.'

'In short, yes.'

'But that is impossible. Peter loved and respected Elijah, he would never have done anything to hurt him.'

'It was in fact you who gave me the initial cause for my suspicion.'

'How could I?'

'You said, when we talked about your feelings towards me, that there was only one other person who knew about what happened between you and Elijah in Liverpool when you were a little girl.'

'And you decided that must be Peter?'

'I thought it highly likely. I knew from your reaction to my affection that you would have rebuffed him as well and you have to admit Peter is a man who is easily angered. I thought he might focus his disappointment on the person who had blighted his chances of happiness by abusing you.'

'That is still ridiculous. If you suspect Peter for that reason you might just as well suspect me. My hopes of happiness in marriage hang by a thread, as do those of any man in love with me.' Then she had paled, staggered a little and sat down on the edge of the water trough to stop herself fainting.

'For the love of God, say you do not suspect me.'

Josiah felt as if he had been hit in the stomach. He took a deep breath. 'I do suspect you.'

'Josiah, I will make any affidavit, take any oath, in any way you require that I had no hand in killing Elijah.'

'Unfortunately, it needs more than an oath from both of you to clear my mind of this suspicion.'

'Then we are lost, for how can anyone prove they have not done something?'

'In the absence of a confession, the law demands evidence, something to connect a suspect to the crime. There is something that I believe is in the possession of Elijah's murderer that would provide such a link. I would like to search Peter's and your possessions and in fact Long Clough in general for this piece of evidence. If I do not find it, then I cannot sustain my suspicion of either of you and I will be satisfied you are both innocent.'

'Peter will not let you conduct a search like that. There is too much animosity between you now. If you found it he would accuse you of planting the evidence on him.'

'I was worried about the risk of Peter causing me serious injury when I embarked on the plan of goading him to fight. I asked a friend to come and be my protector. I think he could tactfully conduct the search under the supervision of one of the brothers or sisters you might pick. I would accept that arrangement. I would not have to be involved in the search and your appointee would watch my associate to prevent any planting of evidence. At present he is the only other person who knows the nature of this evidence. Could you persuade Peter to agree to such an arrangement?'

She had thought for a moment. 'In an attempt to prove to you mine and Peter's innocence I will try.'

'Then I will signal my friend to come here in preparation for a search. He slept last night in the wood. Rachael, if Peter does not agree then I will have to advise Mr Hailsworth, as the magistrate, to order the search. That will be bad for the community even if nothing is found because of the rumours that will start when it is known that a search has been made.'

While Rachael had gone to try to persuade Peter to co-operate, Josiah had gone along the path towards the sawmill and lit a signal fire for Michael. It did not take long until he saw his friend coming along the path. Once Michael had reached him

Josiah explained the situation and they both made their way to the farmhouse.

When they arrived, Rachael was in the courtyard standing by an angry looking but apparently co-operative Peter. Brother James was with her. He stepped forward and intercepted them.

'Constable, Sister Rachael has asked me to supervise the search. I had experience once or twice at sea in helping with searches for contraband aboard ship. She thought that I would make me a good choice.'

'I agree with her. I am sure you will discharge your duty diligently. This is Michael O'Carroll. He has been my friend for many years and knew me as a boy. He knows what I seek.' Michael had shaken hands with James.

'Pleased to meet you. I wish it had been in better circumstances,' said the Irishman.

'And I. Let us get this job done quickly,' replied James.

And now the waiting was over as they all watched as James and Michael made their way towards the house.

Michael spoke. 'We have not found that which Constable Ainscough seeks.' There was an audible sigh of relief from Rachael and the other members of the community who had gathered. Josiah stood up.

'Thank you, gentleman.' But before anyone could say anything else they heard a man's voice from the lane on the far side of the house.

'Hello, is there anyone here? We are looking for Constable Josiah Ainscough?' It was Phelan Hayes.

29

PARTING

Josiah's mind raced. Phelan had said "we", Aideen must be with him. Had Aideen's brother come to confront him about what had happened between him and Aideen on their ride. In which case a defence of "she sent the chaperone away" though true, was going to sound impossibly implausible and ungallant. It was also going to be a very embarrassing tableau in front of the brothers and sisters of Long Clough. But Phelan's voice did not seem to have the tone of a brother about to defend a sister's honour. In fact, Josiah thought that Phelan sounded his usual phlegmatic self.

As he watched Phelan Hayes appeared in the doorway from the house. In the shadows was Aideen's elegant figure. As she came out into the light he could see she was dressed in a dark blue coat and matching bonnet. Aideen and Rachael were now together in the same place. Surely, both would immediately see his divided loyalties, even if no one else in the courtyard saw through him.

Phelan took in the strained expressions on their faces. 'Josiah. What terrible thing have you done to offend these good people?'

At last Josiah's manners came to his aid, at least in getting his voice to work and reducing the possibility that he was standing there with his mouth open.

'Phelan, how pleasant to see you.' Josiah swallowed hard. 'Allow me to introduce you to Sister Rachael and Brother Peter of the community of the Children of Fire.' Peter nodded and Rachael dropped a perfect country-curtsy.

'I am pleased to meet both of you. I know you by your reputation in the Vale and wished we could have more time to become acquainted with you and the rest of the community.' He bowed deeply including all the sisters and brothers into this flamboyant acknowledgement.

He held out his hand to Aideen. 'This is my sister Aideen. It is on her insistence we have come.' Aideen dropped a curtsy of her own to Peter and Rachael. Josiah thought there was not much to choose between her's and Rachael's though Aideen's might have been slower, deeper and perhaps more practised.

Aideen stepped forward. 'Josiah, can I have a word with you?'

'Of course.'

'Aideen,' said Phelan, 'remember that you will have very little time to make the Liverpool train if you are to catch the Dublin packet on this evening's tide.'

'Yes, brother. This will not take long.'

Josiah led Aideen out to the paddock. As he went round the end of the farmhouse he could see Mr Hailsworth's landau. Evidently it had brought her to Long Clough was waiting to take her to the train. She stopped a few yards into the paddock and turn to face him.

'Phelan and I have had some very bad news from Ireland. It arrived this morning by special messenger. Our father is very ill and has taken to his bed, which is very unusual for him.'

She was nervous and clearly distressed, unable to decide if her leather travelling gloves should be on or off.

'His health declined slowly after mother died but he has become very frail in the last year. We fear that he is coming to the end of his life and so we have to cut short our visit.'

'I am so sorry,' said Josiah. He took her hands in his, trying to convey his sympathy; yet another bereavement to be added to her mother's. Though more expected than that death, it would still bring back the feelings she had shared so recently.

'So much passed between us during our ride that I could not leave without parting properly.'

'A note in your own hand explaining would have sufficed. You will be needed at home. I understand.'

'I wanted to be absolutely sure that you appreciated my affection for you. I thank you for the restraint of your own passion in the garden. Looking back, I now see that you were right. It would have been a mistake for us to have given way, though I in no way repudiate my sentiments. I desire you and hope that you desire me in return. But your offer of a proper courtship and time to allow us to know each other more broadly, before any proposal of marriage, was sensible and honourable.'

'Thank you. I do not repudiate my affection for you either, nor do I think any worse of you for your actions.'

'I also want to assure you that I sincerely want you to visit us in Donegal.'

He felt cheered by this invitation but he remembered the words of the song they had sung together at the dinner at Hailsworth Hall. That song suggested affection could be fickle. He hoped he was not as fickle as the character in the song.

'I will come.'

She smiled for the first time. 'I also want to give you fair warning Josiah Ainscough, there is only so much a girl like me can produce in the way of good sense, patience and restraint. If you don't come quickly, you'll find me on your doorstep demanding to know why you haven't been to see me.'

Before he could move, she reached up and kissed him. There again was the softness of her lips, and the smell of lavender water and country air.

She turned away and walked briskly back to the carriage.

Phelan appeared from the courtyard and helped her into the coach. He kissed her hand. Josiah joined him and they watched as the landau drove away. Josiah imagined that they would go through Marple and then on to the railway station Manchester itself. As the landau disappeared out of sight, Phelan turned to Josiah.

'Josiah, you will know better than I what passed between you and Aideen on your ride the other day, but she has been much changed by whatever it was. If I may be so bold, I hope all goes well between you. Let me reassure you that you will be very welcome to visit us in Donegal and while I can't speak for the rest of the family, I will be on your side. Many men have fallen in love with her, you are the first one to whom she has returned the affection. She needs and deserves the peace of mutual happiness.' He shook Josiah's hand.

'Thank you, Phelan.'

'And now I must get back to the Hall. I have to make sure our entire luggage is ready to follow us tomorrow as well as riding to Liverpool to catch the morning tide to Ireland to follow Aideen.'

'Have a good journey,' said Josiah as he shook Phelan's hand a second time. Phelan mounted his horse, that was tied near the chapel, and rode away.

Josiah returned to the courtyard. He tried to get his mind back to considering his position at Long Clough before he got there. He must now make a dignified exit from the community. It was inconceivable that they would want him to stay after placing Peter and Rachael under a suspicion of Elijah's murder. He would pack up and throw himself on the mercy of Mr Hailsworth at the Hall.

As he came into the courtyard the first thing he noticed was Rachael's expression. While waiting for the search to be completed she had remained controlled if stern but when Michael had announced that the search had not found its mark, she had looked the most relieved of anyone. But she now seemed almost as tense as she had been during the search.

Then Josiah realised that he and Aideen might well have been visible to the people in the courtyard, so that Rachael would have seen Aideen kiss him farewell: more confusion, more guilt. All he wanted to do was run away and hide, but instead he walked across and stood, hat in hand, in front of Rachael who did not look at him.

'I am sorry, Sister,' he said. 'I have accused you and Brother Peter mistakenly and I have behaved miserably towards all the Children of Fire, but especially you. I ask your forgiveness and promise to clear my things out of the barn forthwith.'

Rachael looked at him in a rather vague way. 'I'm sorry, Josiah, but I was thinking of something else while you spoke. Did I hear you say you want to leave?'

'Yes.'

She stood up. 'Yes. I suppose that is proper but let us not do so on bad terms.' The focus returned to her eyes and she looked at him with her usual candour.

'It is midday and the rest of the community will be coming in from the fields. Break bread with us once more before you leave. You and Mr O'Carroll must be as hungry as the rest of us with all this waiting and upset. If we all pull together then there can be food for all to eat before we part. A space in which to remember the good things we have shared while you have been here, not just the bad.'

They all rallied round. Bread and butter and cheese were found. The table was laid in its usual way and they were joined by those returning from the fields who had missed all the excitement. They stood together had in hand and sang as always.

James and Michael were in much demand to explain how they had conducted the search. Peter, tactfully positioned himself at the other end of the table from Josiah, who sat opposite Rachael at the top of the table. Elijah's chair was left empty as it had been since his murder. Josiah watched the others and said very little to Rachael nor she to him. She too seemed to have fallen back into a thoughtful mood. He would miss Long Clough and not just because of Rachael. He would miss the whole community and their camaraderie.

When they had finished eating Josiah left the others to clear up the meal so that he could gather up his possessions from the barn. He was nearly ready, when Rachael, Peter and Michael, along with Mr Hailsworth's chief coachman hurried into the barn.

'Mr Ainscough, I have the brougham outside. I am instructed by Mr Hailsworth to fetch you most urgently. I am to say that he is ordering you to come.'

'Of course, I will come. What is the trouble?'

'There has been an accident at the mine, an explosion.'

'Below ground?'

'No, in the forge. Mr McBrinnie has been killed.'

30

A DREADFUL CONSEQUENCE

The brougham clattered along at top speed. Instead of its normal single horse, a pair had been harnessed up, turning it from a gentleman's town dawdler, to an out and out flier, with all the shaking that implied. Even so, on the rough road from Long Clough and the steep climb to the mine, it was still relatively comfortable, giving Josiah a space in which to compose himself.

He wondered what they would find when they arrived. There would be McBrinnie's body, with what it might tell him about how he had died. There would be the forge damaged by the explosion and debris ready to tell its story, if he was calm enough to discern it. But he was far from calm. His mind was a sea of mixed feelings and fears with all that had happened that day. The worst of those fears was that he had caused McBrinnie's death.

The sudden death of the suspect Josiah was most sure had been directly involved with Elijah's murder, meant McBrinnie was now beyond not only justice but also questioning, which led to the thought that McBrinnie been killed to guarantee his silence. In which case, had the nail used on Elijah that Josiah had passed to McBrinnie via Merriman precipitated the killing? Would McBrinnie have understood that the nail's significance or was Josiah assuming too much about the relationship between McBrinnie and his accomplice?

McBrinnie would definitely have known that the nail had not been found by Josiah in the forge but would he have realised that it indicated Josiah's suspicion of his involvement? When it came down to it, Josiah had great difficulty in imagining the dour McBrinnie instigating Elijah's murder in such a dramatic manner. In which case it was McBrinnie who was the accomplice. So McBrinnie might have felt compelled to bring to the attention of the lead perpetrator how the nail had been returned. That person would certainly have realised the significance of the nail and killing McBrinnie out of hand reduced any risk attached.

Josiah had to face the fact that his actions might have caused McBrinnie's death. Although he had not intended such an outcome, he knew he would have it on his conscience for a very long time if that were the case. But thinking that way was of no use and to distract himself he turned to his friend.

Michael, who sat next to him, had volunteered to come with him from Long Clough, an offer Josiah had gratefully accepted. But even Michael seemed lost in his thoughts.

'I think this is the quietest I have ever seen you,' Josiah observed. 'Why so thoughtful?'

'Just thinking how strange life is.' Then he grinned and winked at Josiah. 'As well of course remembering the beautiful and charming young lady in blue.'

Josiah coughed embarrassed. 'You saw us then?'

'Yes, though I think I was the only one; the rest were concentrating on her brother. I must say, Josiah, that for someone who only a little while ago was lamenting his inability to play the game of love, you seem to have learned some interesting gambits in a very short while.'

Josiah blushed and Michael laughed. 'Only teasing, lad. Actually, I was wondering what you knew about Miss Aideen and Mr Phelan in general. Remind me, their family name is Hayes?'

'Yes it is Hayes.'

'Phelan Hayes. You know Phelan's a Celtic name; it means wolf. Aideen is similarly a Celtic name; it means born of fire. It comes from the same root as the name of St Aidan who founded the monastery on Lindisfarne. To top it off Hayes means fire as well. Phelan Hayes is a fiery wolf and Aideen Hayes is doubly fiery. No wonder she came all that way, in such a nice carriage, to give you such a passionate goodbye kiss.'

Josiah blushed again. He did not believe in the fate of names. Many believed that a name conferred almost magical powers and determined a person's destiny or character. In the tradition of biblical names in Methodism, his name, Josiah, was straight from the Old Testament. Josiah was a king of Judah who renovated the Temple in Jerusalem and as a result rediscovered the lost books of the Law of Moses. Josiah had read the story but he did not see much similarity between himself and the ancient king.

'Perhaps that is why Phelan always wears a flame red flower on his jacket,' Josiah joked.

Michael did not laugh. 'I saw the flower. Does he always wear it?'

'I don't know about always but he was wearing one when I met him at Hailsworth Hall.'

The brougham got back onto level ground and soon they were in the yard of the mine. Johnstone was there looking strained.

'When did it happen?' asked Josiah.

'About midday.'

'Anything unusual going on at the time?'

'Nothing. I had spoken to McBrinnie only a few minutes before. We were discussing problems with some of the rails in the deep mine. He said he would go down and have a look later. I watched him walk over to the forge. I even saw him go in through the door. Not more than half a minute after that there was the explosion and the front of the forge disintegrated. Only the stone built walls at the back are still standing properly.'

Josiah looked over. It was difficult at this distance to see much. But there was thin column of smoke rising from the forge into the otherwise blue sky.

'I better get over there.'

'You will find Merriman. He's inspecting what's left. They got McBrinnie's body out about half an hour ago. It was clear he was dead even before we got it out. I've never seen a more horribly disfigured corpse.'

'Is there any reason why Mr McBrinnie would have anything explosive in the forge?' asked Michael.

'None at all,' replied Johnstone. 'Merriman makes it his business to ensure explosives are stored safely.'

'Thank you, Mr Johnstone,' said Josiah. Then he and Michael started to walk towards the forge.

To Josiah the destruction became more shocking the closer he got. Only two days ago every tool had its place, now they had been flung over most of the ground in front of the shattered building. He spotted the hammer that McBrinnie used on the pickaxe blade at his last visit. Quite close by there was the small vice that had held his handcuffs as McBrinnie had repaired them. The only thing that seemed in the same place was the large anvil, so heavy that even the explosion had been insufficient to move it. Merriman was crouched down examining the floor about where the hearth must have been. He looked up at Josiah.

'Over 'ere, lad.' There was a blackened hole in the floor the shape of bowl. It was a bout two foot deep at its centre and six feet wide. 'This is where it 'appened.'

To Josiah it did not seem anywhere near dramatic enough to have caused the destruction around him. 'Is that all there is?' he said.

'The bang when it went off were big enough.'

'But the hole is so smooth. Wasn't the charge drilled into the floor?'

'Apparently not', said the laconic Merriman. 'If it had been then the hole would be deeper and there'd be rock and lumps of earth everywhere.'

So how do you know it was here the explosion occurred?'

'It's the only sign of an explosion and you can see 'ow all the debris radiates from here. Then there's the body.'

Merriman got up and led Josiah outside to where McBrinnie lay covered by a sheet. Michael had raised a corner and was looking at him. Merriman and Josiah joined him.

McBrinnie was in an horrific condition. Even dead and tortured, Elijah had still looked himself; McBrinnie's corpse was unrecognisable. The face was purplish red and black. Patches of skin were missing, leaving seared flesh showing through. The lips had shrunk back from the teeth in a bloody mass. One eye had melted and most of the hair was burned away.

'How could the charge that made that hole do all this to a man's body?' asked a stunned Josiah.

'As I see it wasn't the charge as such that did this,' said Merriman. 'The explosion threw all the red 'ot coals from the hearth into his face. I think he was standing over the hearth when it went off.'

Merriman reached inside the sheet and pulled one of McBrinnie's hands into the light. 'Look here, see 'ow this hand is pitted and blackened. It's his right hand.' He turned it over so that they could see the palm. 'See 'ow it's burnt back and front.

'I'm guessing from what I have heard from Mr Johnstone that McBrinnie 'ad come in 'ere before Johnstone talked to him, to get the fire in the hearth going for the day's work. The men who helped get the body out said McBrinnie had been delayed this morning by having to go to see one of the horses at the stables down the hill. Knowing 'im, he'd have been impatient to get on but 'e would 'ave 'ad to get the hearth working first. Like as not he'd 'ave would have put a few bits of coal on the embers from yesterday, if they weren't 'ot enough. When they were lit he'd have added more and given them a few puffs from the bellows. Then 'e'd 'ave left it to heat up proper like.'

Merriman replaced McBrinnie's right hand and pulled out the left, which was not as badly burned; the palm was intact. 'When 'e came back from seeing Johnstone, the coals should 'ave been glowing well. He'd 'ave taken the rake in his right hand and started to smooth them out. With his left hand he grasped the bellow's chain and pumped to get the temperature up. I think that was when it happened. 'Is left hand was further away from the hearth so it wasn't as badly burned. But the right hand was over the coals 'olding the rake and got the full force.'

'I don't doubt you, Mr Merriman, but do you mind if Michael and I look to see if there's a shot hole you've missed?'

'Go ahead. In fact I'll help you. Three sets of eyes are better than one.'

Josiah reasoned that if there was a shot hole then it might have been under something large, to hide it. There would have been time to put a charge in place while McBrinnie was at the stables. The most straightforward way of setting off the charge was a fast fuse, like the ones he'd seen Merriman use in the mine. If the fuse had been run out of the building, the murderer could have waited until McBrinnie came back and just lit the fuse.

So they looked where larger objects had been. The oil in the case-hardening trough had been ignited by the explosion leaving a black sticky residue on the floor. But there was no sign of a shot hole let alone a crater. They even moved the large anvil in case it concealed where the fuse might have been anchored but there was no sign of a fuse run, though they did find the badly bent rack from the hearth nearby.

'It must have been thrown against one of the beams and come down inside instead of being blown through the roof,' remarked Michael.

Josiah even examined the outside surface of the walls that

were left standing. A fuse lit from outside, might leave burn marks on the stone but there were none.

After about half an hour's searching they had found nothing that undermined Merriman's initial thoughts that the charge had exploded under the hearth. In fact finding the battered rack supported Merriman's conjecture; if that was where the explosion had been, the rack would have been more likely to go straight up and then fall back inside the forge.

'Could the charge have been strapped to the bottom of the hearth itself?' asked Michael.

'That would be very risky if the hearth were too 'ot when you placed it and unpredictable in that even if fitted successfully, it could go off at any time,' said Merriman.

Unpredictable, Josiah turned over the word Merriman had used. If passing on the nail to McBrinnie had precipitated the murder then the target was McBrinnie himself and no one else. If that was the case then the charge had to be triggered by McBrinnie and it seemed that the thing McBrinnie would have been operating when the explosion occurred was the bellows.

'Could you mount the charge on the bellows so that it would go off when McBrinnie operated them?' he asked.

'In theory I suppose you could,' said Merriman.

'But how would you light the fuse?' asked Michael. 'Mr Merriman, could it be lit by touching on the bottom of the hearth?'

'Well it would be hot enough if the fuse were reliable enough.'

Josiah pondered aloud. 'Could the fuse used with the Furness Vale Blasting Cartridges be lit in that way?'

Merriman thought for a bit. 'I think it might but the cartridges are relatively small.'

Michael frowned. 'I have heard the navy use things called bombards on ships. They fire big cannon balls with gunpowder in them that explode. Would they cause this much damage?'

'They're called mortar shells,' said Merriman. 'They're

powerful enough but even the smallest of them contain twenty pounds of powder and have a thick metal casing. They would be too big to get under the hearth assuming you could get one up here without anyone noticing.'

'How thick is the metal casing?' asked Josiah.

'Probably an inch or so. Really can't say.'

Josiah remembered when he had felt the weight of the blasting charges in Mr Bridges office. Then he'd thought they weighed about a pound and a half each. In the mine Merriman had told him, he thought the cartridges were five to six times more powerful than their equivalent in loose powder. If those two estimates were anything like accurate, a grenade with the equivalent explosive powder of a naval shell could be made with two or three blasting cartridges if packed into metal casings about an inch thick. Such a grenade would be small enough to fit below the hearth.

'If you had a something like a naval shell but small enough to fit, could you using a fuse linked to the bellows mechanism to set it off?'

'Say that again?' said Merriman.

'Could you place several grenades under the hearth and then fix the fuses to the bellows mechanism so that it would go up when the bellows was pulled.'

Merriman looked thunder struck. 'Yes, lad, I think you could. Are you thinking that you might make such grenades using the Furnace Vale Cartridges?'

'I am,' said Josiah.

'To leave a hole as shallow as the one we've got, the charge would have to be off the ground.'

'Mounted on the bellows mechanism itself?' suggested Michael. 'Possibly,' said Merriman. 'But we'd need the bellows mechanism to be sure and that must have been destroyed by the blast.'

'But somewhere in the wreckage, there might be pieces of

whatever contained the cartridges. We don't know exactly what we're looking for, but remnants might seem out of place in some way, and we know we're looking for metal about an inch thick. We better search the debris before the light starts to go.'

Starting from the front of the forge they moved out until they had a good idea of the maximum distance that debris had been thrown. Then they formed a short line with about two arms lengths between them. They went back and forward over the field of debris, turning towards the forge on each pass. But while they found plenty of tools, bits of coal and pieces of the roof, nothing seemed out of place and there was no sign of bits of thick metal.

'Better check again inside,' said Josiah. They looked round on both the floor and on what was left of the fittings. It was now rather dark in the forge and they had to light a couple of oil lamps.

'Gentlemen, what is that up there?' said Michael. He pointed to the highest of the roof members still in position. As he moved his lamp Josiah saw something reflect the light. Sticking out of the wood were some slivers of metal. By standing on the large anvil Josiah could reach the objects. They were so sharp he cut his finger as he eased one out of the wood.

'What do you make of that?' he said to Michael handing down the fragment.

Michael turned it over in his hands. 'It's cast iron. Can you get me down some more pieces?' He passed the piece to Merriman. 'Do you cast iron here?'

'Nay, we don't do castin' at all. If we need pieces castin' we order them from a local foundry.' He took the fragment from Michael. 'It's certainly iron and it looks as if it came from something curved.'

Josiah passed down a second piece to them. 'I think I can get at some more,' he said. It took a bit more effort but he retrieved two other pieces. 'There are a few more up there, but we'll need a ladder to reach them.'

They went out into the light to have a better look at the shards. Michael managed to fit all four pieces together. They formed part of what might once have been a tube with an internal diameter of about an inch, same as a blasting candle. They could see that the outer surface of the tube had been notched in places so that it was criss-crossed by knobbly square sections. Some of the pieces of iron had fractured down those grooves between the knobbles. But the complete section of the metal was about an inch thick.

'If there is no casting done here, how did McBrinnie make his horseshoes?' asked Josiah.

'Never 'ad cause to think about that 'till now,' said Merriman. 'He 'ad a workshop near the ponies. Maybe he 'ad a small furnace there?'

'The inside surface of these pieces is blackened,' said Michael.

'What a vicious weapon. Small enough to carry, powerful enough to kill or maim several men, and controllable using the cartridge fuse material,' said Josiah.

They went back to the search. Some digging where the hearth had been yielded some more cast iron shards. Knowing what to look for helped them see pieces on the ground that they had not spotted before. Josiah's thoroughness pushed him in the direction of doing something very macabre. He went back to McBrinnie's body and examined the whole of it, finding more shards embedded deep in his arms and legs. In the end, after some extra help from a couple of Johnstone's men, they collected enough pieces of metal to suggest there had been at least two tubes used. The cartridges must have been used. They retrieved an intact end cap also made of cast iron with a space just right for the fuse for a blasting candle.

The last shift of men from below ground were going home. It was much too late to do any more that day. Merriman had things to attend to and Josiah wished to inform Mr Johnstone that this was indeed a murder but that the body could now be moved indoors.

203

Johnstone took the news well. 'I wish it was not so,' he said, 'but when I saw the explosion, even then it struck me very unlikely that someone as thorough as McBrinnie would have had an accident like that.'

'We will be back tomorrow. We need to find where the tubes for the charges were cast.'

'They wouldn't have been made here,' said Johnstone.

'These were very ingenious devices. I think it very likely that Mr McBrinnie devised and made them himself. Even if they were not actually made here it's the most likely place to find evidence of how they were made,' said Josiah.

31

A Common Past

Having informed Mr Johnstone of the murder Josiah asked the coachman to take Michael and him to Hailsworth Hall. When they arrived, while Michael waited in the kitchens, no doubt using the time to charm some delicacies out of the cook, Josiah was ushered through to the library where he was joined by Mr Hailsworth who interrupted his dinner to talk to him.

'Is it as bad as it appeared?' was his immediate question to Josiah.

'Possibly worse, Sir. It is definitely murder in a particularly ingenious and vicious manner. McBrinnie was the clear target and only McBrinnie, though the murderer could not have known for certain that McBrinnie would be alone when the explosion was triggered.'

'I am very surprised. McBrinnie was such a thorough man and irrespective of professional eccentricities, it seems unlikely he could have had such an enemy? How was the explosion arranged?'

'The murderer used what were effectively grenades made specially to take your son's patent blasting cartridges. I believe McBrinnie designed and constructed those devices but have to prove it.'

'Did he make them on my land?'

'I suspect somewhere within or nearby the mine. I intend to return tomorrow try to find where.'

Mr Hailsworth frowned. 'You will need to question my son Abram at some point, will you not?'

'Yes Sir, but not yet. I would like to have a clearer idea of how the grenades were made. At present it remains as I said when we last spoke. I do not consider Abram a suspect but I do suspect he is much more deeply involved with this matter than appeared to be the case.'

'Thank you, Constable. If there is anything I can do to aid your endeavours you need only ask.'

'Thank you Sir.'

Mr Hailsworth placed a fatherly hand on Josiah's shoulder. 'Josiah, I have every confidence in you.'

Josiah felt a combination of pleasure and sadness. Mr Hailsworth was an upright and kindly man, whose praise he valued. But to see him so distressed about his son moved Josiah.

'I will not fail you Sir.'

The coachman had taken advantage of the stop at Hailsworth Hall to change to a fresh, single horse. The journey back to Long Clough was therefore more leisurely than the outward journey.

'Tell me more about Elijah Bradshawe,' said Michael as the brougham left the Hailsworth estate.

'He came originally from Ireland but never told Rachael where from. When she first met him he was a drunk and taking opium from a woman called Aunty who ran what might loosely be called a house of disrepute. She exploited Rachael. Eventually, Elijah and Rachael came to the Furness Vale and after the previous owner of the farm died, Elijah founded the Children of Fire.'

'Have you got any real idea who killed him?'

'Not really. I know a lot about how he was killed but as to who, I have no clue. I suspected McBrinnie was implicated because the nails used were his design. Now he is dead, any connection of someone else to him seems to have been erased.'

'So you've lost your main suspect and you don't have enough information about what Elijah's life was like in Ireland to pick up a new thread there.'

'That's about the size of it. All I have are bits and pieces, such as what looked like battle scars on his body when I examined it before the funeral. One was probably from a sabre stroke to his shoulder and another, near his hip, from a musket ball. Rachael knew about them but he would never tell her how he had them. It is a fair assumption that they were obtained in Ireland but that is as far I can get.' Josiah pulled out his notebook from his pocket. 'Everything I know is in here.'

Michael took the notebook and started to thumb through it, occasionally holding it up to the window to make the most of the fading evening light. Then he stopped and stared intensely at a single page. He put the book down, took off his jacket and rolled up his sleeve. Then without a word, he presented his left forearm to Josiah. In the middle of Michael's arm was a tattoo. It showed the familiar shape of a celtic harp. The difference between Michael's tattoo and Elijah's was that on Michael's the words below the harp were clear enough to read even in poor light: It is new strung and shall be heard. Josiah looked up at Michael in astonishment.

'Elijah and I seem to have had something in common. I think I might be able to fill in some of the story of what he was doing in Ireland when he got those wounds.'

The coach pulled up; they had arrived at Long Clough. Josiah, his head spinning with surprise that Elijah and Michael should have anything in common, got down.

He had wondered on the way back if he could slink in to sleep and make himself scarce from Long Clough the following morning rather than having to move out at the end of such a hard day. But as he looked up at the farmhouse he saw Rachael standing at the front door. She came towards them. Josiah groaned. She must still be enraged and would now demand he left immediately. He could not really blame her.

'I am sorry, Rachael, I will leave now,' he said, trying to forestall any more upset.

'There is no need for that, Josiah. As I said once before I would feel much safer with you here and that confidence extends to Mr O'Carroll as well.' She looked nervous, even afraid.

'Has something happened while we were away, lass?' asked Michael.

'Only that I have remembered something that frightens me. Come in and I will explain.'

When they were in the kitchen, and she had got Michael and Josiah some food, she sat down to talk as they ate.'

'Josiah you once asked me if Elijah had any enemies. I said no but this morning a face reminded me of an incident that I had quite forgotten. It could be interpreted as showing that Elijah did have an enemy, an enemy who once visited Long Clough.'

Michael stirred in his seat and Josiah, despite his tiredness became immediately attentive. 'What happened?'

'It was twelve years ago. I was ten and Farmer Tremlet was still alive. One day, a day at about this time of year, I was out in the garden playing when a man and a boy came down the path. There was nothing unusual in that nor that they stopped and asked for some water, just as you did yourself Josiah. What was unusual was that the man was blind. I think he was the first blind man I had ever seen, unlikely as that seems.

'I got them a drink and they sat a while and talked. The boy was his son and his guide. He must have been about fifteen. He was a very quiet, attractive boy with intelligent watchful eyes. Josiah who is Phelan Hayes?'

'He is a guest of Mr Hailsworth's. A painter by occupation taking sketches of the Pennines. I met him at dinner the other evening.'

'Where does he come from?'

'The north of Ireland.'

'The blind man and the boy came from Ireland. They said

they were looking for a friend of theirs who they thought might be in the area. They said his name was Fitzgerald. I said I knew no one of that name. They drank their water and went on their way. As I watched them go, Elijah appeared round the corner of the house. Looking back he might have been hiding, watching them without being seen. He was frightened. He asked me what they had wanted and I said they were looking for someone called Fitzgerald.

'Before supper that evening Farmer Tremlet came to me and said that he had sent Elijah to Manchester on some urgent business. He would be back in a couple of days but his housekeeper would look me after while Elijah was away. In a few days Elijah came back and I forgot all about the incident until this morning.'

'Until you saw Phelan?' said Josiah, remembering how distracted she had been while he had tried to apologise and leave Long Clough.

'Yes. Phelan Hayes was the boy who led the blind man. When he came through the door into the courtyard I knew I had seen him before but it took a bit of time to remember exactly when.'

'Are you sure?' said Josiah.

'Absolutely,' said Rachael. 'It was the only time I ever remember thinking Elijah was frightened by anything.'

'Now there's a coincidence,' said Michael. He had made himself comfortable as Rachael had spoken, and got his pipe lit. 'What do you two know about the history of Ireland?'

'I am ashamed to say very little,' said Josiah.

'The same applies to me,' added Rachael.

'You're not alone in that and at least you two have the excuse that for some of the more important parts of the story you hadn't been born. Though I'm slightly disappointed such well-read youngsters as you two don't know more. I'm beginning to think that what is going on in this valley is mixed up with that story. Let's start with the tattoo that Elijah and I shared.'

Josiah interrupted. 'Rachael, it turns out that Michael has the same tattoo on his arm that I found on Elijah.'

'Oh how strange,' she said, immediately following with a flash of girlish curiosity that made Josiah remember why he was so much in love with her. 'Can I see it, Michael?'

Michael rolled up his shirtsleeve and showed her it to her. 'It is the symbol of the Society of United Irishman. I have it on my arm because I was a member. Elijah must have been a member as well.'

'Didn't the United Irishmen lead a rebellion against the British government about forty years ago?' she said.

'Yes and five years after that as well. Rachael, how old was Elijah?'

'Mid-sixties I think but he was as vague about his age as he was with all the other details of his life.'

Michael took a long draw on his pipe. 'They were the best of times in many ways. We looked at what was happening in the American colonies how they had stood up against the parliament across the sea for their right to rule themselves and we thought it was time to do it in Ireland. It was going to be for all Irish people, Protestants and Catholics standing together. The Society was formed to do it and they bridged the tensions between the communities that had been there, well, for centuries. It was a time of hope.' He smiled to himself and took another draw on his pipe.

'It was all about persuasion at first, political action, persuading that parliament to give us home rule. But when that failed the Society led an armed revolt, as had the colonists in the Americas. Elijah would probably have been twenty or so then, just the right to rally to the cause. I was seventeen when I took part in the second revolt. Both were failures and the Society was destroyed.'

Josiah did a quick piece of mental arithmetic. 'Had you and Mary fled from Ireland when I met you as a boy?'

'Yes, lad, we'd been here about two years. Along with a great many others I was a very angry man after the revolt failed. At least I was until I met my Mary. She showed me how ridiculous and stupid it all was, the hate, not the ideals. But I was a wanted man so we came and hid ourselves in England.

'After both revolts the grief of the failure expressed itself in sectarian hatred breaking out again. Groups of Catholics attacked Protestants, Protestants attacked Catholics, especially in country districts.'

'So is that why Irish politics now seem so clearly divided with Catholics wanting freedom from British rule and Protestants supporting the Parliament in Dublin?' asked Rachael.

'Yes that and the since the first revolt British governments have worked hard to enhance those divisions. Have you two never heard of the principle of divide and rule? One of the ways it has been done is by using the Irish romantic love of secret societies and clandestine signs of allegiance. Elijah and I had our tattoos but I saw an exclusively protestant secret sign on the lapel of a young man here this morning, just out there by the pump.'

'You mean Phelan's orange flower, don't you?' said Josiah.

'A sign of membership of one Protestant society of hatred or another. It is an uncommon one in that it is so obvious it doesn't get used much outside staunchly Protestant areas. Where do the Hayes come from?'

'Donegal,' said Josiah.

'A mixed area with Protestants and Catholics, but there are still places where it would be safe to wear the "orange lily" as Phelan does.'

Michael's hand began to shake, his voice became emotional. 'People like Phelan Hayes call people like me Croppies because they reckon we cut our hair short. As it says in one of their favourite songs they will put their feet on our necks to ensure us Croppies lie down and never get our freedom!'

Josiah shivered. He remembered the bruising on Elijah's throat which he thought had been caused by a boot stamping on the neck. 'Easy Michael,' he said. 'Protestants Rachael and I might be but we are your friends. You'll never be a Croppie in our eyes.'

'Thank you lad. I can't help but remember the insults I had when I was young but I also get angry at how easy it's been for a few to stir up hatred among my people.' He calmed himself with another draw on that favourite old pipe of his.

'I can take Rachael's story on a bit further and confirm her identification of Phelan as the boy,' said Josiah. 'Aideen Hayes told me that her father was blind. He was the only man who could woo her mother because she had been disfigured in a terrible fire in the family home in Donegal. Aideen was five or so when her mother killed herself because she had never come to terms with her disfigurement.'

Rachael was frowning in concentration. 'Phelan and his father were looking for someone called Fitzgerald when they visited Long Clough. If Elijah was Fitzgerald could he have had something to do with the original fire Michael?'

'It's possible. Resistance by some rebel groups went on for years. Those groups committed some gruesome atrocities. They were particularly fond of setting houses on fire in the night as a way of murdering the occupants.'

'Aideen said it was a fire set at night or at least in the early morning that maimed her mother,' said Josiah.

'That sounds right,' said Michael. 'Fitzgerald's a Catholic name. Some of the Catholic groups learned that tactic from loyalist groups who called themselves Peek o' Day Boys. If Elijah went on fighting after the first revolt then he could have joined one of those catholic groups. He could easily have got his wounds during skirmishes with soldiers then, even if he didn't get them at the time of the revolt. If Elijah had anything to do with the fire that scarred Aideen's mother then Phelan and his father had a very good motive to search for him.'

'And for killing him in revenge,' added Josiah.

'Remorse for the fire also gives an explanation why Elijah became the wreck of a man who rescued me in Liverpool,' said Rachael. They were silent as they thought through these speculations.

Josiah was the first to speak again. 'But there is still a missing link. What drew Phelan back here? Maybe he realised that Elijah was Fitzgerald by accident and that led to the murder, but why come here in the first place, unless it was the pure coincidence of his being a painter.'

Michael knocked out his pipe into the grate. 'Phelan Hayes may be a painter but the sort of person who wears the "orange lily" in public like that, owes his prime allegiance to the cause of Protestant domination. He'll be a member of some sort of Orange organisation and will do its bidding. I would be willing to bet, one way or another, it was his duty in that direction that brought him here.'

32

FEARFUL DEVICES

Josiah and Michael took an early breakfast the following day and set off to the mine, walking back to Hailsworth Hall and being taken on by coach. As soon as they arrived Merriman joined them and led them down into a wooded valley overlooking the rest of the estate, with the roof of the Hall just visible in the distance.

As they passed the forge, Josiah noticed that the process of stabilising the building and tidying up had begun. Merriman saw his interest.

'Don't worry, Constable, we've been collecting all the bits of metal from the grenades we can find and anything else we thought you might need as evidence. McBrinnie's body is in one of the empty outbuildings near the drift, waiting for the coroner. Mr Hailsworth is bringing him later today.'

Over the lip of the valley the path cut down through some high bracken and then, flattening out, entered a sheltered beech wood. After about a hundred yards they emerged into a series of small flat fields, where several of the mine ponies, not needed for work that day, were grazing. On the far side of the fields were some stables.

'The small forge McBrinnie used for shoeing is near the stables,' said Merriman.

The stable yard was full of activity as ponies were being

harnessed up for the day's work. Merriman pointed over to their left. 'There's a track down from the mine entrances over there by which the ponies go to work.'

The shoeing forge was small. It was not much more that a hearth, a few tools and a medium-sized anvil. But unlike the main forge, in neat rows round the walls were examples of different sizes and types of shoes. In a series of wooden boxes Josiah found various types of nails. He examined the sort used on Elijah. He turned to Merriman and held one up.

'That's as maybe, but there's still a mystery to be solved here,' said Merriman. 'Here is everything that is needed for caring for the ponies, including the shoes and nails. But as you pointed out yesterday, Constable, where is the means to cast them?'

They searched round. The small forge was built on the edge of the valley. At its rear the ground fell away so that underneath the main building there was a large half-cellar accessible through a double door. When they opened it, inside the cellar, to the right of the door was a small furnace.'

'So this is where he did the casting. The doors provide ventilation and it keep the hot work of smelting away from the forge. Typical McBrinnie practicality,' said Merriman.

Josiah looked round. In one corner there was a pile of small pig iron billets for melting. In another were various sizes of crucibles to fit in the top of the furnace, as well as their tongs and carriers.

There were bags of sand and wooded trays for making pressed sand moulds, one under moistened sacking to keep it damp had already been prepared for the casting of six horseshoes.

'Nothing out of order here,' said Michael.

'No evidence McBrinnie made the casings that were used for the grenades that killed him,' said Josiah.

'Looks as if he was expecting to cast a few horse shoes yesterday. You can't leave sand moulds too long before using them,' said Michael. 'They dry out and crumble.'

Josiah was only half listening. Something had attracted his attention to footmarks near the pig iron store. He crouched down and brushed some of the earth away. In the bottom of an impression made by the heal of substantial hobnailed boot was a small piece of iron. It was broken, but not jagged, it had been split deliberately down two of the lines that divided it into two square moulded knobbles. He held it up.

'Mr Merriman, am I right to think that failed iron castings can be melted down again and reused?'

'Yes, provided you use enough fresh pig iron with them.'

'So we wouldn't find any tubes here unless someone happened to drop a piece of an old casing when putting fragments in the furnace.'

Merriman came over and looked at the fragment, tossed it in the air, caught it and whistled. 'Constable, we came looking for a small foundry which we've found. Now we've found evidence that this furnace was used to make the tubing for the grenades. But the most precious thing in a foundry, are the patterns for the items cast, the wooden shapes that are pressed into the sand to make the moulds. They are expensive in time and skill to make. Where are Mr McBrinnie's patterns? There should be one 'ere for 'orseshoes at least.'

They searched again, moving the bags of sand, the crucibles and even the pile of pig iron billet by billet. But there was nowhere the patterns could be. Dispirited, they walked round to the stables for a drink of water and in the case of Merriman and Michael a smoke.

'Perhaps he simply put them somewhere else,' said Michael.

Merriman knocked his pipe out on his boot heal. 'I doubt they would be far from the furnace. He'd want them to hand, especially any private ones.'

Josiah thought for a moment. 'One more search. If we don't find anything then I will put what we have found to Mr Hailsworth and allow him to decide what should be done.'

They went back to the foundry. Josiah cast his eyes over the furnace itself. It was no more than waist high, bellows to one side and place for stoking with coal at the front. At the top was a space for the crucibles to be dropped in over the fire. All was mounted on a slab of solid Peak District grit-stone. There was a metal gantry above it to allow the crucibles to be raised on a chain pulley. A very well designed arrangement.

He now had a plausible account of what had happened. Phelan with the help of McBrinnie had killed Elijah in revenge for the death of his mother. McBrinnie had told Phelan about the nails and Phelan had killed him to shut him up. But there were still questions to be answered. What was Phelan doing in the valley? Why had McBrinnie made the grenades? Josiah became aware that Merriman was looking up at the gantry with him.

'Does that piece of gubbins worry you too?'

'No not really. It seems very neat to me. As you said early typical McBrinnie practicality.'

'But unnecessary. It don't need a chain hoist to move the crucibles this furnace takes. The ones over there,' he pointed to the crucibles and tools, 'can be handled between two men for pouring or even one man at a pinch. It is also very unusual to put a furnace on a slab of stone. Hard baked clay is normal. Eventually the stone will crack with the heat.'

Having had his attention called to the stone Josaih looked at it more carefully. On the right front corner there was something metal in the dust. It would be very useful if it happened to be another piece of grenade tubing. He stooped and brushed the dust way. Attached to the corner of the stone slab, facing horizontally to the right was a heavy metal eye-ring. Merriman saw what he was doing and started examining the stone on the left side. There was an identical eye-ring on the left corner. They circumnavigated the slab. In all there were four eye-rings one at each corner.

Merriman let down the hoist and attached four hooks he found on the end of its main chain, one to each eye-ring. Then with Michael's help they hauled the furnace into the air six inches and pulled it away to one side.

They looked in astonishment at a large-brick-lined cavity that had been concealed by the furnace. Josiah lit his small police lantern, gave his hat to Michael, and went down into the hole. It was about seven foot deep. To his left, sloping downwards, was a cramped tunnel about three feet high which ran for about five yards. This ended in a small chamber in which were three small chests. In one were the wooden patterns for several different designs of horseshoes as well as others for miscellaneous parts McBrinnie must have cast for use in the mine at odd times. In the second there were two sets of patterns for the grenade tubes and caps. In the third there was a supply of Furness Patent Blasting Charges along with two reels of fuse.

Josiah dragged the chests back to the opening to be hauled. Though they had been looking for the patterns, seeing them in the light of day was still a surprise. No one knew quite what to say. Michael finally broke the silence by saying the obvious, 'McBrinnie made the grenade tubes.'

Merriman was looking at the grenade tube patterns. 'Designed and made but I bet he didn't stop at making just a few and the fact that the patterns are still 'ere suggests 'e was go'in to mek more.'

'But there are no more here,' said Josiah. 'Mr Merriman, please can you examine the blasting charges? Are they from the mine's stores?'

Merriman looked carefully at several. 'No, Constable, they ain't. These 'ave different batch numbers to the ones we received from Furnace Vale.'

'So that connects Phelan Hayes and McBrinnie directly to the powder mill. I am willing to surmise that Mr Abram Hailsworth can enlighten us as to the nature of that connection.'

They replaced the furnace and closed up the foundry. Merriman spoke to the senior miner at the stables who agreed to make sure no one went in or out until a carpenter was sent to secured the door. Then they started back up the path, Josiah carrying the grenade patterns personally.

When they got back Mr Hailsworth was waiting, having brought the coroner. Josiah gave Mr Johnstone a quick report before Johnstone went to see the coroner about the details of the inquest. Merriman went back to his duties. When they were gone Josiah reported to Mr Hailsworth.

When he had heard the whole account Mr Hailsworth sighed. 'You and I Josiah urgently need to ask my son some significant questions do we not?'

'Yes we do, Sir. Do you know where he is at this moment?'

'I left him at the Hall taking coffee with his mother no more than half an hour ago. We will go directly there. Will you need Mr O'Carroll, if so he can come with us?'

'No, but with your permission I would like to send him back to Long Clough using the brougham. I take it Phelan has left the Hall?'

'Yesterday.'

'Then we have no real idea where he is. It is possible that since Rachael recognised him he may have recognised her and could seek to silence her to prevent the connection to Elijah bringing him under suspicion of the murder. Michael can make sure she is safe.'

33

CAT AND MOUSE

Mr Hailsworth's landau swept up the approach to the Hailsworth Hall but this time Josiah had neither the heart nor the time to enjoy the view of the house. Once in the courtyard they went up the back stairs and came out close to the library. Abram was still talking to Barbara Hailsworth in the library alcove. He looked up, pleased to see his father, a pleasure that vanished when he saw Josiah a few paces behind.

Steven Hailsworth spoke gravely and directly to his wife. 'I am sorry to interrupt your conversation, my dear, but Constable Ainscough and I have some very important questions to ask Abram. I am afraid that we will have to ask you to leave us.'

Barbara Hailsworth got up with dignity and left without saying a word. Her only acknowledgement of Josiah was a slight, cold nod as she passed him.

Mr Hailsworth sat down on the red-plush seats facing his son. 'Abram, Constable Ainscough has unearthed some information that involves you directly in his investigation into the death of Elijah Bradshawe. As the Chief Magistrate in the district he has asked me to sit in to witness his interview with you about these matters.'

'Father, is this necessary? Can't you let this matter drop?' The voice was mildly irritated, as if the whole thing where a bore or inconvenience but Josiah fancied there were more serious tensions in the background which Abram's manner was trying to hide.

'No. As magistrate I could not let it drop under any circumstances, doubly so because you are my son. I am sorry Abram this will be as disturbing for both of us but it has to be done. I will now leave the field free for Mr Ainscough.'

Josiah took out his notebook and looked Abram in the eye. 'Mr Hailsworth, when did you first meet Phelan Hayes?'

Abram shifted slightly in his seat. Josiah's question had surprised him and he had to pause before answering. To Josiah's surprise Abram did not obfuscate. 'Nearly two years ago.'

'Abram!' said Steven Hailsworth. 'In March, when Phelan Hayes presented himself here as a painter you never indicated you had met him before!'

Abram backed off slightly. 'I am sorry that I was less than forthcoming. It did not seem an important connection at the time.'

Josiah proceeded. 'How did you meet him, Mr Hailsworth?'

'In the Lake District while I was buying some equipment from the powder mills in the area, he was making illustrations of the fells. We passed some days together while I was waiting to hear from two of the mills about bids I had made on some of their presses and the weather was too wet for him to get out to paint. When I finished my business and was leaving I suggested that if they ever came to Derbyshire he should be sure to look me up and that we would be able to give them lodging at the Hall.'

A plausible answer though Josiah, but he still felt there was more to it. 'Did he know why you were in Cumbria?'

'Yes, I made no secret of my plans to start a gunpowder mill.' Momentarily Abram looked sheepish. 'I may have somewhat boasted about the matter. At the time I was attracted to Aideen and I may have tried to impress her by inflating the prospects of my new business.'

Again plausible. It agreed with what Abram had said about

Aideen when Josiah had seen Abram at the powder mill but the matter was still worth a bit more pressure.

'You were infatuated but it did not last. Is that a fair assessment?'

'I suppose you might put it that way.'

'Can you tell me more about what you mean by that?'

'When I got back I simply realised I loved my Elizabeth more than Aideen. Indeed I doubted if I had ever really loved Aideen at all.'

Abram was being commendably open and there seemed to Josiah to be no inconsistency worth probing further with him about Aideen. He changed tack; it was Abram's dealings with Phelan that mattered. 'What about your relationship with Phelan?'

'A pleasant enough acquaintance, nothing more.'

'Are you sure of that. If I suggested I observed tension between you and him the night of the dinner. Would that surprise you?'

'Yes. I would say your observation was in error.'

The way Abram had fended off this small suggestion of tension between him and Phelan suggested to Josiah that Abram was uncertain in how to respond. He would return to it again but first make it look as if he was satisfied with Abram's answer. It was time to play one of the hidden cards in his hand and change his line of attack.

'When I talked to you at the powder mill I asked you whether you used sulphur in making your blasting powder. You told me that you did not – is that still you answer?'

'We do not use sulphur in either the mixtures for the blasting cartridges or for the powder in the fuses.'

'Then why did I find a sample of flowers of sulphur spilled on the tramway near to a locked storage building at the mill. Would you swear that your mill has never made blackpowder containing sulphur?'

'We have never used sulphur in any of our products.' Abram answered carefully and confidently but his lips were pursed and tense.

Josiah pressed him. 'That is not what I asked; it might not have to be for a product, it might just have been a test batch for comparison.'

Abram looked even more uncomfortable and was excessive excessively emphatic in his reply, 'Never!'

Why had Abram not taken the escape route he had offered him, thought Josiah. Josiah paused and Steven Hailsworth interjected, 'Constable, is there any evidence that there is sulphur in the products?'

'No Sir. In fact Mr Merriman confirmed that there is, in his opinion, no sulphur in either the charges or the fuses. As I understand it there is only one market that would insist on sulphur being used and that would be loose powder for military applications where the sulphur would reduce the risk of misfire.'

As he said this Josiah watched Abram's expression from the corner of his eye. He expected Abram to be relieved but if anything he looked more not less tense. Something in what Josiah had just said had disturbed Abram more than anything else Josiah had asked up to that point. Time for another card from his hand.

'Mr Hailsworth, we now know for certain that Mr McBrinnie, the farrier at your father's mines, was murdered. More than that we know that it was done using cast iron grenade charges which McBrinnie designed and made to utilise your blasting cartridges. We found a supply of those cartridges charges that had come directly from the powder mill in a secret hiding place at his foundry, along with wooden patterns for the tubes. Both are now in my possession. I also know that he supplied the nails that were used to crucify Elijah Bradshawe, a murder for which we believe Phelan Hayes had a personal motive.'

Abram Hailsworth finally lost his composure. 'Good God man do you think I helped kill Elijah!'

'No, Mr Hailsworth, I do not! What I think is that there is a link between you and Phelan Hayes that led to you to supply McBrinnie with a stock of blasting cartridges. I believe Phelan Hayes is somehow at the bottom of the succession of killings that have taken place in this valley. Those murders probably include those killed in the explosion at the powder mill earlier in the year!' Josiah went back to his friendly tone. 'Why will you not tell me what that link is?'

Abram looked trapped. He paused and started to speak but broke off, coughed and tried again.

'Please, my son. I know you too well for you to conceal your feelings from me. What are you hiding?'

Abram cleared his throat and whispered, as if he feared to be overheard even here at the heart of Hailsworth Hall. 'Because he will kill her!'

There was silence. 'Mr Abram, who is threatened?' asked Josiah.

'Elizabeth and her son. Phelan is holding them hostage.' With the uncleared coffee cups there was a jug of water and two glasses, Abram filled one. His hands were shaking. He took a sip of water before speaking.

'When Phelan arrived here on the doorstep in March he immediately took me to one side and made it clear how pleased he was that my mill was up and running. He told me he had an agent working nearby who had kept a careful watch on our progress. He also made it clear that if I did not make him a quantity of military grade powder for use in muskets there would be consequences. He wasn't explicit what those consequences would be but he forced me to be silent about my having met him in Cumbria by implying a threat of harm to you Father,' he looked at Mr Hailsworth, 'and Mother.'

Steven Hailsworth muttered something Josiah thought might have been, 'Oh my God.' Abram took another sip of water.

'I tried to resist him but the explosions at the mill followed immediately after I made a concerted attempt to deny him. After that Bridges and I bought in the sulphur a bit at a time so as not to arouse interest and with the help of three men who we could trust, ran secret batches of the powder incorporating sulphur through the mill.'

'How much did you make?' asked Josiah.

'What he demanded: five ton, enough for a small army. We finished last week. Ironically, two days ago if you had forced me to open that store you would have found one hundred barrels of blackpowder that invented mill records would demonstrate were being stored for a Cumbrian mill owner.'

'What is in that store now?'

'Nothing. There is nothing in that store now. Phelan came and took all of it this evening at six. He warned me not to think I could stop him. He has Elizabeth and her son under guard in her house in Hayfield. They will be killed if the shipment does not get at least twenty-four hours head start from possible pursuit.'

'How are they transhipping the powder?'

Abram was stony-faced he took a deep breath. 'I won't tell you.'

'Then I will ask Mr Bridges.'

'He does not know. The only chance you have of stopping them is if I tell you how they are getting the powder out of the area and I won't tell you that before Elizabeth is safe.'

'What about the grenades?'

'Phelan demanded four hundred and fifty cartridges as well as a suitable quantity of fuse. Bridges glimpsed the grenade tubes while the black powder was being loaded. He said there were about hundred to a hundred and fifty of them. You have made it harder for them to make the extra tubes to convert those charges into grenades by finding the patterns but they could use one of the metal tubes as a guide to make new patterns once away.'

That was the last thing of substance Abram Hailsworth was prepared to say. Even though Steven Hailsworth and Josiah, pleaded with him to tell them where the powder was going he would say nothing more. They even asked Barbara Hailsworth to implore him to co-operate but she refused, saying as a mother herself she would not help them endanger Robert, Elizabeth's son.

By evening it was clear that a rescue of Elizabeth and her son was the only way they could induce Abram to tell them how the powder was being moved.

34

To Arms

It was a night of frantic preparation. All the servants of the house were set on various tasks and errands. Steven Hailsworth sent a note to the head of the small detachment of local militia in Hayfield instructing him to rouse two or three of his best men, arm them and meet him just outside the town at dawn. The note stressed that they should assemble discreetly and without fuss so as not to attract any attention to themselves.

Realising she could not dissuade her husband in a rescue attempt of Elizabeth, Barbara Hailsworth turned herself to assisting the effort and organised the female servants to ensure that there were enough bandages and dressings available to go to Hayfield with the men. A groom was dispatched to Long Clough to fetch Michael. When he came back Rachael, Peter and James were with him. Rachael set to work helping Barbara, and Peter and James made themselves useful in preparing a couple of carts with the supplies, tools and assorted weapons assembled during the night, taking them off in the direction of Hayfield as soon as they were ready. Rachael went with Peter, and Agnes, the maid Josiah had met the night of the dinner, went with James. Even if they were observed they would appear to be roving traders off to sell their wares in Hayfield.

Josiah came across Abram preparing a brace of pistols and a couple of fowling pieces. He took him to one side. 'I know your instincts and your honour make you wish to lead this rescue; after all you love her. But I do not think it is wise for you to lead the charge. Your courage and passion does you credit but this is going to require guile and cunning if we are going to get them out alive.'

'You'll not be able to stop me coming!'

'I will not try. Your role will be vital, you are the only one with detailed knowledge of Elizabeth's house but I would ask you not to be too forward in any attack. I do not want to rescue Elizabeth only to find the man she loves dead in a pool of blood.'

'Do you not trust me, Josiah?'

'As well as I would trust myself in your position. There is one person I think we will need before this day is done. Explosives have been at the heart of this matter and I would like to have Mr Merriman with us, as an expert on blackpowder and your blasting cartridges. Can you get him to the rendezvous point?'

To Josiah's surprise ten minutes afterwards he was seeing a calm Abram off from the courtyard with no more argument. He ran into Michael on his way back.

'I heard your pretty speech to Master Abram. Remember to give yourself the same leeway you've given him. This is the first time you've ever been in battle.'

'I will try, Michael. With God's help, I will try.'

'I've also got some news for you. When Phelan left he did not take his luggage with him. He left instructions for it to follow him to the Liverpool boat by carrier. The luggage should have gone yesterday but there was a mistake and it is still here. I wonder if he might have left that shirt in it?'

They found the luggage which consisted of three trunks and a couple of large valise. At the bottom of the second trunk, which contained Phelan's clothes and painting materials, they found Elijah's torn and blood stained shirt.

'That confirms it,' said Josiah. 'Phelan murdered Elijah with the help of McBrinnie, as well as being responsible for the explosion at the powder mill. Then he killed McBrinnie. Michael, he has killed seven people in cold blood. We must make sure he doesn't kill two or more before we stop him.'

They let the wagons get an hour's head start then, with the eastern sky only slightly lighted they mounted up. Steven Hailsworth travelled with his wife in the brougham. The best shot available with a fowling piece, the head gamekeeper, joined the coachman on the box, and Michael and Josiah went on horseback in front.

They left the Hall on one of the tracks that led to a gate in the estate wall. They looped south using a couple of lanes known to the gamekeeper, wide enough to take the brougham, coming out at the rendezvous point on the road to Chapel-en-le-Frith, south of Hayfield

The wagons, which had been brought over by James and Peter, were discretely tucked away in a small copse. Three men of the Hayfield militia were there with their sergeant. They came smartly to attention as Steven Hailsworth got down from the coach. Gallantly, Michael helped Barbara Hailsworth out of the brougham and they joined Mr Hailsworth as he went across to brief the sergeant. Josiah went over to Rachael and Peter.

'Have you seen anything?'

'Not a thing,' said Rachael. 'No one passed us. We found the militia easily.'

'Has Abram Hailsworth arrived?'

'Yes. He brought Mr Merriman with him about half an hour ago. They have gone off towards the house so that they can see how the land lies. Brother James has gone with them.'

Josiah's first thought was that of alarm. Would Abram be able to contain himself? But even as he started to worry, three figures broke cover on the other side of the road and, bent double. ran across to them.

'I am heartily glad to see you safe and sound,' he said to the small group. We had better join the militia men so they can get the benefit of your scouting efforts.'

Abram walked over with Josiah. 'I bet you wondered if I would be hot-headed when you found I'd charged off.' he said.

'It did cross my mind.'

'Not to worry, Mr Merriman and Brother James were caution itself. We thought it a good thing to take a look at the house as soon as possible.' They reached the group around Steven Hailsworth.

'Abram, good we are all met. Good day to you, Mr Merriman, I am glad you could join the party. What is next, Constable Ainscough? Sergeant Olds here will take his cue from you.'

Josiah tried not to show the panic he felt. He had thought older and more experienced heads, more used affairs such as this, might now take over but there was no time to argue about it.

'Abram, what did your scouting party find?'

'In short everything is quiet. The house is over there near the river about five hundred yards away. From where we came out just now, there is a path across the fields that leads to a garden gate at the back of the house. Between that gate and the house itself there is a small orchard and then a formal garden divided from the orchard by a thick hedge of about six feet high. If we approach that way then we can probably steal up to the back of the house using the cover afforded by the trees and the hedge. That will be greatly helped by the fact that there is a thick mist over the river on that side of the house.'

'Is there a similar well covered approach to the front of the house?' asked Sergeant Olds.

'In principle, yes,' said Abram. 'Further up the road there is a track that goes down to it but that path is rather open. Brother James reasoned that if they have set a guard, that was where it would be but as far as we were able to see there is no one on the road or at the front of the house.'

'What about upper windows?' asked Michael.

'No sign at all,' said Merriman.

'At the back?'

'Arder to say.'

'But there are no lights visible anywhere,' added Abram.

'Abram, how many servants does Elizabeth keep?' asked Barbara.

'A maid and housekeeper.'

'The housekeeper would be up by now setting the range fires. There should have been some activity. Any smoke out of the chimneys?'

'None,' said Brother James.

Josiah pondered what these last remarks meant. Potentially there were four captives in the house. Up to that point he had assumed he would find Elizabeth and her son in the same room under a single guard. But the two servants complicated the matter. They could not rule out the possibility that the guard would split the group up making rescue more difficult. But to him, the safety of the servants were no less a priority than that of Elizabeth and the boy.

'So there's no sign of any activity at all?' remarked Michael. 'I would have expected there to be something to suggest there were guards present no matter how secure they felt about the control of their prisoners.'

Josiah looked at his friend. Michael had something on his mind. 'What are you thinking, Michael?'

'That there may be no guards at all. That this is a blind.' As Michael spoke the first direct rays of sun came over the hills to the east. The sun would disperse the mist quickly losing them that advantage.

'How early would an Irish tinker call to see the housekeeper about pots to repair?' asked Josiah.

'If he had a tip there might be good pickings to have, easily as early as this,' chuckled Michael.

'Would you be prepared to play the part, Michael?'

'Yes. Mr Abram, is the track big enough for one of the wagons?'

'I think so. I'd take the smaller one to be certain.'

'I'll come with you, Mr O'Carroll.' It was Agnes. 'Many of the tinkers who call at the Hall have wives or daughters. It will look less suspicious if I come.'

Barbara Hailsworth looked worried. 'Are you sure, Agnes?'

'Quite sure, ma'am.'

Josiah went back to giving orders. 'Michael and Agnes, get the cart ready. Brother Peter will help you. He'll also hide under the cover behind you in case it develops into a fight.' Josiah grinned at Peter who unexpectedly smiled back.

'Sergeant Olds take your men round the back of the house. Mr Abram and Brother James will show you the way. Get as close as you can without being seen but don't attack until I give a signal. Then force your way through the doors with all speed. Abram, you know the inside of the house. Wait behind the militia. Help guide them in searching the rooms if it comes to a full assault.

'Mr Merriman and I will follow the route of the wagon from cover. I'd like your head gamekeeper to come to protect us if that is alright, Mr Hailsworth?' Steven Hailsworth looked over to the man who nodded his assent.

'Please bring him back in one piece, Constable, or I'll have no grouse to shoot next year.'

'Noted, Sir. If we get a chance to enter quietly from the front we will. Let's hope this door is ready to be pushed open or at least carelessly guarded.'

The militia formed up and Abram led them round the back. As soon as Josiah knew they were well away on the path, he gave the nod to Michael and Agnes to set off. The cart made its way up the road and he saw it make the turn into the lane. Then he led Merriman and the gamekeeper across the fields to intercept the line of the approach.

They got to the track a little in front of the cart and watched as it ambled past their position. Agnes with a shawl over her head and Michael were singing. Presumably, Michael thought that it would keep Agnes's spirits up. But though the tune was beautiful, the few words Josiah could catch were too wistful to be really cheering. They followed the wagon on their side of the hedge.

There was no sign of anyone and no challenge. Michael pulled up in front of the house and got down. Josiah positioned himself as far forward as he could so that he would be able to hear anything that was said if the door of the house was opened. He kept Merriman beside him and gave the gamekeeper instructions to guard Agnes who looked exposed and rather frightened sitting out in the open on the top of the wagon.

Josiah heard Michael knock on the door. There was a pause and then he knocked once more. Then he began to sing again, his Irish voice sounding natural and cheerful in the gentle morning sun. Then he knocked again and shouted, 'Any pots to mend?'

35

DESPERATE MEASURES

Josiah could just see Michael's silhouette against the lightening sky. He watched as his friend looked through the front windows of the house and then went round both sides of the building. He came over to the hedge behind which Josiah and Merriman were hiding and knocked out his pipe. As he did so he whispered to Josiah. 'I can't see any life at all.'

In reply Josiah and the others climbed out of hiding and ran quickly to the main door.

'Can we get in from here?' he said to Michael.

'I think so, lad. Give me your truncheon.' With its butt he deftly cracked the glass in one of the leaded lights in the front window and opened it. Josiah climbed in. He found himself in a comfortable sitting room. Making his way carefully over to the door to what must be the hallway, he listened. The house was quiet. He opened the door, peeked into the empty hall and went through it making for the front door. The bolts were drawn back and the key for the door on the floor. The door was unlocked and he simply opened it to let the others in.

Slowly they went through the downstairs rooms. The kitchen was empty and the range cold. Only the sonorous ticking of a grandfather clock disturbed a second sitting room. Michael and Peter went down into the cellars from the kitchen while Josiah, Merriman and the gamekeeper climbed the stairs. Three doors ran off from the landing. The first led to what looked like a child's room, which was empty, but the bed had been slept in. The next, led to a lady's bedroom and dressing room. This too was empty but the bed was undisturbed. They were about to go into the third room when they heard the only sound so far that might be a sign of life. Someone or something was knocking rhythmically on floorboards above their heads.

They backed up and found the narrow stairs that led up to the attic rooms. Josiah signalled that the gamekeeper should go first with his gun at the ready. The drumming had stopped but one of the plain boards on the stairs creaked. Immediately it started again, this time with greater intensity.

There were two rooms off the attic landing. It was clear that the noise was coming from the one at the end. Quietly Josiah opened the door.

Tied hand and foot under a large window opposite were three women and a boy. Two, one older than the other, were dressed in black dresses with white aprons. The third woman wore a smart silk dressing gown. The young boy was also in nightclothes.

They all had their mouths silenced with cloths and their hands were bound. They were hog-tied and their bonds were fixed to the floor so that they could not shuffle about. As soon as they saw Josiah the two younger women and the boy started to make muffled cries. The older woman, presumably the housekeeper, made no effort. She appeared to have fainted.

Josiah stepped into the room. As he did so the urgency and volume of the captives' noises got louder and it was accompanied by them widening their eyes. They seemed to be nodding furiously towards his feet. He looked down but there was nothing there. He took a second step. The prisoners went wild, struggling and throwing themselves about as much as their bonds would allow. Then, against the black leather of his boot he saw it. A strong linen thread about six inches above the floor. On his left it was fixed to the wainscoting with a hook, on the other side of the room it was fixed to a weight on a small see-saw. This was balanced by a lighted candle held over a pile of blackpowder from which a trail led to a short fuse on a grenade behind the door he had just opened.

Gently he moved his boot back from the thread but the designer of this deadly trap seemed to have thought of everything, for the line was sticky with resin. There was a clunking sound from the sea-saw; the weight was now half over its edge. The cord tightened further, the weight fell off the sea-saw and there was a blinding flash as the black-powder ignited.

He had not expected to feel his body hit the floor but he did. He even coughed as the smoke from the powder got to into his throat. He looked up and saw Merriman ripping the fuse out of the grenade.

'Stop having a bloody rest, lad! Get up and give me a 'and with this abomination!'

There was a pounding of feet on the stairs and into the room charged Abram, Michael and Rachael.

Rachael ran over to Josiah and helped him up from the floor. Her face was white and she was out of breath. She put her hand up to his forehead and pushed back a few strands of hair that were over his eyes. 'Thank God you are alright,' she said. 'I thought… well, we all thought… just… well… thank God everyone is alright.' Then she looked embarrassed and went to help the housekeeper.

Josiah opened the window. 'Agnes,' he shouted. The young woman appeared in view in the garden. 'Tell everyone that we are alright, including Elizabeth, her son and her servants.' He was pleased to see that Agnes gave a little jump for joy at the news before shooting of to spread the word. He shut the window and saw another heart-warming scene of Abram embracing Elizabeth while being hugged by Robert.

When the cloth was out of the housekeeper's mouth, to

Josiah's great relief, she started to recover. The maid had bad bruises round her ankles and wrists but could walk when she had rubbed some life back into her numb feet. She got down the attic steps by herself only taking Michael's arm for steadiness on the larger stairs down to the hallway.

Elizabeth wanted to do the same, but Abram would hear none of it. Picking her up in his arms he carried her downstairs. Josiah heard the cheers as they emerged through the front door. Rachael took Robert down by the hand.

'Are you one of the Children of Fire?' said the boy.

'Yes I am. I am Sister Rachael.'

'I thought so; I have seen you when Mummy has taken me to hear Brother Elijah preach.'

With everyone gone Josiah was left alone with Merriman. Josiah offered his hand to the powder man. 'I, well we all, owe you our lives.'

'It were my life too lad and I 'ad the advantage of knowing the fuse on the grenades where the weak link in McBrinnie's infernal device. But I wouldn't have been 'ere if you 'ad't had the foresight to send Master Abram to fetch us. Reckon you saved your sel' there.'

'Thanks anyway.'

They went down stairs. Outside Mr Hailsworth had brought the brougham down the lane. Elizabeth and her son were being attended by Barbara Hailsworth. Rachael was making the maid and the housekeeper comfortable on the wagon. It was clear that they were all being taken back to Hailsworth Hall so that they could be looked after.

Josiah walked over to Elizabeth. She stood up as he came towards her. 'I believe I owe you thanks for my own life and that of my son,' she extended her had to Josiah. 'Thank you, Constable.'

'It was my duty, ma'am. There are a few things you could tell me if you have the strength.'

'Anything.'

'How long were you held captive?'

'From late last evening until you rescued us.

'How many of them were there?'

'Just two.'

'Would you recognise either of them again?'

'No, they wore masks at first and made their desires clear more by gesture than speaking. They blindfolded us at times, presumable so that they didn't have to do everything with their masks on.'

'How did they get in?'

'They simply knocked on the door. When Mary, my maid, went to answer it they seized her. Then they charged into my room and look me captive, then they woke Robert. They caught Mrs Jones, my housekeeper, off guard downstairs in one of the storerooms. Then they took us upstairs at pistol point and tied us up. Finally, they rigged the explosives and left almost exactly at midnight, the grandfather clock struck, just as they left. I suppose they even locked the front door after them.'

'They didn't bother. The door was open.' Josiah turned to Abram. 'Mr Hailsworth, I have kept my side of our bargain. How is the powder to be moved?'

'Using the canal,' said Abram. 'They would not be able to move that amount of powder very far by wagon. It took three wagons to get it from the mill but a barge could take that amount of powder easily and still leave space to hide the barrels under other cargo. Also Phelan boasted early on, that the powder was only part of the plan. There was a shipment of muskets and small arms on its way to them. It is pretty clear that was coming by canal as well. I am sorry, Constable, but it looks to me that Phelan Hayes has got clean away.'

36

Taking the High Road

A swell of dissatisfaction came over Josiah as he watched Brother James at the reins of the wagon, accompanied by Agnes and the gamekeeper leaving for Hailsworth Hall. Elizabeth's servants were safe on the back, being cared for by Rachael.

He ought to feel elated, after all they had saved Elizabeth, but he felt that they had completely failed. Phelan was gone and hundreds would die if the powder got to Ireland.

Merriman came over to join Josiah. 'Good night's work, Constable.' Michael and Brother Peter strolled over to join them.

'Mr Merriman,' said Peter, 'I have to take the second wagon back to the Hall and pick up Brother James and Sister Rachael. I have time to take you back to the mines and give your pony a rest.'

'That's 'andsome of you, brother.' Merriman shook hands with Michael and Josiah, and then accompanied Peter across the fields to the copse where the other wagon was still secure.

'So that's that,' said Josiah.

'Know what you mean. It feels as if we've only done half a job,' said Michael. Josiah looked at his old friend. 'Do we believe that what Phelan told Abram was the truth?'

'About moving the powder by canal?' said Michael.

Finally, Josiah's frustration got the better of him 'Oh rats! Phelan wanted twenty-four hours head start according to Abram.

We've cut that in half, there must be more we can do than stand here like idiots.' He started to walk briskly in the direction of their horses. 'Let's see if Mr Bridges thinks they really are taking the powder by canal. We'll ride to the powder mill.'

Fortunately, they made good time on the road from Hayfield towards Macclesfield. Josiah shouted to Michael as they rode.

'The gang was never large. Phelan, McBrinnie and a third member who was away dealing with the arms. When Phelan killed McBrinnie, he was on his own until the arms arrived. The fellow who came with them must have helped Phelan capture Elizabeth but there was still the job of getting the powder away.'

'So a trap and no guard,' shouted back Michael

They swung into the powder mill, which was just waking up to the day's work. Mr Bridges was in his office. He leapt to his feet as they came in.

'Is she alright?' he said immediately.

'Yes, she wasn't guarded. There was an explosive trap set for anyone trying to rescue her but Mr Merriman defused it,' said Josiah.

'Thank God for that,' said Bridges. He sank down in relief. 'I hated this business from start to finish but felt I had no choice but to co-operate with Mr Abram. Ask what you need to know. I will help you any way I can.'

'What Phelan told Abram was that the powder was going by canal. Is there anything you saw when they took delivery that might contradict that?'

'Not really. Canal would be the best way to tranship that amount of amount of powder to a port. No one said, but given Phelan's nationality, I always assumed it was to go to Ireland and that means going by sea. They could put the whole lot on a barge and though it would take time they could take it quietly and reliably to several ports.'

'How many?' asked Josiah.

'In practical terms three: Elsmere Port or Runcorn on the Mersey, Connah's Quay on the Dee.'

'Why not Liverpool, it the biggest?' asked Michael.

'All the canals that can be used to get to Liverpool, run through Manchester. It's a long way round and risks a number of inspections of cargo at junctions between canals run by different companies. There are toll charges due at such junctions.'

'Why would inspection be a problem? Isn't gunpowder transported by canal?' said Josiah.

'Not usually. The laws that govern how blackpowder can be transported were drawn up before the canals. The law prohibits taking large quantities within a mile of any parish church. The clause was a legal trick to keep large quantities of explosives away from towns or larger villages. Canals link towns to towns. Even in the country they pass close to many parish churches. If powder was found at an inspection, it would mean paying a risky bribe or the game would be up. The three ports I suggested are on quiet canal routes with small numbers of junctions and no long tunnels either; there are often inspections at tunnels as well.'

'So they went a couple of miles to the canal and loaded a barge and must be headed towards Marple,' said Michael.

'Hang on,' said Bridges, 'I didn't say that. I heard the drivers with the wagons talk among themselves. They were going through Disley, so they must have used the Macclesfield canal.

'How long would it take them?'

'It wouldn't be easy. The road across the top from here is steep. The further south they aimed to go the longer it would take.'

Annoyingly, Mr Bridges paused, some might have said for dramatic effect but Josiah thought it more likely that Bridges was just trying to make his estimate as accurate as he could.

'Ten, even twelve hours, if they go south as far as Bosley and avoid the turnpikes so as not to attract attention.' Bridges looked at his watch. They could well be loading the powder on the boat about now.'

'Mr Bridges, did Mr Abram tell you Phelan had demanded twenty-four hours without pursuit?' said Michael.

'No he didn't.'

'We think they kidnapped Elizabeth to guarantee it,' said Josiah.

If they did they would have had plenty of time to get to the very far end of the Macclesfield canal. From there are several different routes they could take and plenty of traffic to hide in. They'd be nigh impossible to find from there,' said Bridges.

On fresh horses from the powder mill, Josiah and Michael rode on. If their surmising was right, they had an advantage over Phelan in that they could use the turnpikes. They had to make that advantage pay if they had any chance of capturing the blackpowder.

It took them about an hour and a half to get beyond the ridge between the Furness Vale and Cheshire Plain to the west. The turnpike brought them out above Bollington and then descended towards Macclesfield. They found a country road going south, so that they could see the line of the canal below, as well as skyline of the escarpment to the west. That way they could keep a sharp eye out for boats on the canal below and wagon's coming over from Furness Vale.

The day was beautifully clear. Easily visible on the canal was a succession of barges going both north and south. They could even see boats moored at mine wharves in the direction of Poynton.

They pressed on more slowly, intent on observation rather than speed, hoping against hope for something that looked out of place but there was nothing. They were about to cross the road which linked the quarry at Teg's Nose to Macclesfield, when Michael suddenly stopped. From inside his coat he took out a small telescope and pointed it at a spot on the ridgeline. Josiah looked in the same direction. There was a dot on the horizon. It would have been difficult to see except that it was silhouetted against the sky; a figure on a path coming down from the ridge.

Michael handed the telescope to Josiah. 'What do you think?'

Josiah found telescopes difficult to use. Eventually he got it steady. It looked like a man. As he watched, the track turned and it was clear that he was driving a wagon.

'He's coming from the right direction but surely he's way too late to be one of the wagon drivers from the mill?'

'I agree but it's a very lonely track he's using. Maybe he's seen something on his travels that might help us. Why not ask him?'

They held their course. The track the driver was on seemed to be coming down to their level. As it got lower views of the driver became less frequent due to the lushness of hedgerow and bracken. Then from their left a rutted way, eroded by wagon wheels came in from the left.

They waited. In a few minutes they heard the crunching of hooves and wheels. Someone was whistling but they would not see anything on the trackway until whoever it was reached the junction.

'Easy boy,' called a voice. A horses head appeared at the junction, followed by wagon shafts and finally a clear view of the driver. It was Brother Peter.

37

TAKING THE LOW ROAD

Michael kicked his horse forward, snatched the reins from Peter and brought the wagon to a sharp stop.

Josiah and Peter starred at each other. Josiah had no idea what his own face conveyed. But after his initial surprise, Peter's bore a rather self-satisfied and complacent smile.

'You should see your face, Constable, it makes a very satisfying picture. He said it would when you found me. He was right.'

'You're doing this for Phelan Hayes, aren't you?' said Josiah fighting the temptation to launch himself at Peter and throttle him on the spot in rage and frustration.

'Yes. Now and last night, though you were such a right bunch of fools as you scurried around being so self-important.'

'You knew all along Elizabeth was not guarded.'

'Yes. Your airs and graces and the action of your performing bog-trotter over there, or should I say Croppie, were very comic.' Michael growled under his breath.

Peter chuckled. 'I still remember what you did to my shoulder, boyo!' Michael got down from his horse. Josiah wondered if he was going to hit Peter but the Irish man held his temper and contented himself moving to inspect the back of the wagon.

'Did you know about the explosives in the room?'

Peter looked slightly guilty at that point. 'No,' he said. 'Phelan didn't tell me that part. He just told me not to be too keen on playing the hero.'

'Would it have made any difference if he had told you?' shouted Josiah.

Peter grinned and shook his head. 'No, I would have been pleased if you had been blown up, but making a fool of you was enough.'

'How would you have felt if Rachael had been with me!'

Michael had pulled back the tarpaulin that covered the back of the wagon. It had a great many lumps and bumps in it as if it was concealing barrels of explosives or boxes of cartridges. In fact there were no explosives, just empty crates and other bits and pieces. Pleasure in even this tiny ruse made Peter laugh loudly.

Josiah felt cold with rage. 'You're a snivelling coward Peter and you'll deserve the hanging that's coming to you!' Peter stopped laughing.

'Hanging? What hanging?'

'Peter you really are a very stupid man,' said Michael. 'You think you can help Phelan and not stand in danger of your own life. He's a murderer several times over, but more than that he's a traitor to the crown. As a result you're at least a conspirator in sedition, probably a traitor in your own right as well.'

Josiah rubbed the lesson home. 'By sending you as blind to draw us off and keeping his secret last night when you could have warned us you're a co-conspirator. Putting you in the position you're now in is as good as giving you up to the law. If he succeeds and gets clean away you'll be the only one left to stand trial and when you're found guilty the judge will make as dramatic and public example of you as he can.'

'You know,' said Michael, 'you hang for murder but I've an idea they can still do more than hang you for treason.' As it had been in the sawmill, Josiah watched as Peter tried to understand but this time he failed.

'I'll spell it out, Peter,' continued Michael. 'Ever heard of the traditional punishment for traitors: hanging, drawing and quartering? I think that is still the punishment but what does an ignorant Croppie like me know?'

Something was rattling around in Josiah's mind that he had heard, even said, but no quite understood. Then he got it. 'Where is Phelan?' he asked.

'How should I know?' said Peter.

'Because this isn't the wagon I saw you use to take Mr Merriman back to the mine.' This is one of the wagon's from the powder mill. You left us, took Merriman home, doubled back and picked up this wagon to execute Phelan's little subterfuge. Which way are they really taking the powder?'

'Speak up, lad,' said Michael to Peter, 'it may be you're only chance of avoiding the drop or worse.'

Peter paused. 'They loaded it on the barge on the Peak Forest. Then Phelan paid off the other drivers before he sent me off.' Then he grinned at Josiah.

Josiah got down from his horse and pulled Peter off the wagon and sent him sprawling in the dust. He seized Peter by the shirt before he could get up and starred, teeth clenched, right into his eyes. 'I'll ask you one more time,' he said quietly. 'Where are they really talking the powder?'

Peter's complacency turned slowly to fear. He did his best to cower but Josiah's grip was firm. Peter swallowed hard. 'They're going through Manchester. Phelan said it was the last thing anyone would expect, "even that bastard Ainscough" as he put it.'

Josiah let him go and stood up. Peter fell back on his elbows. 'Peter, I arrest you in the name of the Queen. Take off your boots and stockings. Michael if he doesn't obey you take them off for him and I don't care how permanent is any damage you have to do to him to get the job done.' Peter looked at Michael and started to comply. When Peter was barefoot, Josiah picked up the boots and hung them over the saddle of his horse. 'Michael unhitch the wagon horse and make sure it runs off towards home.'

When the horse had gone. Josiah hauled Peter to his feet with Michael they pushed him back onto the wagon. They tidied Peters arms to the back of the seat and Josiah made sure there was no chance he could get away by hand cuffing Peter's hands for good measure.

Josiah and Michael went as fast as their horsemanship allowed to get back to the turnpike.

'Phelan will have to go down Marple Locks to get to Manchester,' Josiah shouted to Michael as they rode. 'We'll split up where the road to Marple goes off. Can you go back to the powder mill and get some of Bridge's workers out to help capture Phelan? Bring them to Marple. It will need reinforcements to take Phelan. Tell them were after the man who killed their work mates in the spring. That should make them keen enough. I'll go to Marple and do my best to hold him there.'

They joined the turnpike and canter was turned to gallop. Josiah swung north where the turnpike split and Michael went straight on. By the time Josiah had passed the small Methodist Chapel at Marple Ridge, his horse was lathered and sweating.

He leant forward and stroked the horses neck. 'Not far now boy, not far now. One more effort.' Pulling up outside the Navigation a groom was alerted by the clatter of hooves. He came out and looked at the horse and rider in astonishment but took the horse with no question asked.

Then it was up to speed of Josiah's own legs. He ran back to the top lock of the flight. He doubted that Phelan would be in the limekilns basin but his thoroughness and method had got him to the brink of capturing a murderer and he was not going to abandon it now.

He searched quickly but thoroughly. As expected there

was no sign of Phelan or anyone who looked like Phelan in disguise in the basin. To save time he ran over the Top Lock gate, balancing on the beam a good fifteen feet above the empty lock. There was a barge entering from downstream and he had to leap the ropes being used by the pony to manoeuvre it into the lock.

'What the bloody hell do you think you're doing!' shouted the barge woman who was steering the boat. 'You'll break you're bleeding neck, you stupid sod!' But some of the younger bargees gave him a cheer.

There was no sign of Phelan between the Top Lock and the Buxton road down which he'd just galloped. The canal was hemmed in here, congested with traffic using the tightly packed locks and negotiating moored boats across from the towpath. But there was a convenient path from which Josiah could check each barge without being seen.

He was beginning to ask himself what Phelan's reaction would be if he caught him before Michael arrived with reinforcements. Whatever the details it would be violent and Phelan would be armed whereas all Josiah had was his fists and his truncheon. He must keep the element of surprise in whatever he did and that meant not being seen.

The next landmark was Mr Arlon's transhipment warehouse just before the bridge that carried the Glossop Road. From the top of the bridge he surveyed the canal as it swung right in a slow curve to the next lock half hidden by trees. There was no barge going down on this stretch unless it was in the lock. But the only usable path was the towpath which he used to approach the next lock which was empty. From it he could see most of the locks left in the flight. There was a barge was entering the next lock down and behind it a butty steered by a woman. Standing on the side of the lock was a man in the dress of a bargeman complete with a working man's cap but this was no bargee but Phelan.

38

CHECKMATE

Josiah realised that if he was catch Phelan or at least stop the powder getting away this was the best place to do it. He needed to trap the barge in the locks at the very least. He needed to out flank Phelan and to do it he must get <u>passed</u> without being seen. His looked over the stone retaining wall that supported the towpath where the ground fell away steeply towards the Goyt. Below him was some sort of rough path through the trees next to the wall. That would have to do. He found a point where he could jump down and started to fight his way along through the undergrowth where he thought he had seen a path.

He came to a place where there was no tree cover and the path was clearly visible from the canal for a good twenty yards. He was considering running this gauntlet but stopped when he heard Phelan's voice from no more than three feet above his head. He must be just below the lock he had just seen the barge entering. Josiah was not the only one feeling the strain; Phelan's voice was tense and tetchy.

'Damn it, Fergus. How many more locks! By my reckoning we've already come through ten!' Fergus must be the bargeman.

'This is number seven.'

'God's blood, man, at this rate we'll not get through before nightfall!'

'Try to remain calm, Mr Phelan. It will take the time it takes.

The more angry and impatient ye get, the more chance there'll be an accident or some other mistake that will cost us even more time. They count the locks from the bottom upwards so after this there's six to go.'

'It's alright for you to be calm, you've not got as much as I have riding on the success of this mission.'

'I suppose they'll 'ang you if they catch us but it will be just as bad for me and my family; I'd expect a one way ticket to New South Wales and I doubt I'd ever see Jane or me boy again. Now stop griping and help me with this jammed gate!'

There was grunting and sounds of effort and a heavy bang as the gate was swung back. Josiah flattened himself against the wall and inched his way towards the cover of the trees beyond the gap, praying that all eyes above would be focused on the barge as it moved out. When he reached the trees he felt sick but there had been no cries of discovery or worse.

Further on he found another path that came down from the canal which emerged next to a lock below which there were only two more locks left in the flight. Fifty yards upstream he could just make out the lower gates on a lock at an angle to his. As he watched he saw Phelan's pony come into view as it pulled the barge into that upper lock.

Josiah ran across the small lock bridge and waited, crouched in a damp field of large plants with big umbrella shaped leaves, so he could see how Phelan was doing and give himself time to think.

It was quiet, this far away from the kilns. The sounds of the wind in the trees and the scattered song of small birds had replaced the noise of the hammering of the limestone. It was quiet enough that, as the barge got into the lock, he could clearly both see and hear Phelan and Fergus.

'How long before we are safe?'

'I reckon, when we're across the aqueduct. Then there'll be fewer eyes to see us and more traffic to hide us. We should be there in about an hour.'

'Anywhere else we can be delayed?'

'There no locks from here to Ashton just a few bridges. Not much risk of delay until we're close to Manchester.'

Josiah looked down towards the bottom of the flight. By the very last lock was a cottage, out of which came a man. He walked up to the penultimate lock and started inspecting the gate mechanism. This must be a lock-keeper and Josiah was very glad to see him. Here was someone with the knowledge and authority to bar Phelan's way.

Before the voices could get closer, Josiah broke cover and ran down the twenty yards of towpath towards the man. The lockkeeper looked up as Josiah skittered to a halt in front of him.

'Can you make this lock impassable?'

'What!'

'Can you make it so that this lock cannot be passed by the boat that is coming down behind me?'

'Why in God's name should I do that?'

'Because I am a policeman and I need to trap that boat,' He stabbed his finger towards it, to make his point, 'between here and that other lock.'

'So it may be, but that don't give you the right to order me about!'

'On the contrary, Sir, it does. I can order you to help me in the Queen's name and if you refuse I can, and will, bring you before the magistrates in Stockport for your obstruction of me in the line of my duty!'

The lock-keeper hesitated and looked a bit uncertain. 'What's so urgent about that barge?'

'It is carrying a hundred barrels of gunpowder and other explosives. Its butty is carrying an equivalent in muskets and small arms. I also have evidence that one person on the barge is guilty of seven murders. Will you help me?'

There was water in the spillway; another lock was being emptied. Phelan was probably in the lock immediately above where Josiah was.

Finally, the lockkeeper made up his mind.

'Suppose I'll have to help you then,' he said with ill-grace but it was too late. There was a shout from behind Josiah.

'God damn you, Ainscough!'

Phelan, having assisted with getting the barge through the lock must have come to its edge and seen Josiah and the lock-keeper. As Josiah watched, Phelan took out a pistol from his coat. Josiah saw a puff of smoke, heard the report and the crack of the ball hitting the lock gate.

'Christ!' swore the lock-keeper. He started to run and shouted over his shoulder. 'I'll try to jam the bottom lock.'

The barge was now more than halfway across the water between the locks and Phelan was running towards Josiah down the towpath. But the shot had frightened the pony and the barge was out of control. Fergus was at the tiller but without the pony to pull back on the rope he could not control the barge. Its prow hit the top gate of the lock beside which Josiah stood, a shuddering blow. Fergus jumped off and went to help the boy calm the pony.

Josiah retreated to the other end of the lock and took his truncheon out of its pocket. He was frightened but resolved. As well prepared as he could for the coming encounter. Phelan was still running but when he got to upper gate of the lock, he stopped and faced Josiah, taking a second pistol from his coat.

'Give up, Phelan,' Josiah shouted. 'Even if you get away you will not be able to take the blackpowder and the weapons with you. Whatever you came from Ireland to do is at an end.'

'Josiah, I admire your tenacity in doing your duty at the risk of your life. I missed you just now but I will not miss from this range.'

'Then why don't you kill me and be done with it?'

'Because, at this point, it is not my duty. You see I am doing my duty as well.'

'I find that difficult to believe. What duty could demand you set a trap to kill Abram Hailsworth, three innocent women and a boy, just so you could win yourself a few hours to get away?

'You found them? Can I ask if they were alright?'

'No thanks to you, they are all well!'

'Good. Though I did my duty in that case it sat heavily on my heart. I am a soldier, not a murderer of children.'

'Soldiers do not murder their own men.'

'McBrinnie? I did not murder him.'

'How can I possibly believe that?'

'I cannot tell how or what you believe, Constable, but I did not kill him, though I would have done if it had been ordered.'

'Ordered? You are the commander here. Surely, the only orders you have to follow are your own?'

Phelan laughed. 'I am just a soldier and like all soldiers, and policemen, my duty is to obey orders. I have only done what my captain has ordered me to do.'

'Phelan, I do not understand what you hope to gain by this sort of fiction.'

'He is not spinning a fiction, Josiah, but stating the plain truth.' The voice nearly stopped his heart. The figure that had emerged from the barge's cabin, was pointing a small double-barrelled pistol at him. He watched as, with its free hand, it took off its worker's cap and shook out a beautiful cascade of red hair.

'Do not move, Josiah. As much as I love you I will not hesitate to shoot and as my "lieutenant" will tell you I am as good, if not a better, shot than him. It is my duty to do all I can to get what this barge contains to Ireland. Like you I will do my duty or die in the attempt.'

'Aideen,' was all Josiah could whisper.

39

THE COST OF DUTY

Fergus had got the pony back under control. Aideen shouted at him. 'Back here now. Get the lock filled while I keep Constable Ainscough quiet. Help him, Phelan.'

'I sent the lock-keeper down to obstruct the next lock. You are trapped.'

'Look behind you, Josiah. While you and Phelan were talking, the lock-keeper's cowardly legs carried him to safety. Not everyone takes duty as seriously as you and I.'

Phelan and Fergus were operating the sluice paddles to fill the lock. When Fergus had raised one of the paddles Aideen shouted another order.

'Back to the other lock and get the butty through it. The Constable is on his own; the odds are in our favour.'

Fergus trotted back up the towpath. Phelan finished opening the second sluice paddle. The force of the water was at its maximum and Josiah could hear it as it streamed into the empty lock. The barge, with its nose still against the upper gate, was being pulled about by the strong current created by having the sluices fully open.

'Quicker, Phelan, quicker. Open the central paddle on the upper gate. Come on, man!'

Phelan obeyed. The rumbling of the water increased and spray came up from the depths of the lock. The barge started to buck. Josiah remained still, conscious that, even while standing on the moving deck, Aideen seemed to have little difficulty, in keeping a steady aim at him. She looked as she had when jumping the stream and wall on the way up Kinder: magnificent, fearless and dangerous. Then he saw a figure two locks upstream. It was waving and shouting but could not be heard above the noise of the water pouring into the lock. He would have known Michael O'Carroll anywhere.

Now the tables were turned. While Josiah had been unable to see the desertion of the lock-keeper, Aideen and Phelan could not see what was happening upstream. Two large men were fighting with Fergus and his wife for control of the butty. The boy deserted the pony and went to join in.

Another man, with Michael and Mr Bridges were running towards the lower lock. Phelan saw them as he looked up from finishing opening the central paddle.

'Aideen, behind you!' She swung round and fired both barrels at the man, who was fifteen yards away. He took the shots in the legs and went down but Michael and Bridges ran on.

Josiah took the opportunity of the distraction to launch himself at Phelan. He grabbed the Irishman and they toppled over the balance bar of the top gate. Josiah's truncheon and Phelan's pistol were knocked out of their hands.

They rolled to and fro on the ground as Phelan tried to break Josiah's grip. Josiah's hat came off and rolled away. Once Josiah nearly managed to stand but Phelan kicked his legs away and they were back on the floor grappling for any advantage. Dangerously they rolled towards the filling lock but somehow missed going over the edge. Then Josiah found himself on top and free. He staggered backwards, grabbed his truncheon from the ground and before the Irishman had time to get up properly, knocked Phelan cold with a crack to the head.

Mr Bridges and Michael arrived, intending to board the boat to subdue Aideen but it was not to be. Josiah saw Michael hold his arm out to stop the Mr Bridges moving towards the boat. Aideen had made desperate use of the time Josiah had been fighting Phelan. She was now standing near the tiller trying to strike a match. On the top of the cabin she had placed one of McBrinnie's grenades with a short fuse.

Josiah eased himself forward while her attention was on the grenade. The first match she had tried had gone out in the breeze. She was fumbling with another.

'Do not do this, Aideen. It is over.'

'Never,' she hissed. She was still beautiful but no longer in charge of her emotions. The second match flared up. Cupping her hand to protect it from the wind she brought it towards the fuse.

Josiah jumped onto the side of the boat as fuse took light and she held up the grenade ready to throw. He collided with her and together they went overboard.

Submerged, his ears were full of the rushing sound of the water cascading into the lock. He surfaced. Aideen had fallen nearer to the front of the boat and was already in trouble in the current generated by the open paddles. Josiah grabbed one of her flailing arms with his right hand and caught hold of the sleeve of her jacket but the cloth was waterlogged and slippery. He clung on as the current drew them both towards the gate, fighting the current by sculling upstream with his free arm and kicking his legs.

Then his right hand began to slip until he could not hold onto the cloth. He managed to re-establish his grip on her wrist but his hand was aching and he did not have the strength. In seconds he was holding only her palm and a few second latter all that was left were hooked fingers. He gave up struggling against the current and reached to get his other hand on her wrist. They went under and then resurfaced together.

He was desperately close to getting a new steady grip on her wrist when a pistol went off somewhere above him, a terrible pain shot down his back and he was fighting to hang on to Aideen as his strength ebbed away.

'Mother!' she screamed before the current broke Josiah's hold and dragged her under; then his consciousness dissolved.

40

Bread and Jam for Breakfast

Peaceful lights flickered in the darkness: blue and green…

… A little while later there were more, this time tinged with sharp pain: blinding red and yellow.

… Again terrifying lights and sounds: a woman screaming; the roaring of animals?

… Body floats. Water trickles down my throat. Words 'Josiah drink.'

… Whiteness, eyes hurting, a moving shape, a voice. 'Josiah. Josiah. Can you hear me?' I open my eyes, blink and tried to put my hand up to shade them from the sunlight. Pain. Pain in my back. Blink again. Gentle fingers pushing back hair on my forehead. Only one word I remember. 'Mother?'

… Voice, 'Josiah, do you know me?' I know the voice. I am awake.

'Rachael? Where am I, Rachael?'

'Long Clough. I am caring for you.'

Desperation, panic. 'Must get up.' Pain. I grip her arm and try to pull myself up. 'Must hurry. She is going. Must save her.' Roaring in my ears starts again.

'Lie back and rest,' soft hands, cool pillows. 'That time has passed.'

'Where is she?' Cheeks are wet. Why am I crying?

Josiah woke up clearheaded. Through leaded windows he could see trees swaying in the breeze. There were sounds of activity from the courtyard and birdsong. He could not move his left arm. It was not painful, it just did not move to his bidding, not even the fingers. His right arm was stiff but manoeuvrable. He felt his left shoulder with his right hand. It was heavily bandaged and it was very tender to all but the slightest touch. The door of the bedroom swung open and Rachael came in.

'At last, you are awake,' she said and smiled. 'That's very good to see.' She had a tray with her on which was bread, butter and jam, and what looked suspiciously like a china teapot.

'Do you think you could manage some breakfast today? The bread and butter are ours, the jam, or rather conserve, from Barbara Hailsworth. But the pièce de résistance, as I believe the French say, is from the landlady at the Navigation. She has sent you one of her teapots, a matching cup and saucer, and as well as a quarter of her best tea. Also she sends a message that you will be welcome to a ham sandwich on the house but only when you can walk over to Marple to eat it.'

Rachael put the tray on a table and pulled up a chair near his bed. 'Tell me what you will start with and I will pass you what you need and help you to eat it.'

'First a question? How long have I been here?'

'About three weeks.' The happy façade slipped just a little and she looked seriously at him. 'What can you remember?'

He could see Phelan pointing a pistol at him. Then he was falling into water with Aideen. 'I can remember the water rushing and,' He could feel the wet cloth slipping from his fingers, the terrible pain and a scream before the blackness. Then he remembered it all.

He wept. 'She is dead. I failed her.'

'It is alright now, Josiah. At least you are safe. Have your breakfast then I will get Michael and he can tell you everything.'

Josiah could not believe it. 'Has Michael been here three weeks?'

'He had to give evidence at the trial and go back to Stockport a few times to see that Mary was managing but apart from that yes.'

'Do my guardians know I am here?'

'Rev. and Mrs Cooksley have visited often, as has your brother John who has called every time he has had to come to the chapels out this way. You have been asleep when they have come so I have had more pleasure from their company than you. But enough of this, eat your breakfast or I will eat it for you. Barbara Hailsworth's jam is most excellent and this batch of bread is one of my best, even if it is immodest of me to say so.'

They played and laughed like brother and sister, Rachael preparing morsels of the bread and jam, and Josiah making messy attempts to get them to his mouth. Eventually she forbade him to try to feed himself for fear of having too many crumbs in the bed and too many jam stains on the sheets. She resorted to feeding him herself as she might have a small child. He tried to take the teacup at one point but as soon as his hand had to support even that small weight it started to shake.

He had never seen Rachael so happy. Before there had always been an element of sadness in her but that was not evident now. He wondered what had changed. Time would tell and he would let it tell him. He had no strength to hurry and no will to try.

When the breakfast was finished she plumped up his pillows, tidied the bed and smoothed the sheets. 'Now if you are sure you have the strength then I will get Michael.'

'I do not know if I have the strength but now I am awake I need to know what happened to stop it preying on my mind.'

Michael looked rather sheepish as he came in. He looked down at Josiah with eyes that smiled but lips in a pensive line.

'Good to see you awake, lad. There were a goodly number of candles lit and prayers said for this result.' He pulled up a chair and sat on the opposite side of the bed to Rachael. 'What can you remember?'

'We were pursuing Phelan, but Phelan wasn't in charge, it was Aideen. We went over the side of the boat and I, I couldn't save her.'

The Irishman sighed and looked at Rachael to see if she approved. She nodded and he began.

'When you and Aideen fell into the canal, Mr Bridges and I jumped onto the barge.'

Immediately Josiah was agitated; he interrupted, 'She shot one of the powder mill men! Is he alive?'

'Her pistol was loaded with small shot. It caused many cuts to his legs and he lost quite a bit of blood but it didn't break any bones. He was back at work in a week.'

Rachael intervened. 'Josiah, let Michael tell you the story all the way through. That way you will be able to conserve your strength.' Josiah nodded and tried to relax.

Michael continued. 'At first we couldn't see either of you, then you surfaced and we realised that the strength of the current from the water pouring into the lock was pulling at Aideen. It was clear that we needed to stop both of you being drowned.

'Mr Bridges found a rope, intending to get in front of Aideen so she could hang on to it. When you both surfaced again we were ready but we had forgotten Phelan. Behind us he had recovered from the blow you gave him, found his pistol and shot you in the back before we could stop him. We subdued him and pulled you out but Aideen had been sucked under. She never came up. We recovered her body later. It was wedged under the paddle on the top gate. She didn't stand a chance.'

'How did I survive? I was in the grasp of the same current.'

'I caught onto you alongside the barge and we lifted you out. You coughed up a lot of water but remained unconscious but rapidly we became most worried about your wound.

'We carried you and Mr Bridges' man to the Navigation and called a surgeon. He packed the powder mill fellow off after cleaning his wounds and applying a few bandages but he didn't want you moved very far. The pistol ball was deflected by your shoulder blade and stopped when it hit your shoulder joint. He was worried that the ball was near your lungs. Rachael can take up the story from there.'

'We got a message from the Navigation that you were seriously wounded. Could we get you to Long Clough? James and I came over with a wagon and brought you back here along with the surgeon. He found and removed the pistol ball from your shoulder but the wound went bad and you started a fever. Your life hung in the balance for days. Even when the fever broke but you were still only half-conscious. It has taken a week for you to wake up properly.'

Michael moved forward on his chair. 'The surgeon thought that there might have been permanent damage done to your shoulder. Can you move your arm?'

Josiah shook his head. 'I can't even move my fingers.' Rachael stood up and quietly stroked Josiah's forehead. 'Is that a bad sign?' he said to her. 'Tell me the truth for I will only imagine the worst.'

'It is likely that you will never be able to use that arm again,' said Michael.

Josiah was shocked but tried to put on a brave face. 'At least I am still alive thanks to you my friends.' He paused before going on.

'What happened to Phelan?'

'With the help of a local smith we shackled him and the barge crew together and Bridges marched them back to the powder mill. They had to leave Peter out all night but retrieved him and the wagon in time for Sergeant Smith to turn up at the Mill with some men and drag them all back to Stockport.

'The barge and butty were put under guard by soldiers from Stockport armoury. Mr Prestbury had sent them after receiving a message from Sergeant Smith that he was going to arrest Phelan with a detachment of police.

'And that is all I think you can cope with for now,' said Rachael. 'Rest some more and you might be able to have some more food later if you feel up to it. In the meantime, I need to tell the surgeon that you are conscious so he can examine your arm.'

'One last question. Where is Aideen's body?'

Michael and Rachael looked at each other. She spoke. 'Her body was kept in the stables at the Navigation until the inquest but when that was over. I begged the coroner to allow me to take charge of her since there is no family, even in Ireland. Her and Phelan's father died three years ago and there is no one else.' She looked slightly embarrassed and fidgeted with the edge of her apron. 'I also felt that it might be important to you.'

'She is in Steven Hailsworth's icehouse on his estate,' said Michael. 'The community have agreed to bury her as an act of Christian charity, there being no church or burial ground that will take her.'

Josiah asked a few more questions but tiredness overcame him and he started to fall asleep. They made him comfortable and then left him in peace.

Josiah's strength returned quite steadily as he ate and slept normally. Two days later he asked Rachael if he might get up. She thought carefully.

'Yes you may, but only for an hour or two to sit in the sun. How about after you have had some food at midday?'

She was good as her word. After bread, meat and tea, Brother James came upstairs to join Rachael and under their watchful eyes, Josiah got out of bed and stood up under his own steam. Standing up he was dizzy and felt weak but the main problem was his left-arm. It hung limp and useless, contributing nothing to helping him balance. He looked down at it sadly.

'Mmm, I supposed that might be a problem.' She went downstairs and came back with a large square of white linen.

'James, can you see if you can find a walking stick for Josiah,

I think there's an old one of Elijah's somewhere in the barn. It will give him more confidence when he has to try the stairs.'

She made the linen into a triangle and, tying the corners together, passed the loop over Josiah's neck. Then she took the lifeless arm and passed it gently through so that the triangle formed the perfect sling. She was close to him and as she smoothed out the cloth, her hair brushed his cheek. He could not bear the sensation and looked away. In his mind and emotion she stood simultaneously for herself and for Aideen. He felt ashamed of his selfish emotional confusion between them.

She saw him look away. 'Do not worry, Josiah. You must grieve for her. It is natural. But things can change. Look.' She placed her hand on his check and gently turned his head round so he was looking into her eyes. 'Do not move or try to embrace me, I am not ready for that,' then she kissed him full on the lips as her hand caressed his cheek. 'Even pistol rounds can trigger feelings that offer all sorts of healing,' she whispered before stepping back and finishing the sling.

'Now I know you cannot feel anything in the arm but trust me it is secure against your chest, and will not impede you.' James came back with the stick.

With help Josiah clambered down the stairs. There was a bad bruise somewhere on his back, which made it impossible for him to put his feet down more than a single tread at a time. He was also much more dizzy on the stairs than he had been on the flat floor of the bedroom. As a result he went down very painfully and slowly.

The courtyard was bathed in sunlight. As he came out into the warmth of the sun he saw that all the community were there. When they saw him they broke into clapping and singing.

Rachael and James steered him through to the paddock where a comfortable seat of hay bales, pillows and a blanket had been made underneath an oak tree. He sat down and looked across the Furness Vale.

In the distance was the smoke and steam from the Marple kilns, to the south-east more smoke from Arlon's mill. He could also make out where the gunpowder mill must be.

But the overwhelming impression was not of industry but of nature, of green trees and fields under a blue sky with occasional white clouds. A valley where peaceful animals grazed and folk moved about their lives undisturbed except for their private concerns and worries. A small brown bird fluttered off the stonewall at the end of field. It hopped along the grass and took off, circling upwards and singing. His arm was damaged and might never move again but he was alive and simply glad to be thankful and praise God.

He had nodded off under the tree when Rachael's soft voice woke him.

'Josiah, you have visitors.' Standing in front of him were Thomas and Martha Cooksley. He tried to get up.

'No, my boy, stay where you are,' said Thomas. 'We would have gone without waking you, glad simply to know you were up and on the mend but Sister Rachael insisted. She believed that she would never hear the last of it from you if she did not rouse you to greet us.'

'I will leave you together,' said Rachael. She turned to Mr Cooksley. 'If you could spare the time before you leave, I would be grateful if I could ask your help once more. I think I have made my decision but I want to be sure that my reasoning is sound.'

'Of course, Sister.'

For the next half an hour there was much smiling, holding of hands, kissing of brows, especially by Martha Cooksley, and general signs of relief and gladness. There was very little of serious Methodist discourse.

'I should come home,' Josiah said at one point.

'Of course we would wish you to come home but we are

aware that there are matters you may feel you need to resolve here after such a dreadful ordeal. Come back when the time is right, not just to make us happy. We could not care for you better than Rachael and the community have done and here you have the advantage of good clean air to help your recovery,' said Thomas.

'How is John?'

'He promises to come later when he has to come the Marple Ridge meeting. He will be bringing many greetings from your friends in the market and several offerings of vegetables, fish and fowl would not surprise me. Now before we go I must speak with Sister Rachael. Do not fret, Josiah. God has looked after you well and he will continue to bless and keep you.'

After Thomas had left Josiah with Martha, Josiah was able to ask what he had been curious about since he had heard what Rachael had said to his Guardian. 'What is it that Sister Rachael needs to discuss with father?'

'Mercy me, you always were the most inquisitive child; it is no surprise to me that you turned out to be a good detective. It is a confidential matter between them. All I can say is that I know Sister Rachael has an important decision to make. She and Thomas have got on so well while we have been visiting you, that she asked his advice, which he has been happy to give.

'Now don't be so over curious. Behave yourself, do not be a nuisance to these good people and above all get better quickly so I can have my chance of making a fuss of you as soon as possible.'

41

THE CONDEMNED CELL

Rachael and Josiah stood in front of the wicket gate in the squat round tower at Chester Castle Gaol. They knocked for admittance.

Josiah was wearing his uniform, with his lifeless arm carefully strapped under the coat and the empty left sleeve tucked into a jacket pocket. Rachael was dressed in her Sunday best, with a black bonnet and dark cloak.

They had come in response to two letters, one for each of them that had arrived the day before by postal rider. They were from Phelan, awaiting execution in the gaol, requesting they would come to see him.

The reason Phelan gave for his request to Josiah was so that he could answer any questions the Constable might have about how his and Aideen's crimes had come about. To Rachael he said he could supply information she might value about Elijah's life in Ireland and that he wished to ask her forgiveness concerning Elijah's murder.

'Will you go?' asked Josiah.

Rachael hesitated. 'I think so. I cannot deny a fellow creature making whatever peace he can. Peter is also in the same gaol. It may be I can see him for the last time as well. I will have no other chance.' She looked very sad as she said this but went on. 'What will you do?'

'I will come with you. I am still not altogether clear about why these crimes were committed. Above all I do not know why he shot me when I was trying to save Aideen.'

When the gate opened and they were admitted they were shown to the stark cellblock. A prison officer in a blue coat and trousers, with a simple fob cap and a large bunch of keys, introduced himself and showed them into a poorly lit corridor that smelt of urine and excrement. He led them down some stairs to a lower level. There was a distant scream from somewhere above, answered by another much closer, but down on this lower level it was quiet.

'These are the condemned cells,' said the officer. 'It tends to be quieter down here than in other areas of the prison.'

There was an iron gate across the corridor that the officer unlocked and then locked behind them. As far as Josiah could judge, there were about six cells. All had doors of open iron bars. There were high oval windows, also barred, at the far end of each. These windows let in light without affording any view, except of the sky. Below the window was a flat wooden bed, at one end of which was a built in cylindrical wooden pillow.

'Hayes is the only prisoner at present,' said the officer. He stopped in front of the third cell on the right. 'You can speak to him from here, you're not allowed inside. You have half an hour.' He turned and walked away.

Phelan was sitting on the bed. His hands we shackled to a chain round his neck. He looked thin and gaunt. When he looked up at them they saw that his eyes were tired and red, with dark rings round them. He was badly shaved and he seemed to have initial difficulty in understanding who they were. It took several seconds for him to recognise them.

'You came,' he said in flat voice which tailed off. 'I had thought you would not.'

'We received your letters,' said Rachael. 'What do you wish to say to us?'

'It all seemed much more logical when I wrote,' he said. 'Now it doesn't seem to be as clear. It is the darkness that looms and it occupies so many of my thoughts now that I have difficulty thinking of anything else.'

Josiah could see how the wreckage of the man that she saw before her moved Rachael but she was determined and forced the conversation forward.

'In your letter you told me that you knew something of Elijah's life in Ireland.'

'I assume you already know he fought with the United Irishmen in the 1804 rebellion under his original name of Fitzgerald?'

'Yes,' said Josiah. 'We also know you came to Long Clough with your father looking for him.'

'I thought you remembered me when we met at Long Clough. Elijah was one of those who fought after the rebellion was crushed, though it was probably more running and hiding than fighting. I think that he was probably trying to break from the group he was with when he met my mother.' The vacant look came across his face again but after a moment it passed and he resumed.

'They fell in love but her father had his own history of violence before and after the rebellion and had been responsible for several anti-Catholic attacks. Despite this, about the time Elijah met my mother, her father was being actively canvassed, as a respected protestant loyalist, to lead a new Orange Lodge. Even though Elijah was not a Catholic, when Elijah's affiliations emerged, my grandfather lay in wait for him one night when he came to the house and took a horse crop to him. He promised my mother that he would do the same or worse to her if she dared see Elijah again.' Phelan sighed. Again, the blank expression on his face and a second pause before he spoke again.

'But fate had not finished with them. I think Elijah must have been seen visiting my mother so they decided to test his loyalty by forcing him to be involved in setting the fire at my grandfather's house. The deaths of my mother's brother and her injuries sickened Elijah and to make sure he could escape completely from the rebel group, he came to England.'

'Her wooing by our father and our births should have ended the bitterness but it simply changed it. Every day they lived my father and mother poured into Aideen's and my ears the hatred and fear of the rebels. They bred me to be a soldier for the cause, and so I became, but Aideen was prepared from birth to become some sort of avenging angel for the disfigurement of our mother. When mother killed herself she guaranteed Aideen's fanatical zeal. When she was dead, her sister took over Aideen's "education" in such matters and in her terms she did a perfect job.'

'Are you a zealot as well?' asked Rachael.

'No, I am a soldier. I wanted to kill Elijah for what he had done but if left on my own I would simply have called him out and shot him in a duel.'

'But Aideen was different?'

'Yes. She was in many ways a better soldier than I, better rider, better shot, better tactician in the field. I suppose she proved that by being appointed as my senior officer for our task in England. But the fact was she was not so much a better soldier but just much more brutal and resolute than me.'

Josiah frowned. 'Had she killed in cold blood before the attack on the powder mill?'

'She did not see it as cold blooded murder but simply a military necessity. But the answer to your question, Constable, was yes. She killed three times in attacks on Catholics before we came here. You were very lucky to survive your encounter with her that day in the wood.'

Rachael looked at Phelan intensely. 'What military necessity did the murder of Elijah satisfy?'

'None. In fact you would never have caught us if she had

not killed Elijah in that ridiculous manner. Aideen's anger and passion, combined with my duty to her meant I went along with her plans. It is not forgiveness for killing Elijah I want you to grant me if you can, Sister Rachael, but my part in the manner of his death. It was a blasphemy and I repent it before God.'

Rachael was squeezing the bars of the cell door hard so that her fingers were white as they had been the night when she had told Josiah of Elijah's abuse of her in Liverpool but as then she was in control of her feelings. Her voice was steady as she answered Phelan.

'Thank you, Mr Hayes. I understand. I cannot find it within my heart to forgive you at this moment but I will pray that in time forgiveness of you may be possible and will be acceptable to God. I will pray for you.' She turned, leaning against the door of the next empty cell to be out of Phelan's view, leaving Josiah a space for his questions.

'What was your primary task in England and who sent you?' asked Josiah.

'Our primary task was obtain stocks of powder and arms to equip a secret militia in the north of Ireland to attack Catholics.'

'Why did you come to the Furness Vale?'

'By chance. Our first targets were the powder mills in Cumbria. They had the advantage that if we obtained the powder and the arms we could get them away by sea from a number of ports.'

'What went wrong with that plan?'

'The Cumbrian mills are all well established and work closely with the military. We could not hope to intimidate them to make them cooperate. We needed someone new to the business, preferably with an incentive to cut corners.'

'And you met Abram Hailsworth.'

'Aideen spun him along, she enjoyed playing the femme fatale and Abram was easily impressed.' Just as she played me, thought Josiah.

'When we failed in Cumbria we took the opportunity to place McBrinnie in Steven Hailsworth's employment, by a combination of threatening and bribing the blacksmith they then had. McBrinnie reported to us regularly and as soon as he told us that Abram had the capacity to supply our needs we came to Long Clough and like two good cuckoos, joined him in his comfortable nest.'

'When did you realise that you had been to Long Clough before with your father?'

'Immediately. I also quickly realised Elijah was Fitzgerald but I did not tell Aideen.'

'Why?'

'Because of her obsession. I wanted to focus on the main objective of our mission. I knew that once she knew about Elijah she would become blinded by revenge. So it proved.

'Come now once she had turned her femme fatale act on me surely then you must have felt safe?'

'Nearly killing you in the wood she thought would deal with the threat you posed. When she failed she became more subtle and started watching you closely, especially when you were revealed as a policeman.

'Remember when she encountered you on the Long Clough track just after you had visited the powder mill? She had watched you all day and was making sure you did not go back to the mill, while I was there seeing Abram to find out what he had told you.' Josiah must have looked abashed.

'Her love for you was not a lie, Josiah. I think she saw in you real hope in what had been a hopeless life. Someone who she could love and respect. I think she dreamed that in marriage to you she could find a way to get out of the cycle of hate and death. She had become tired of it, just as Elijah had been.'

Josiah remembered what Aideen had said in the hidden garden about forgetting duty. He should have realised then that she had been strangely desperate about her dream of living there with him, but his emotions had been clouded by Rachael's news about Liverpool and the memory of his dalliance with Maria. What Phelan had said put a different complexion on what had happened that day.

Aideen had wished to use him to end the burden of her duty to the loyalist cause but he had pushed her away because of his duty to find Elijah's killer, who was standing in front of him and who he had embraced. At that point she must have despaired of ever being free.

'I have one last question. Why did you shoot me?'

'I was not trying to kill you, and am glad you are still alive. I knew instinctively we were done for, the moment I saw you standing by that lock. I did it for Aideen. If you had saved her, she would have only been brought to a place like this, waiting for the baying mob that will watch me slowly strangle on the end of a rope. Drowning seemed kinder.'

There was a rattle of the gate at the end of the corridor; time was up. Josiah offered his hand to Phelan through the bars. In his palm, there was the small envelope Michael had slipped to him. Phelan took it from him.

'That is from Mr O'Carroll. He asked me to tell you that if he was to have to travel your path he would want something to remind him of where he had come from and the old country. He hoped you'd accept whatever it is, even though it comes from a Croppie.'

Phelan opened the envelope and emptied it into his hand. It was a small orange flower. Phelan stared at it, put it back in the envelope and tucked the envelope out of sight before the guard came.

'Thank him from me. I have a gift for you as well. In my sketchbooks, you will find some recent drawings of Aideen. If you can bear to, I would like you to have them. You will be able to remember her when I cannot.'

'Time is up Miss, Constable.' The prison officer was back.

They turned and silently filed out behind him aware that Phelan was standing at the bars of his cell watching them go.

When they were outside Rachael turned to the prison officer. I believe there is someone else here who was involved in this crime,' she said. 'May I see him?'

'You mean the so-called Brother Peter. I'm afraid it's too late Miss. He left for Liverpool docks this morning. He's on his way to Botany Bay by now.'

May I ask something, Officer?' said Josiah.

'Of course, Constable.'

'Mr Hayes seemed to indicate that he will be executed in public? Is that true?'

'That's correct. We believe in the old ways here. We use a gallows on the north gate of the city and encourage as many of the public to come and jeer as possible.'

'Poor Phelan,' said Josiah.

'Oh, that's just the start, Sir. When he's dead then we'll wrap him up snug in a winding sheet, cover him in tar and attach chains. You'll be seeing him for the next two years dancing on gibbet near where he committed his crimes. Just to remind everyone the consequences of doing the same.'

They would be the last two human beings Phelan Hayes would ever see who held any genuine empathy with him and saw him as more but than a monster deserving of a violent and degrading death.

42

A New Beginning

The meeting with Phelan made Josiah wanting to return to the familiar. The need for him to be in the Furness Vale was over and he started to be feel sick at heart about all the death, sadness and unhappiness he had seen. Things were coming to an end and even though he would be unable to return to duty because of his arm, he needed to leave.

The next day Michael said that he would be heading back to Stockport that morning. 'Mary has been coping well but it is time I went. You will do well enough without me now.'

'How would I have managed without you?' Josiah said.

'Well you are just about the most inventive chap I know so I daresay you would have managed somehow, lad.'

After he had seen Michael off, Josiah sought out Rachael. She was doing the washing.

'You are looking much stronger, Josiah,' she said as soon as she saw him.

'Yes. I am surprised how well my body stood up to our long journey yesterday. I have been wondering...'

'Whether it is time to go home? I agree the things of this phase of our lives are ending but, if you can, please stay until Sunday. When you came, I promised that we would send you back onto the road with our prayers and blessings. I hope that Sunday will be a chance to do that joyfully.

'There is an important meeting for all the Children of Fire and their friends this evening which you may find of interest. And there is one much more solemn task you and I must attend to.'

'The matter of Aideen's burial? That is also on my mind.'

He sat under the oak tree and read "Paradise Lost" for the rest of the afternoon. He'd never really finished it at school and he had asked John to bring him a copy so he could remedy this gap in his education. But reading about Satan put him in mind of both Aideen and Elijah.

For most people Aideen was a villain and Elijah a saint. But Elijah Bradshawe had not been a saint. Indeed if they had known the details of his life, many would consider him a monster beyond God's redemption, for having put such stumbling blocks of abuse and murder in the way of the children Rachael and Aideen once were. But his founding of the Children of Fire had been a good action, as was his care for Rachael and his scheme to help run away apprentices. Josiah could see them as actions in atonement for his earlier sins.

In the end Rachael was the only person alive who had any clear right to speak for or against Elijah Bradshawe and she forgave him. That would have to be enough for Josiah Ainscough as well. He would extend his forgiveness to Aideen and Phelan in the same spirit.

They buried Aideen's body near the Forester's cottage. Peter and James dug two graves on Rachael's instructions. A simple wood coffin was provided by the Hailsworth estate. Josiah went over on the Long Clough wagon to bring her back to her last resting place.

When they took her body from the ice house, she was already in the open coffin. Her corpse was pale and deathly but the hair was still red and beautiful. Josiah took a red rose from the garden at the Hall and placed it between her fingers before they fixed the coffin lid down for the journey. While at the Hall he took the opportunity to take from Phelan's luggage the sketchbook, which contained the last drawings of Aideen by her brother.

Steven and Barbara Hailsworth followed Josiah in the brougham as he drove the cart with the coffin slowly back past Long Clough and then up behind Pulpit Rock. Rachael and James were at the grave. The inscription of the small tombstone simply said:

Aideen Hayes
1816–1841
Rest peacefully

Bible passages about hope and forgiveness were read over the grave. Rachael summed up their thoughts.

'I never spoke with Aideen Hayes but from what Josiah has told me and what I heard from her brother in Chester, Aideen could have had very little hope of choosing a less murderous path than the one she walked. As a child those who should have cared for and nurtured her through the loss of her mother poured hatred and desire for revenge into her; she was made into a weapon. We lay her here without condemnation and offer her up to God, as the only proper judge of the choices she had and made. Her brother's body now swings on a gibbet in this valley but today, in hope, we open a grave for his bones too so that when they can be retrieved he may lie here in peace with her.

With James's help, Josiah threw in the first shovel load of earth onto Aideen's coffin. Then all those present shovelled in some more earth until James took the spade and closed the grave.

That evening, the Children of Fire filed into the chapel, reminding Josiah of the evening he had presented himself to explain his presence in the community. That had been on the day Elijah's body had been found. But this evening he did not have to let himself in and no one turned to stare as he entered; he was an accepted member of the community. All he had to do was withstand a battery of sympathetic questions about his arm and wait to see why Rachael thought this an important meeting for him to attend.

There was a pause and then, in single file, Elijah's inner group entered. The oldest male member of the community, Brother Simon, headed the procession with Esther, James and Louise. A few steps to the rear came Rachael, a black bible in her hand. The inner group lined up at the front and Rachael sat alone in a front pew.

'Would Sister Rachael please stand forward?' said Simon. Rachael stood facing him. 'Sister, a month ago the community called you into this chapel and presented you with our view, arrived at after much prayer among us, that you should become the leader of the Children of Fire to succeed our founder Brother Elijah Bradshawe. At that time you asked a month for prayer, personal reflection and study, to discern whether this was truly a calling placed on you by God. This day, that month is up. Have you come to a decision?'

'I have,' said Rachael. 'I have thought, prayed and considered this very carefully. At first I did not know if this was what God wanted. I felt too young and inexperienced. I felt I could not possibly bring the fire to preaching that Brother Elijah brought. I have also wondered if a woman can lead a community such as this, given the times in which we find ourselves.

'Then, unexpectedly, God placed me in the way of a helper. As Constable Ainscough, our friend Josiah, lay with his life in the balance, his guardian Rev. Thomas Cooksley came to see his adopted son, waiting patiently at Josiah's bedside, never trying to wake him, though as any father's heart would he yearned to see Josiah well. He had the strength to simply wait in hope and prayer. As I watched with him, I saw a man of God and after hesitating I told him of the choice I had to make.

'First, he reminded me that very few who God calls do not doubt themselves at first, but one serves as a leader not in one's own strength but in God's. He advised me to read the experiences of the Prophets to see that.

'Second, he showed me that while women do not lead churches in this day and age, the Bible has many stories of women called to lead communities, even nations, in God's name. He reminded me that though in the church he serves only men are ordained, that today there are hundreds of women leading Methodist meetings and societies up and down the country. God has called them to leadership just as much as he has called any man.

'I have pondered what I have learned in this month and the promptings of my own heart. I will serve as leader of the Children of Fire, relying on the help of God and on your love.'

'Alleluia! Alleluia! Alleluia!' Josiah was on his feet shouting at the top of his voice in an outpouring of praise that he had not felt since a child. In normal circumstances, he would have been embarrassed at such a display of enthusiasm, but everyone around him was doing much the same in joy, hope and faith in the future.

Then suddenly and perhaps too soon, it was Saturday evening and the last opportunity Josiah would have to help Rachael clear up in the kitchen and share with her the day just past.

'One last drink when we have finished?' he said as he put cooking pots on the high shelves she had difficulty reaching.

'Yes,' she said, 'and as it is a significant evening shall we have tea?'

'That would be splendid. You rest and I will brew up.'

He made the tea and brought it over to where she was sitting near the window. He poured it for her.

'Thank you,' she said and took a first sip. 'I will miss the washing and the duties I have here in the kitchen. Sister Louise will be taking over from me as housekeeper. My time will be taken with the study and the relationship of the community with the outside world.'

He sipped at his own tea. 'Are you content with your choices?'

'Yes.' She hesitated slightly. 'Nervous of stepping into Elijah's shoes, particularly those concerned with preaching but yes I am content.'

'I am sorry that you found out from Phelan about the affection that had grown up between me and Aideen. I should have told you myself.'

She laughed. 'Oh really, Josiah, for someone who has intuition in abundance yourself, you underestimate intuition in others. I realised that something was happening between you and Aideen before I met either her or Phelan.'

'This may be impertinent but I need to ask, when you were considering succeeding Elijah did you consider if we had a future?'

'Of course. Every time I looked at you in that bed or tried to get you to drink or to take the smallest amount of food or heard you groan in pain when we changed the dressings, I wondered how I would feel if you died. I was afraid that in some way my coldness had driven you to be reckless and that in confronting Phelan and Aideen you had hoped to die. I also worried what would happen if you woke, were healed and then rejected me.

'But when you woke up I realised that what I felt was a dream. You had your path and choices to follow and I mine and that they do not run together, at least not at this time.

'Josiah, you are called to be a policeman. Do not lose that thought. There was a desperate need for you to be among us at Long Clough at this time. You will be needed elsewhere in the future.'

'I shall not be of any use to the police with only one arm.'

'Then there will be another path for you.'

The next day James walked up the path to Pulpit Rock and, for the first time since Elijah's murder, the warning bell rang, announcing that a sermon would be preached that afternoon in the name of the Children of Fire. Josiah waited with Thomas and Martha Cooksley for Rachael to lead the community out for she had decided to take the head of the procession and not make a dramatic appearance on top of Pulpit Rock as had been Elijah's custom.

Rachael was dressed in a leather belted cassock but unlike Elijah's hers was a deep, vibrant green. She did not wear the white tabs or a clerical collar but she had her own embroidered preaching cloak. On it was a tree with all types of birds singing in its branches. There was a picture of children piping and playing games in a dusty street. There were pictures of lilies, and corn growing at the borders of fields. A rich man was begging to be allowed to enter a castle keep through a small door but he would not leave his riches behind to find safety, and an old woman having searched a house for a lost coin, was holding it up in joy. There was a sad looking young man eating with the pigs and also being embraced by a man who was his father. As she passed Josiah he saw that on the back was a green hill, with a man in the far distance standing before a hopeful sky talking to a great crowd and in the foreground, there were children playing round an empty tomb in a beautiful garden bringing gifts to the same man whose garden it seemed to be.

He and the Cooksleys fell in behind the community. A little way on they passed Abram and Elizabeth with Robert. Frederick was there with a man who bore a striking resemblance to Mr Bridges as well as the same mix of old and young, poor and well off as Elijah had drawn. The last face Josiah saw before Rachael and the inner group started the climb to the top of the rock was Sarah Arlon with her maid.

They found a comfortable place to sit at the foot of Pulpit Rock and waited. The bell rang again twelve times then Rachael walked slowly to the edge of the rock. Only one thing had changed in her appearance. When she had been in the procession, her hair had been contained in a bun. She had unpinned it and it flowed as free in its gold as Elijah's had done in its white. There was to be no doubt that it was woman who was preaching. There would be no confusion on this matter. Those who thought a woman could not command the authority of a man were welcome to depart; she would be heard in the name of her God and her convictions.

'My brothers and sisters, welcome.'

The voice was clear and demanded attention. She could not dominate with her volume like Elijah but the wonderful acoustics of the rock brought her words to all as if she had been sitting next to them.

'This is an important day. No one has spoken to you from this place since Brother Elijah Bradshawe was taken from us. In these weeks, it has been unclear as to whether the Children of Fire would be able to survive after his passing. But little by little we have regained a measure of confidence and I have acquiesced to the request of the other members of the community that I lead the Children of Fire, in succession to Brother Elijah.

'Friends I do not do this for my own aggrandisement but because there are so many matters in these times of change we live in that require to have shone upon them the light of the truth of God. I take up this challenge, not in my own strength but in the strength of God who has called me forward. I offer my service to you in humility and modesty, for I am resolved to be a faithful servant to you and this community.'

'And we'll do our best an' all!' shouted a man at the back of the crowd who all laughed as Rachael smiled at the remark.

'And even before I made my choice to serve, it seems the Holy Spirit was moving in front of me. When Brother Elijah preached his last sermon from here, he condemned Mr Abram Hailsworth for the pollution entering the river Goyt from the powder mill. Mr Abram has promised to stop that pollution and the fish of the river will be safe again. We praise God for this change of mind and we pray for Abram and his new wife Elizabeth in their future life together.

'But God's providential action did not stop there. The Children of Fire have always held caring for children as important.' She held up her left hand in which was the black bible that she had carried from Long Clough. It was open and she offered to them the word contained within.

'Here in Luke's gospel Jesus reminds us of our responsibility to children: "It were better for him that a millstone were hanged about his neck, and he cast into the sea, than that he should offend one of these little ones."

'Children suffer everywhere in our land, in lightless mines crawling through the dust pulling trucks of coal, in the factories where their young lives are stolen for profit amid the clatter of deafening machines, in nameless places where they are forced to satisfy the lusts of the depraved by violence, poverty and need. In this valley, we will make a sanctuary for children who need us.

'In partnership with the Hailsworth family the Children of Fire will build a school for those in need. There children who are abused will find a shelter and there they will breathe our clean air. They will be taught to read and write, they will be taught trades so they can build better futures for themselves. But above all they will be loved!'

Rachael seemed to have grown taller as she spoke. 'brothers and sisters, join us as you can in this calling. They are our neighbours, we see their need and we hear God calling us to help them. Give yourselves now to that call. Let it be our crusade!'

Her hands were now raised above her head and she looked ecstatically towards the sky. As she finished, an intense stabbing pain shot down Josiah's left arm, he called out and clutched it with his right hand.

'What is it, Josiah? Hold me if you are faint,' said Martha Cooksley.

Josiah took a deep breath and looked down at his arm. Where the lifeless fingers projected from the sling there was a slight movement, as his left forefinger twitched. Thomas slipped his hand over it.

'Thanks be to God,' he said as he and Martha hugged Josiah and Rachael's congregation cheered, praising her gift and challenge.

HISTORICAL NOTES

When an author sits down to write an historical novel, it's a case of running along the border between the two worlds of fiction and fact, keeping both in balance.

The 1840s was a time of great change. It was the beginning of the Victorian period, but much of what we think of as being typical of that period was not yet in place.

The Queen herself was still young and not necessarily the universally praised mother of the nation she was to become. This is illustrated by the four attempted assassinations on her life from June 1840 to May 1849.

Irish politics was volatile. The rebellion of the United Irishmen in 1797 was a fresh memory and it involved tactics that we might well consider terrorism today. The last manifestation of organised rebellion was in 1804 when the resistance of James Corcoran collapsed. In the 1840s, Irish resistance was exemplified by the Young Ireland whose activities eventually led to a further uprising in 1848. By then divide and rule policies from London had hardened the sectarian divisions of Catholic versus Protestant.

In the period the symbol of the end of the Napoleonic War in June 1804 at Waterloo, is balanced by the Peterloo Massacre in June 1816. They represent the struggle between the old political order and the new economic order of the industrial cities that plays out in tension over constitutional change. The result was that Chartism emerged as the most popular political movement.

In terms of physical settings of the book, there are several buildings that exist today that make appearances in *Children of Fire*.

The Packhorse Bridge, known nowadays as the Roman Bridge, crosses the river Goyt as described a few miles upstream of Marple.

Until recently there really was a giant-sized cross on the north ridge of the Goyt Valley, my Furness Vale. There will be again when the local Churches Together get it repaired after damage in a storm.

There is no Long Clough or Pulpit Rock, though there is a story that John Wesley preached from a rock when establishing a Methodist Society at Marple Ridge. But Long Clough Chapel exists, complete with its dedication tablet. It is Hollinsclough Methodist Chapel in Derbyshire.

The lime kilns at Marple were real, as is the canal and the locks of the Marple flight on the Peak Forest Canal. Coal mines were common in the area towards and beyond Poynton.

But the real scene stealer is Hailsworth Hall, in reality Lyme Hall (a National Trust Property) displaced a few miles. Much of the internal and external details of Hailsworth Hall are taken from Lyme Hall including, paintings, carvings, and especially the library and the dining room.

All the inventions in the novel were either current at the time or could have been made with the current technologies of the time. The compressed blackpowder in the blasting candles of the Furness Vale Powder Mill could have been produced at the time and were produced in the early 20th century in response to the convenience of using dynamite but by then the market was already lost for blackpowder blasting.

The most significant question must be this: would there have been a religious community like Children of Fire? I have no direct evidence of such a community but it was a time of religious change. The Irish workers coming into the growing industrial towns like Stockport, brought Irish Catholicism with them. They were matched by a second group of immigrants from the countryside, who were Protestant. The church that rose to fill their needs was the Methodist Church.

The Oxford Movement was just around the corner; this would lead to the Anglo-Catholic movement in the Church of England.

The Primitive Methodist Church used meetings in the countryside as well as building chapels a model that was mimicked by the Chartist and emerging Trade Union movement. There was plenty of room for a self-styled prophet like Elijah and a female religious leader like Rachael.

But as I said *Children of Fire* is a novel not an history book; it's a tale meant to entertain. Enjoy.

For those wishing to visit sites used in the novel there is a guide on Paul's website at www.paulcwbeattysbooks.co.uk

ACKNOWLEDGEMENTS

There are too many people who have helped me with this book for me to thank all of them individually, but special thanks are owed to:

Staff of the Police Museum Manchester for advice about the status of the new Borough Police Forces in the 1840s, like the Stockport Force.

Ian Tyler, responsible for the initial idea behind *Children of Fire*, through his book *The Gunpowder Mills of Cumbria: A History of Cumbria's Gunpowder Industry*, Blue Rock Publications, 2002, reprinted 2010, ISBN 0 9523028 8 8

Dr Francis Mair, Senior Lecturer in Chemistry at the University of Manchester, for explaining the details of the production and action of gunpowder to me.

And last but by no means least, *Writing Magazine* and The Book Guild Publishing for putting up the prize which has enabled *Children of Fire* to be published.

NOTES FOR BOOK GROUPS

For those reading *Children of Fire* in book groups, free notes to aid discussion written by the author are available at www.paulcwbeattysbooks.co.uk